THE
LITTLE
BROTHER

THE LITTLE BROTHER

Bill Eidson

HENRY HOLT and COMPANY New York

Published by Henry Holt and Company, Inc.,
115 West 18th Street, New York, New York 10011.
Published in Canada by Fitzhenry & Whiteside Limited,
195 Allstate Parkway, Markham, Ontario L3R 4T8.

Library of Congress Cataloging-in-Publication Data
Eidson, Bill.
    The little brother / Bill Eidson.—1st ed.
      p. cm.
    ISBN 0-8050-1236-2
    I. Title.
PS3555.D487L5   1990
813'.54—dc20   89-20013
                                                        CIP

Henry Holt books are available at special discounts for
bulk purchases for sales promotions, premiums, fund-
raising, or educational use. Special editions or book
excerpts can also be created to specification.
For details contact:
Special Sales Director
Henry Holt and Company, Inc.
115 West 18th Street
New York, New York 10011

First Edition

BOOK DESIGN BY CLAIRE M. NAYLON
Printed in the United States of America
10 9 8 7 6 5 4 3 2 1

Quotations from Cyrano de Bergerac by Edmond Ros-
tand, translated by Brian Hooker, copyright © 1923,
1937 by Henry Holt and Company, Inc., and renewed
1951 by Doris C. Hooker, are reprinted by permission
of the publisher.

I would like to thank Catherine Eidson,
Rich and Sheila Berry, and Frank Robinson
for their help and good advice along the way.

THE
LITTLE
BROTHER

"LISTEN, I'VE GOT some questions." He glanced over his shoulder into the empty backseat. "What did it feel like? Did you know it was me? Did it hurt?"

He waited.

No answer.

Wiping his mouth, he felt the familiar anxiety bubble in his stomach, tasted the sourness of his breath. He tried to relax the muscles in his back, rolling his head and exhaling purposefully. *I've been here before*, he thought. *He'll talk. They always do.*

Prologue

It was after midnight on a Tuesday morning in July. The traffic was minimal, and the car was beginning to feel good to him. As he headed west on the Massachusetts Turnpike, the lights of Boston disappeared from his rearview mirror. At Route 128 he turned south and, twenty minutes later, took the exit for Route 95 to Rhode Island. The green dashboard light highlighted his chin and threw his eyes into shadow. High cheekbones were offset by a softness in the chin, making him look younger than twenty-four. His mouth was wide, with full lips. Hair cut short above the ears.

He didn't get an answer until he was halfway to Providence. Leaning against the armrest with the cigarette glowing in his cupped hand, he heard the faint voice, and the tension in his shoulders eased. He took his foot off the accelerator, let the car slow down to exactly fifty-five, and set the cruise control.

Where am I? the voice asked.

"Where do you think?" He exhaled the smoke slowly after speaking.

You did this? You?

"Take a look for yourself." He could feel the other look into him, a frightened understanding beginning to dawn. A smoldering rage other than his own flared.

"Get it?" he said.

You bastard! You shitter, you fucking didn't have the right!

He looked into the mirror. "I decide what's right."

The other's hot despair blasted through him.

"Come on, answer my questions," he said. "It won't be like this for long, and I want to know what it felt like. Did it hurt? You knew it was me, didn't you?"

For a moment, he thought he was going to learn something.

Instead, another enraged question: *What am I going to do?*

"Uh-uh," he corrected. "It's what *we're* going to do. I guarantee, you'll be amazed."

■ ■ ■

The dashboard clock read 2:25 A.M. He parked at the foot of the Jamestown Bridge, on the mainland side. A few lights winked on the opposite shore. Five minutes passed before a car came over the top of the bridge into his view. He looked at his watch as the car rolled down the steep incline and swept by. Ninety seconds. He figured it would take about the same for a car to climb from the opposite side to the top; that was all he could count on for privacy once he was up there.

He slipped the car into gear and drove up to the top of the bridge, checking the rearview mirror along the way. Nobody was behind him. He peered down the opposite side. No one in front. He turned off the lights and started counting. "One thousand one, one thousand two, one thousand three . . ."

He opened the trunk. The smell of feces swept up into the clean night air. Though the dead man was over six feet tall, he had the small, damaged look of an animal killed on the road. His naked legs were white in the glow of the bridge lights.

"One thousand nine, one thousand ten, one thousand eleven . . ." He hauled the body up by the shoulders to the lip of the trunk. Dead more than three hours, it was already quite cool. Squatting down, he draped the dead man over his back and stood, groaning with effort, pushing with trembling legs. As soon as he was standing it was easier. He hurried over to the railing and dropped the body onto it, belly down.

"One thousand thirty, one thousand thirty-one, one thousand . . ." He got three cinder blocks and a length of heavy chain from the trunk. Standing the heavy blocks on end, he strung them together with the chain, then wrapped an end of chain around each leg and tied them off with an awkward square knot. He finished by hooking the S-shaped ends into the links.

There was enough slack in the chain for him to balance the cinder blocks on the edge of the railing, which he did. Then, bending down, he lifted the body's legs and set himself to shove hard.

No! the voice raged. *Don't. You can't do this!*

He hesitated, then said, roughly, "You'll see." The blocks slid off the railing and clanged against the stanchions. He pushed harder, and suddenly the body flipped over the railing. It hit the bridge once on the way down, then for a time it was just a light falling spot against the black water below.

The voice screamed all the way down, until the body finally hit,

3

with a white splash he couldn't hear. He gripped the railing with all his strength, sweat pouring off his face.

"Damn," he said, softly.

The voice fell silent. It was still in him, though. Watching, changing.

"See, Tony," he said. "You didn't need that body, did you?"

JUST BEFORE 4:30 he wedged the Thunderbird into a tight space in front of the South End apartment building. He sprang up the stairs, not tired at all, hungry to be in his own place. Stepping inside, he turned on the light and looked around, taking in all that was now his.

Same old place. But not the same old me.

It was the top-floor unit in a building where the rent was paid by mail. The rest of the tenants were a good deal older than he and Tony. The only contact they had ever had with anyone was the occasional rapping on the floorboards when Tony played the stereo too loud. The apartment had been renovated years ago, a haphazard job that had turned a large one-bedroom into a cluttered two. A huge wooden spool turned on end and stenciled BOSTON EDISON served as a coffee table. Across from the nonworking fireplace was a black velour sofa covered with imitation sheepskins. Underneath the bay window was

a blond wood cabinet that housed the stereo, Tony's pride. Floor speakers stood waist high.

He walked over, flipped the power switch on, and stabbed the tape play button with a rigid forefinger. Hard-driving music filled the room. Quickly, he turned down the volume. *No visitors tonight*, he thought, shivering with pleasure. *Soon, but not tonight.*

He hurried back to the doorway of his new bedroom, but didn't go in. He inhaled the scent of after-shave lotion. Suddenly, the feel of his poorly fitting clothes became unbearable.

"I'll be right back," he whispered.

In the bathroom, he showered quickly. Steam billowed as he reached out of the shower for a bottle of hair color hidden in the towel closet. He looked at the label. It was the stuff advertised to change your hair color "so gradually no one will notice."

Tony noticed, he thought. *That and a few other things. So what? Tell it to the fish.*

Putting on a black terry-cloth robe that was hanging from the door, he picked up the after-shave scent again, mingled with the tang of perspiration. Padding quietly through the kitchen, he flicked the lights off and drew the shades on the bay window. In his old bedroom, he pulled the shade and turned on the overhead light.

A box spring and mattress lay along the far wall of the narrow room. The walls were bare except for the Grand Prix poster Tony had stuck on his wall with a thumbtack. "Have some art, for Christ's sake."

In the closet next to the bed, he pushed aside several neatly hung white shirts and pairs of pants to reveal a blue case sitting on the side shelf. He carried it close to his chest over to a caramel-colored writing desk with a mismatched wooden chair. After turning off the light, he shut the door and sat down, closing his eyes.

A tickle of anticipation ran up his spine. He stayed in the same position for a full minute, savoring the feeling.

He opened his eyes and unlatched the case. Light spilled out from a series of tiny bulbs around the mirror in the lid. His shadow appeared as a great hunched bird on the wall behind. Framed by his wet hair, which looked black in the meager light, his face appeared as stark as a vampire's.

6

Give the hair a little time, it'll look black at noon on a sunny day, he thought. He splashed on some after-shave, then massaged a thick blob of setting gel into his hair and drew it back into slick lines with a wide-toothed comb. The sweet scent of the gel competed with the lotion, filling the room. He rubbed bronzing cream into his face, neck, and arms, knowing that his two sessions at the tanning center the previous week were no competition with Tony's beach time.

Carefully, he wiped his hands clean. The cream wouldn't take effect for several hours, so he darkened his face with powder and brushed it smooth. In the corner of the makeup case was a stack of five contact lens cases. He took out the one marked with a green dot, leaned back into the chair, and dropped the soft contacts into his eyes. He kept his head back and blinked until his vision cleared. The room fell into darkness when he eased the lid of the case down. He sat back for several minutes and closed his eyes, ears tuned only to his own steady breathing.

He leaned forward and opened the case. In the mirror, a black-haired man took his measure with a direct, green-eyed stare. He gave a slow grin, his mouth lifting to one corner just so.

"You're back," he said.

■   ■   ■

It was just before sunup when he pulled the shade in the master bedroom. Wearing a pair of black bikini underwear taken from the chest of drawers, he crawled into the king-size bed. He burrowed his face in the pillow, happily unable to distinguish his own scent from that which was already there.

Groaning with heavy-eyed pleasure, he rolled onto his back, leaving a smudge of brown makeup on the gold pillowcase. He wasn't sure he would be able to sleep at all, he was so excited.

It was like that night with his brother.

Different, but the same. Even though Tony had been asleep when the ice pick had slid into his heart, he had wakened with that same look on his face, the one that said, "Not to me. Not from *you.*"

2

THE FIRST THING he did when he awoke that afternoon was look up the number for the small media representative firm where Tony worked. He wrote it down, then took a cassette from the blue case in his bedroom and slipped it into the tape deck. He kept the volume low and stopped the tape frequently to repeat a phrase aloud. It was a pleasure to use the speakers instead of the headphones, as he had been doing for the past few weeks, for fear that Tony might walk in. Now he made fast progress; his mimicry was near perfect.

Ostensibly as a joke, he had cajoled Tony into recording some of his exploits, saying he could sell the tape in the back of *Penthouse*, as an instructional aid on picking up women. He'd asked an occasional question to glean the information he needed, but it had been easy—Tony had gone for it completely. He was half drunk on four cans of beer, and always willing to give advice. "Confidence," he said. "That's what I've got, and that's what you need." Tony had filled both sides of the cassette.

Tony responded to a question about the women at work by discussing the secretary in detail. Karen was a good-looking woman in her early thirties who alternately flirted with and disapproved of him. As he often did with names, Tony shortened hers, calling her simply "Kare."

That type of information was useful to the man who was listening to the tape. He had recognized early on that most people judged how well they knew others by how well others knew them.

When he felt he could repeat Tony's sleepy yet resonant voice perfectly, he erased the tape and dialed the number.

"Boylston Advertising Sales," a woman's voice answered. "Can I help you?"

"You could, but so far you haven't," he said. "When are you going to drop that loser, Kare?"

"Tony? Is that you?"

"You forgot me already? I saw you yesterday." He chewed on his lower lip. That was stupid. What if Tony hadn't?

"Yes, well, don't talk about Donny that way. What I said that time at lunch, I didn't mean to have it thrown in my face."

"You wouldn't have said it if it weren't true."

She gave a short laugh. "Maybe so. Even more reason not to throw it at me. Anyway, I was just about to call you for Jerry. Are you sick or what? Your voice sounds kind of funny."

"I've got a cold coming on."

"You better think up something better than that. Did you just forget all your appointments? We expected you in this morning, and when you didn't show, we figured you went directly to the agencies. A Mr. Piedmont from Johnson & Cleary just phoned wanting to know why you stood them up for your three o'clock. Jerry took the call."

"Uh-oh," he said, grinning.

She caught the tone. "It's not funny, he's furious."

"Hey, that rhymes, kind of. Anyway, put him on. See if he can give me rabies over the phone."

She was silent for a moment. Then, "Oh, Jesus. Just when he thought you were going to work out."

"I've been working out for two years too long," he said. "So save the lecture, okay?"

"Listen, stop that and be nice," she whispered fiercely. "He's been good to you. Why such a wise guy, anyway? You got a new job or what?"

"A whole new life," he said. "You wouldn't believe it. It's a shame you don't get to be part of it."

"This is getting tired," she said, coldly. "Jerry's here now. I'll put you through."

"Good-bye, Kare," he said, cheerfully.

"Uh-huh."

The phone clicked, and he was kept on hold for almost a minute. Karen had surprised him. He'd thought she'd be more upset. She was probably in Jerry's office now, bleating out their conversation. He considered hanging up. But they would just call him back, so it was better to deliver the message when he was ready.

They would have been getting this call sooner or later, he mused, even if he hadn't killed Tony. More than once Tony'd said that he was on the verge of starting his own rep firm, that the time spent working under Jerry was just good experience.

Finally the connection went through and a raspy voice said, "You better be calling from the hospital, telling me both legs are broken and all your fingers too. Not going to your appointments, not even calling. How long you been doing this? Is this just the first time we found out?"

"Manners, Jerry, manners. Is that the way to answer the phone?"

"What's going on with you?"

"Good news."

"What?"

"A big career change. More money, more fun. Fact is, I was just wasting my potential working for you. Guy offered me a new opportunity and I had to take it."

"Who?"

"You don't know him."

"If it's Haskins, have the balls to tell me now."

"Like I said, you don't know him. Relax, Jerry, I'm out of the whole space-sales thing. Moving back to New York, closer to my family." His lips twitched. "You know how it is. I got to thinking, I'm going to die someday, and looking back and seeing all the ad space I sold just doesn't seem to cut it."

"What the hell are you talking about?"

"I'm quitting."

"Just like that? No notice, just don't show up for your appointments, then cancel out two years with a phone call?"

"That just about covers it. Just do the direct deposit with the last two checks, okay? I figure that's what I got coming, including vacation."

"Screw you."

His voice took on a sharper edge. "What's that mean? You sending the checks or no?"

"It means screw you," Jerry said distinctly. "Goddamn it, Tony, people quit jobs every day. It doesn't have to be like this. Of course I'm going to send you your checks. I do what I say. I thought you were like that, too. Yeah, a wise ass who chases skirts up and down Newbury Street, but I thought still you knew the right thing to do. I put in too much time with you, too much effort, for you to just quit with no notice."

"I'm crying," he answered. "But send the checks anyway." Then some of Tony's regret began to seep into his consciousness and in a confidential tone, he added. "Honest, Jerry, I had to take this position. No choice. Besides, you're old enough, you ought to know. People are never what you think." He hung up.

■ ■ ■

Several hours later, he put on Tony's clothes: a tan linen suit, a blue shirt with button-down collar, a burgundy tie with navy stripes, and black shoes with leather tassels. He slipped on the heavy gold watch he had admired for so long.

Tony stared back at him from the huge mirror over the black

11

dresser. The bronzing cream had darkened his skin, but not quite enough. He rubbed on more makeup. As for the hair, the black wig he had bought the week before would do the trick for tonight.

He worked on the voice again. "Looking good, Tony. No punkers or B.U. girls tonight. Pumping some convention lady it is." He held his gaze, smiled, then turned out the lights. Outside, the summer mugginess covered him like a sweat-soaked blanket. He considered going back for an even lighter suit but decided against it. They kept the rooms air-conditioned at the Westin.

He left the building and turned right onto Columbus Avenue. Many of the buildings along the street were gutted and boarded up, although here and there he noticed real-estate signs. *Tony would be good at selling real estate*, he thought. More money in that.

Moving at an easy pace, he took the time to savor being Tony. The clothes were comfortable and fit well. Most people looked away if he looked at them directly. And when a tough-looking black youth stared back at him defiantly, he didn't feel even a tickle of the fear that normally would have twisted his stomach into a sour ball. Tony had that confidence, that arrogance, wherever he went. People recognized it; in particular, women recognized it.

A block ahead, a derelict sat on the steps of an abandoned building, babbling an angry litany. He rocked back and forth, clutching his knees. At the end of each breath he would rear back and yell an unintelligible word, then start over.

The man dressed as Tony found himself matching every fourth step with the bum's punctuating yell. When he got closer, he stared directly at the old man, willing him to look away.

But interest flickered in the man's milky eyes. Stained teeth flashed between his fast-moving lips. Drool had formed twin streaks of yellow down his beard, and at a distance of six feet the urine smell was overpowering. As his babbling wound up to another conclusion, he took a deep breath and screamed, "Liar!"

Tony faltered. Or rather, the man wearing his clothes faltered. He reached for a jagged-edged brick by his right foot. The derelict reacted immediately, scuttling back up the stairs, bellowing, "Go 'way, go 'way. I didn't do nothin'."

12

Tony immediately settled back into place. He grinned and made a show of pulling his sock up instead of touching the brick. He turned his back on the man and continued down the street; he even laughed when the old man began to yell after him from a safe distance.

Turning left up West Newton Street, he noticed the urban transformation was more complete. If he decided to take Tony into something more lucrative, like real estate, he would want a new apartment, maybe in Back Bay or on Beacon Hill. But for now, everything was just fine. So much potential.

Ten minutes later, he was riding up the escalator in Copley Place. The feeling of being watched and admired only increased as he walked into the lounge. "Dewar's on the rocks," he told the bartender. He sat back in a tall gray-and-chrome swivel chair and checked out the four waitresses. All wore the same uniform: a tight green dress with a slit cut up to midthigh on the right leg. The material was supposed to look like silk, but he was sure it was polyester. *All the better*, he thought.

One of the waitresses looked great: tall, early twenties, with bright blond hair that hung halfway down her back. When she raised the drink tray over her head, the thin material hugged tight under her breasts just like his hand would do. She looked over and caught him watching. He smiled calmly. So did she.

Just a day in the life, he thought, watching her take an order from two older men in business suits. She leaned back, hip cocked, one smoothly muscled leg exposed. On her way back to the bar, one of the men said something to the other and they laughed. She looked at him, at Tony, rolling her eyes. He shook his head; couple of old losers.

He checked his watch. 9:00 P.M. Waiting for her to get off would take too long. He decided to try to connect with somebody else first. If nobody good showed, he could go away and come back an hour before the lounge closed. *An hour should be plenty of time with her*, he thought, *the way she's looking for it*. He sipped his drink and considered the other women in the bar.

Most were already with men. Lots of name tags on lapels, a convention crowd. The men dressed in conservative suits, a few with

13

bright yellow or red power ties, practically glowing in the dark. He closed his eyes. It was the women he could hear, chattering, light sounds over the rumbling voices of the men. With Tony inside him now, it was hard to imagine the excruciating pain women's voices had been able to deliver in the past.

He opened his eyes abruptly. One woman he could have been interested in was guarded by her friend, a woman so fat she should be wearing a WIDE LOAD sign. The only woman actually alone at the bar looked fortyish and tough. Not what he had in mind at all. So he waited.

Two drinks later, a woman who looked to be in her late twenties sat down two chairs away and ordered a glass of white wine. She had brown hair with blond streaks and wore lipstick a bit too vividly. The electric blue of her dress made him expect blue eyes, but when she glanced his way, he saw they were brown. She wore a white convention tag over her left breast with the name SUSAN printed in red capital letters. He found her attractive, not gorgeous but attractive. She would be lucky to sleep with him, he decided.

He looked at the mirror behind the bar and found he had a good view of her, right between the Chivas and the Jack Daniel's. When her head turned in his direction, he glanced her way, did a mild double take, and said, "So, Susan, you need a break from the hospitality suites?"

Smiling, but looking confused, she said, "Oh, I sure did. How much talk about employment can one person take? Plus all those pushy headhunters, trying to get your business." Suddenly she put her hand to her mouth. "You're with an agency, aren't you? With my mouth, you've got to be. You know the saying? 'Open mouth, insert foot,' that's me. I'm sorry."

Laughing, he put up his hand. "Calm down. I'm not with an agency, whatever kind you're talking about. I'm not even with the convention. I just figured you might be tired of running around to the hospitality suites. This hotel always seems to have something like that going on."

Her brow furrowed, and then she clutched at her name tag. "I get it, you're just trying to pick me up! Here I thought I was supposed

14

to know you. You'd think I'd be used to it by now, everybody running around peering at each other's chests and using first names only."

"Sounds like a vacation I had in the Bahamas once," he said and then tensed. Where in the Bahamas?

She giggled. "I've had a few like that. So what are you doing here tonight?"

He moved to the seat next to her. He smiled, warm but still distant enough to be polite. "Up until now, just killing time. I'm in from New York. Tomorrow morning I have to make some presentations to the ad agencies around here."

"What are you presenting?" She giggled again. "You a male model?"

"Hey, flattery," he said. "*I'm* supposed to do that. But anyhow, what I do is work for publications, sell their ad space to ad agencies. But I think I'm getting out of that, maybe doing something more interesting, like real-estate development. Make more money, too."

"Money and interesting usually do go together," she mused. "At least that's what I've noticed in my travels."

"Ah, you should have said so up front. I would have told you I was a rich Californian in town to sell my vineyard for ten million dollars."

She petted his hand lightly. "I'm from California, so that would have worked really well on me. We could go back, I could quit work, and we could be rich together."

"Well, see, I've got the right attitude. That's got to count for something."

"Just about everything," she said, into her wineglass.

He signaled for another round of drinks. "So tell me about yourself."

And she did. About the convention. About her job as a recruiter for a growing San Jose high-tech manufacturer. About her boss, whom she was close to slapping with a sexual harassment suit. About her lover, whom she had just dropped. After an hour, she had had three drinks to his two.

"Don't get me wrong," she said. Her leg was warm against his.

15

"I'm not a prude. I just don't like to do it on command. And I especially don't want to do it with my boss." She slapped the bar. "His belly sticks out to here! It's disgusting. Why doesn't he get the idea?"

"Listen," he said, putting his arm around her. "I can see why you're not interested, but if I were him I'd be chasing you around all day too. You're a good-looking woman. You've got to expect it."

The giggle. "If you were chasing me all day, I'd let you catch me."

"Susan, I've been chasing you all night."

"I noticed," she said. "Catch."

■   ■   ■

He caught a glimpse of his face in the lobby mirror as they walked around an older couple on the way to the elevators. Being Tony was strong in him now, and he hurried Susan into a waiting elevator and pushed the door close button. He drew her into the corner and kissed her on the mouth.

"Hold the door, please," the old man said, irritated.

But he left his finger on the button and said in Susan's ear, "The hell with him, he's already got his own girl." The door slid shut. Her breasts felt firm and ample against his chest. He touched his tongue against hers and got an erection.

"Nice," she said, pushing her hips forward. He ran his hands over her silk—real silk—dress, feeling the panty-hose line at her waist, then cupping her cheeks. Her skirt was slit on the side too, like the waitress's. He put his hand on her thigh and started to run it up her leg slowly. "Careful," she said. "The door might open, and much more of this, I'm not responsible."

"Okay." He emphasized the huskiness of his voice, stepping away from her slightly. She blinked, then smiled. "You're different than you seem at first," she said.

"How so?"

She laughed. "Well, you *stopped*, when I asked you to. That

16

doesn't happen too often." She added quickly, "Not that this happens to me all that often."

His face suddenly felt wooden, but his voice sounded easy enough, saying, "Well, when you're right, you're right. We don't stop, there could be some old geezer waiting for the elevator who'd kick off when the door opened, the way we're heading. That would slow us down for sure, waiting for the ambulance and all. And I don't want to wait. How about you?"

Smiling, she said, "No, what I mean is first you come off as this slick type of guy. You know, pick me up two minutes after I sit down. Usually guys like that talk about themselves the whole time, but not you. You let me talk, and, God knows, give me a chance, I'll talk."

"So why are you saying I'm not what I seem?"

The elevator door opened and she stepped out, taking a key from her purse. "Don't get me wrong," she said as they reached her room. "You're beautiful. I like you better this way. You know, a nice guy, not just a stud." She cocked her hip against him and said, "Though I'm sure that, too. Want to come in and show me?"

She went in ahead of him and flipped the light switch. He blinked in the harsh glare, and when she turned, he mentally pushed her age up another few years. Looking at him, her eyes narrowed and her mouth opened, then snapped shut.

"What?"

"Nothing." She looked in the mirror and said, "Oh God, this light stinks, it's not doing us any good."

Us? he thought, and started to touch his face, but stopped. He waited while she turned off the light and drew the curtains back. The John Hancock tower stood like the blade of a colossal sword stuck into Copley Square. Her room was smaller than he had expected and dominated by a huge bed.

Kicking her shoes off, she stretched across the width of the bed easily. "The room may not be big, but it's got all the furniture we need," she said, patting the mattress.

He could barely see himself in the mirror with only the moonlight

17

illuminating the room. He wished he could see Tony more clearly, putting it to this girl Susan the way she wanted it. Was the wig on straight? Why had she looked at him like that when the light was on?

"Come on," she said, "I want to see you without those clothes . . . and show you me, without mine."

He knelt beside her on the bed, leaving one leg on the floor. "Hey." She picked at his sleeve. "Clothes. Leaving your suit on comes under the heading of wham, bam, thank you, ma'am." She slid her hand over his chest and down. His penis wilted. She touched him, and the room wasn't so dark he couldn't see her frown.

"I'm just what I appear to be," he said, hating the quavery sound of his voice. *Goddamn Tony.*

"What?" She sat up. "Wait, I didn't mean to insult you. Don't get mad."

"Well, why did you have to go say that?" His voice was rising. "We were doing fine, then you go say I'm a fake, start looking at me like something is wrong."

She crossed her arms. "I didn't say you were a fake. So I just noticed the makeup, okay? I wasn't going to say anything, it doesn't matter. We're just here for one night. So lighten up."

"Nothing is the matter with me," he said savagely. "I was doing fine, then you screwed it up."

"Right," she said curtly. "My fault. You're wearing a wig, and makeup, and you can't get it up. And it's my fault."

He broke her nose. Howling, hands covering her face, she fell back onto the bed under him. She tried to roll, but he got his hands underneath her arms, grabbed her by the throat, and dug in with his thumbs. He twisted his legs around hers so his groin pressed hard against her belly. She tried to scratch at his eyes, but he jammed his chest against her face, buried his head in the pillow, and rode her as she tried to buck him off.

And then the feeling came. It was always a surprise. She was hot and sweaty beneath, and she had hurt him just moments before. She had only known him for a few hours, yet she still felt that woman's compulsion to cause him pain. But as her life pumped against his

18

hands, he was suddenly touched by a love for her, and with it, he was hard again. A flickering sense of jealousy that she had had other men passed through him, and then he forgave her as her hot twisting below rubbed him hotter and hotter. When he climaxed, the muscles of his arms and chest swelled, and something cracked in her neck. She twitched and then was silent. He lay on top of her until finally he realized the only beating heart was his own.

Leaning back on his right elbow, he looked down at her staring eyes. "You shouldn't have made me do that," he said.

■ ■ ■

He sat in an armchair looking out the window, disgusted. Her body had become incontinent. Fucking Tony had lasted less than two days. He kicked the armchair across from him suddenly, knocking it over.

There had been times when he'd been somebody else for over a month, and without having to kill any women. Now he had to start all over again.

Nobody had pounded on the door to save this Susan. He assumed that if anyone outside the room had heard the noise, they would figure it would be an embarrassing mistake to knock and ask what was going on.

He yanked the spread out from under her and put her on her side, facing away from the door. Grabbing a handful of hair, he pulled her head up and put a pillow underneath. Then he covered her with the spread, so only a shock of her hair was visible.

Surprise, surprise for the maid.

In the bathroom he checked himself for cuts. She had gouged his right temple, but it wasn't bleeding very much. He went back into the bedroom, found the wig on the floor, and brought it into the bathroom. It covered the cut easily.

Taking a paper towel from the dispenser, he wiped down every surface he thought he had touched. He didn't really know much about it, but he didn't think his fingerprints would do the police much good. He had never been in the military, had never been fingerprinted by the police anywhere. And so what if the police picked up a print down at the bar or up here in the room? They could keep it, as long as they didn't have him.

Using the paper towel, he opened the door and left the DO NOT DISTURB sign on the knob. He walked down the stairway for two floors before taking the elevator. In the lobby, he kept his breathing steady, met no one's eye, and walked out of the hotel. Walking away from the South End, he took a left at the Boston Public Library on Boylston Street. He continued past a multicolored glass window of an English-theme pub and took another left. Twenty minutes later he was going up the stairway to Tony's apartment. He let himself in and leaned back against the door, eyes touching on the cheap furniture, the posters without frames. He spit on the floor.

In the master bedroom, he turned on the light to see what Susan had seen. The makeup line was obvious near his eyelashes. There was bronzing powder on his shirt collar, and the wig was slightly askew. Sweat had drawn streaks through the makeup on his face. He closed his eyes and almost vomited.

After a few moments, he raised his head and opened his eyes. Only a foot away, on the dresser, was a picture of Tony sitting in the Thunderbird when it was new. A blond girl in a blue tank top was kissing his cheek, her eyes on the camera. Tony was grinning, his left hand out the window, thumb up.

"Bullshit!" He threw the picture into the mirror, shattering his own image. He pulled the suit off as quickly as he could. Stumbling when he reached the pants, he fell onto the bed, then jumped off as if burned. He threw the black briefs along with the rest of the clothes onto the bed.

He hurried into the bathroom and showered. Some of the black hair color flowed down the drain with the shampoo. He dried off with his own towel and then stuffed it into a garbage bag with his dirty clothes. In his room, he dressed quickly in tan polyester pants and a white shirt. He returned the contact lenses to the blue case. In the mirror, his face looked narrow and his lower lip trembled. He slammed the lid down. Tossing the rest of his clothes into the garbage bag, he took his belongings into the kitchen and left them by the door. Glass crunched under his shoes as he walked into Tony's room. Tony's wallet was on the dresser. He stuck it in his back pocket, then stepped up onto the bed, unzipped his fly, and urinated over clothes and pillows. "You're useless," he said.

■ ■ ■

He stayed in the car on a side street in Brighton for the rest of the night. It was hot and cramped in the backseat, and his skin stuck to the vinyl. Breathing through his mouth, he tried to relax. But as he began to fall asleep, his arm, shiny with sweat, slid off the rounded edge of the seat and thumped on the floor. He rolled over and pushed his face where the seat and the back met, rubbing it in a way he found soothing. Closing his eyes, he began to hum quietly, steadily. For a long time, his thoughts turned to gray cotton, nothing.

Suddenly he knew that Tony was in the trunk and tearing through the seat to get at him. The car was careening around corners, and he was jammed, helpless. He could hear the ripping of foam, and feel the touch of Tony's dead fingers through the vinyl, brushing against his own cheek.

He tried to scream but couldn't get anything out. He rolled onto his back but couldn't get up; his arms lay paralyzed. Above him, the seat bulged tight over the outline of a face, like that of a baby suffocating in a plastic bag. Then the bag ripped and Tony's head burst through. The right side of his face was crushed, one eye swollen shut. Tony reached out to clutch his throat, and suddenly they were underwater, chained together and weighted by cinder blocks. He held his breath as long as he could, then finally, blood pounding in his forehead, he opened his mouth wide to the black water.

He awoke. His face was still jammed in the corner, and his arms had fallen asleep beneath him. Turning over on his back, he gasped in the stale air of the closed car. It was morning. He sat up, pushed the front seat forward, and dragged himself outside. The sun was covered by a hazy cloud. It hurt his eyes to look anywhere.

Sensing that he was being watched, he turned quickly to find a little Oriental boy in the yard of the house he was parked in front

21

of. A chain-link fence separated them. "Did you sleep there?" The boy pointed to the car, his high-pitched voice amazed. "All night, did you sleep there?"

He almost didn't answer, then knelt by the fence, smiling, and said, "Do you know what wonton soup is?"

The little boy said, "Wonton."

"Well, that chewy part in the center tastes like pork. Know what it really is?"

The boy shrugged.

"It's little boys who don't mind their own business. We put them in a grinder and let the rest of their family eat them in soup. You think about that before opening your mouth about somebody else's business, okay?"

The boy backed away from the fence quickly. "Hah," he said, but he looked scared.

"You talk about me, your mama-san and daddy-san will be eating you before they know you're gone."

The boy's lower lip stuck out, and he crossed his arms and backed away. "Hah," he repeated.

The man got in the car and drove off thinking both he and the boy were lucky. If the little kid had been a crier, he could have been in the house by now screaming about the man out front who tried to grind him up. Then again, if it had looked like that was going to happen, who knows? He could have been over that fence before the kid hit the porch. Why did he do stuff like that? He started a little joke, and it could have gone all wrong. Last thing he needed was to have to explain *anything* to the cops right now. Especially why he twisted some kid's head around for looking at him funny.

At a convenience store in Kenmore Square, he stopped and picked up the *Boston Phoenix* and the *Globe*. There was no mention of Susan, dead Susan, but it was too soon anyway. He thought about it sometimes, why he always wanted to read about it in the paper the next day. Like on television, the SWAT team comes bursting in on some sicko, and he's got clippings of his victims on the wall. He didn't do that nonsense. But he *did* need to know what the police knew, just so he didn't get caught. Logical.

22

Crossing the street to a bank, he took Tony's cash card up to the machine and punched in the code, "Stud." Sure enough, Tony's big mouth hadn't lied. Three hundred dollars was the daily limit, and he planned to hit a different branch each day for the next few days until the meager account was cleaned out. Beat working. And it was a lot safer than hanging out in the park at night, trying to avoid getting mugged by the other muggers.

At breakfast, the young waitress tossed her hair impatiently while he stumbled out his order. His face turned stiff. He didn't know what to do while waiting, where to look, what to do with his hands. He started to read the paper, like the man in the booth across from him, just as the waitress brought back his French toast. She made a small irritated noise when he knocked the pepper shaker off the table. He bent down to pick it up and envisioned taking the steak knife from the table, ramming it up under her chin, and twisting. Instead, he smiled politely. "Sorry."

After she returned to the kitchen, he sliced the French toast into small chunks, poured on a stream of sugar from the glass dispenser, then topped it off with maple syrup. He ate ravenously, pushing new forkfuls of the sopping bread into his mouth before he'd swallowed what was there.

When he was done, he looked through the *Phoenix* for a furnished room and found one listed with an address nearby, on Massachusetts Avenue. The waitress was back in the kitchen, out of sight. He left a five-dollar bill in the puddle of syrup on his plate, wiped the steak knife off carefully, and slipped it into the back of his pants. It was good to be ready.

He drove down Massachusetts Avenue past Symphony Hall and parked the car in the South End. With Tony's resident sticker, it should be there whenever he wanted it. He walked toward Commonwealth Avenue, carrying the garbage bag of clothes and the makeup case, thinking about the chances of the police looking for him. The real question in his mind was whether they would look for Tony. There was no reason to look for *him*.

He didn't have black hair and green eyes. The person who'd killed Susan did. The bartender knew that; the blond waitress, probably, too. Maybe even the old geezer and his wife who'd been shut out of the elevator. He'd picked the Westin because it had seemed like Tony's type of place, but Tony had never talked about going there.

He'd talked about places like the Lion's Den on Stuart Street. "You should see it," Tony would say. "I walk in and Louis at the bar points them out and I take what I want. He says I'm good for business, I keep the babes coming in."

The more he thought about it, the more he realized how full of it Tony was about everything. Tony hadn't brought a girl home once all summer. He always made a big deal about how he would go to girls' apartments so he could leave whenever they tried to crowd him. Such bullshit.

He glanced at his watch. Tony's watch. He covered it automatically with his right hand, then relaxed. Far as he knew, nobody was even looking for Tony yet. And if they were, how could *he* be traced to Tony? He had never said so much as hello to the neighbors. The rent was just a cash deal with Tony.

And Tony didn't even know his real name. Loser. That's what he and the girl in the hotel were. A couple of losers.

■ ■ ■

"It ain't a hotel and it ain't your apartment," the old man said. "So don't be calling me for ice, and keep the TV down after eleven."

He nodded. "How much?"

"One forty-five a week, plus a twenty-five-dollar deposit on the key." The old man's stubbly chin stuck out defiantly. "Some people come in here and leave me with a kitchen full of dirty dishes and take the key. Then I got to go cut another one. I can't make my nut if I got to pay for a key every time."

"Yeah," he said, handing over the cash in exchange for the famous key. "I'll get it back to you."

The old man grunted. "That's the way it starts. Anyhow, come on, I'll show you the room now. You don't like it, good luck finding something better."

The landlord, wearing baggy brown pants and a yellow Ban-Lon shirt, shuffled ahead of him down the narrow hallway. The building seemed to be decorated to the old man's taste. Fiberboard hid what were probably nine-foot ceilings. The walls were painted an institutional beige, like in high school.

"Last person here," the landlord said, as he opened the door, "loved to eat cabbage and fish. Must've ate it every day. So don't worry about that smell, it'll go by tomorrow. Damn cabbage stinks." A cockroach scuttled across the opposite wall, onto the nightstand, past the telephone, and down to the floor. "Life in the big city," the landlord said. "Can't do nothing much about that. Find a can of Raid under this sink, if they give you the heebies."

He crossed his arms and said, "I'm not going to be here long. That phone hooked up?"

"For local calls," the landlord looked at him warily. "You got to go through me to place long distance."

"No problem. I can find what I need here."

Alone, a few minutes later, he brought the telephone stand closer to the table, opened the newspaper, and started ticking down the "Apartments to Share" column with a pencil. He quickly scratched out the ads for women, or those with multiple roommates. His nose wrinkled when he read a listing stating that the present occupant was gay, ". . . but you don't have to be." He read it again, glanced toward the window, then scratched a big X across that ad. He did the same with all those requiring someone older than thirty. About a dozen possibilities were left. There were more in the *Globe*. He started dialing.

3

WHEN THE PHONE rang at Boston Divers, Leo looked at his watch and said, "That's probably Gary. Minimum, it's going to cost us two grand. Two grand we might as well have swirled down the toilet."

Rod picked up the receiver and kept his face blank while the mechanic gave him the price. "Twenty-three hundred," he repeated into the phone.

Leo overheard. He stalked away from the display case and began carrying rental tanks into the back room.

Rod said quietly into the phone, "Gary, what's the soonest I can have those outboards working? I've got to get that boat back in the water. If I can't schedule some dives soon, I'll need to find a new partner. Leo is not taking my little escapade too well." Rod rubbed the bridge of his nose as he listened. "Okay, Gary," he said, "see if I ever come to you for good news again."

After he hung up, Rod helped Leo with the tanks. Rod swung the heavy bottles with long-practiced ease. His arms were muscular, and his hair was bleached sandy white from the sun. His eyes were sharp blue, a particularly vivid shade against his ruddy complexion. Right now they were staring at his partner's back. Finally, he said, "You want to say something, say it."

Leo was smaller than Rod, twelve years older, and bald. Very wiry, with enough black hair on his arms and chest to cover two heads. A heavy gold chain glinted in the V of his green cotton shirt. He set a tank down and faced Rod. "When?"

"Not until next Tuesday."

"No dives this weekend."

"That's right."

Leo stared at him. "No boat dive revenue for a prime week of the summer, plus twenty-three hundred bucks. I hope she likes you."

"Bette wasn't too impressed, believe me."

Leo snorted. "Why should she be? Racing that idiot, Latta, into port. What the hell were you thinking?"

"How many times, Leo, how many times are we going to go through this? I was a jerk. I was racing Latta, and the kid in the Whaler cut us off, and it was either hit him, or go up on the sandbar. Latta wasn't budging."

"Neither did the rocks on that 'sandbar.' "

"Look, I'm going to take care of this."

"Meaning what? You'll call the insurance company?"

Rod set the last tank down. "The hull repair I'll do myself. And I'll pay for the lower units."

Leo looked directly at Rod. "With what? I know your finances. You're always just a few hundred away from being broke."

"I'll reimburse the store. On an installment basis, once a month."

"How?"

Rod shrugged. "I'll figure something out."

"You going to try and get Latta to kick in?"

"No. It's not his boat."

Leo turned away. "Okay. You're learning."

An hour later, Rod looked at the options he had listed on yellow lined paper. He was alone in the store, sitting on a three-legged stool behind the display counter, waiting for the first customer of the day. He made another entry at the top of the page, underlined it, and called Bette at the Newbury Street clothing store where she worked as a buyer. Her voice filled the line, giving him an automatic lift.

"I've got two questions for you," he said. "First off, are you going to sue me or the store?"

"You? I know how much you've got—why waste my time? The store, now, you must have liability insurance, right? Something to compensate a woman dragged out on a boat, only to have it run into the rocks."

"It seems the insurance company and I are not talking these days."

Her voice lowered. "Really? They won't cover it?"

"Not if they don't know about it."

"Meaning?"

"Meaning Leo and I discussed it, and I'm going to pay for the damage out of my own pocket. Something about me gaining maturity."

"Oh, Rod, sounds like hard words. Now you're getting it on both sides, from him and me." Her voice lightened. "What was your second question?"

He took a deep breath. "On the top of the list of options I have a sentence that says 'Bette moves in with me.' "

"Oh."

"Oh," he repeated. "Listen, hardwood floors, love, reasonable rent. It *is* my top option."

Her voice was cautious. "Thank you, Rod, and maybe—probably—someday yes, but for now, draw a line through that choice, okay?"

"Done."

"Rod?"

He didn't answer for a moment.

"You're angry, right?"

"A little. But the timing's bad; crack you up on the rocks one day, ask you to move in the next."

"Oh, come on, it's not just that. I've got a lease. I can't just walk out on Lori and besides . . . I mean, we just haven't talked about it enough. I can't just move in with you like that. Let's go out on Saturday, okay? I really want to see you."

"Sure," he said. "Bring your car, though, unless you want to ride around in a van that smells like seaweed."

"Rod?"

"Yes?"

"Come tonight, too."

"Sure," he said. "I'll bring an overnight bag."

■ ■ ■

Rod put the phone down quietly. He looked at his list, then called the *Phoenix* and placed an ad for a roommate. He gave the store phone number and included his first name in the ad. "Make sure you put it in the right column," he said. "Last thing I need are those weirdos from the personals section. In fact, put that in the ad: 'No weirdos need apply.' "

4

BETTE PICKED UP her roommate at the airport on Saturday morning. "Oh, damn," Bette said, brushing back her red hair. She could read Lori's expression a dozen car lengths away. Bette was a tall woman with high cheekbones and light, freckled skin. Her eyes, like Rod's, were intensely blue, a feature that made some people think they were related.

She unlocked the passenger door. Lori threw her bag into the backseat and said, "Let's get the hell out of here and home. I want this trip to be *over*."

"That good?" Bette started down the ramp.

"Don't ask." Lori crossed her arms and looked out the window. She wore tight jeans, black boots, and a red knit blouse. Men and women noticed Lori when she walked down the street, her small body opulent in miniature. She had a wild tangle of black ringlets and emerald-green eyes. Now her lower lip extended a little farther than usual.

Bette sighed.

"You want to say something?" Lori snapped.

"No, but you do. Save us both some time and say it."

Lori didn't answer until they reached the tollbooth at the Sumner Tunnel. Then, "Poor Thomas moves to big bad New York and feels lonely. Calls me on the phone late at night. Fool that I am, I fly down at my own expense, because he's too strapped what with the outrageous cost of apartments in New York, let him tell me about it one more time, I'll scream . . . and he dumps me."

"Thomas dumped you?" Bette said, unbelieving.

"Well, it goes sort of like this. We spend a week together, and it starts off okay, but then, you know, some of that dead feeling starts creeping in. Like, do I really know this person I say I love and all. At first, I thought it was just me and I felt guilty. So I say something and he agrees, he knows what I'm talking about. Naturally, I start getting all insecure—'What do you mean you know what I'm talking about?'—you know. So anyway, we have these long, late-night talks. Long-distance relationships are hard, but we can work it out . . . love will prevail, blah, blah, blah. You know. So I'm putting all this effort in, feeling lousy about the situation, but at least feeling good we're talking. Then Friday night comes. Knock knock on the door, I open it, wearing only my bathrobe, because it looked like things were finally working out with us, if you know what I mean, and this blue-eyed bitch is standing there, looking over my head, jangling her keys, asking if Tommy is in."

"Tommy?"

"Goes well with Jennifer." Lori extended her lower jaw to say the name. "Tommy introduces me, his face all white and sweaty-looking." She hit the dashboard with a red-nailed fist. "Damn him! The bastard introduces *me* to *her*—you know, 'Jennifer, this is Lori.' Like he's more worried about what she thinks of me being there than what I think of her."

"What did he say for himself?"

"Oh, he let her do all the talking. 'So sorry to interrupt, didn't know you had company. Just stopped by to invite you up for dinner at Daddy's tomorrow night . . . but if it's a problem . . .' "

31

"What did *you* say to all this?"

"Be quicker to tell you what I didn't. To him anyhow. I'll lie awake nights thinking about things I should've said to her, but I was too stunned. I just gave her a little push and locked the door behind her and started bawling. She was too civilized to put up a fight. Just went downstairs, got in her little car, and drove off, mission accomplished."

"She knew you'd be there?"

"I don't doubt it for a minute. The girl wanted a stockbroker named Tommy, and now she's got one."

"I'm so sorry, Lori." Bette was silent for a moment, then said, "Maybe you don't want to hear this now, but if he'd do something like that, then he's not worth fighting for."

Lori laughed shortly. "Don't worry. I reached that opinion while I was pushing the iceberg out the door. He's welcome to what he gets—her telling him to 'do it my way' from now on. Besides, she spends too much time in the sun on Daddy's boat, you can tell. Five years from now, she'll have crow's-feet as deep as rain gutters. Where will he be then? I hope he marries her."

She straightened and said briskly. "Let me tell you, I'm not going to sit around feeling sorry for myself. I had enough of that, sitting up all night in his bed while he slept on the couch. And I do mean slept—I had the door locked, and I could still hear his snoring. It made me so mad." She touched Bette's arm. "Thank God you were in when I called this morning."

Bette waved her hand. "I wasn't too perceptive. I thought something was wrong, but you didn't say a thing."

"I didn't want to give him the pleasure of hearing me cry. Which I would've done, then, if I'd started talking about it." She slapped her hands sharply. "Then. As for now, it's time for me to meet more men, and you're going to help me. And I'm going to have a good time. God help the one that tries to mess up my head like this jerk Tommy. That's the way I think of him now—Tommy. Little baby."

She crossed her arms and looked out over the Charles River as they sped along Storrow Drive. After a few minutes she said in a calmer tone, "Tell you the truth, even when I was ranting around calling him a bacteria, I felt a little relieved."

"I was wondering when you might get to that," Bette said. "You didn't seem all that excited about going. More like something you felt obliged to do."

Lori nodded. "I had been planning on it for a while. And then I felt so guilty when it wasn't much fun. It just doesn't seem like much of a relationship, a weekend here, a weekend there. You know, sometimes you just want to go out on a Tuesday night for pizza, and say 'Have a good day at work' in the morning. Not have to fly to New York every time. Plus the fact that he could move to New York without either of us talking about marriage or anything says it all."

Bette switched to the left lane for the Kenmore Square exit. "You've never been lonely for long. I don't think you're going to start now."

"Better not," Lori said darkly. "I'm ready to get out tonight. No sense staying at home while he's minding his table manners in Connecticut. So let's go out dancing, see who I can meet."

Shaking her head, Bette said, "I'm sorry, I can't tonight."

"You're going out with Rod? Take me with you, I like him."

Bette smiled. "Sorry, not this time."

"Come on, Bette, don't make me beg. Look, I *love* Rod, okay? If he wasn't yours, I'd be knocking on his door. Or convincing him to knock on mine, actually."

"I'm going to have to keep you away from him. The fact is, he asked me to move in with him this week."

Lori's face fell. "No, my week can't go this badly. You're moving out on me? I mean, I want to be happy for you, Rod's a great guy, but the timing—"

Bette put her hand over Lori's mouth. "I said no, Lori. No for now."

Lori bit Bette's hand. "That was dumb. Good for me, but dumb for you. Tell him I'll move in."

Laughing, Bette said, "Let me tell you what prompted the big romantic invitation." She described how she and Rod were cruising around the harbor up in Stoneport when another diver cut across their bow, covering them with a sheet of seawater. How Rod returned the favor, and the two of them raced for the red nun into the harbor.

Lori pealed with laughter. "He's a nut! He ran right up on the rocks?"

Bette glanced at her roommate. "Lori! He did it to avoid the kid in the little Whaler. It's not that funny, the kid could have been hurt, and it'll cost Rod a couple of thousand dollars out of his pocket."

"Funny, no. Crazy, yes. Lori, Rod's a wild man, and he loves you all the way, I can tell, just the way he looks at you."

"Right. That's why he waited until he was desperate for my rent money before asking me."

"Picky, picky." Lori shoved Bette's arm playfully. "You don't believe that. You know it's just a good excuse for him. Don't get me wrong—you showed real character by refusing to dump your room-mate. You're lucky my character wasn't put to that kind of test. I'd've rented a U-Haul by now. He's the kind of man I'm looking for— someone who's crazy and crazy about me."

Bette put her arm around Lori. "Don't worry, you'll find one."

"Oh, I know." Lori sighed. "But what about tonight?"

HE WALKED INTO the lobby of a red-brick apartment building near Coolidge Corner and rang the bell for apartment number four. It was his second appointment of the day, and he had the new issue of the *Phoenix* under his arm. The listings from the previous week had been a waste of his time. Although he could usually judge from a few minutes of conversation over the phone if the person was gay, boring, or, worst of all, lonely and looking for companionship, he'd been completely fooled by a guy he had called the day before. Deep voice, solid-sounding. Good sense of humor. Didn't sound like a queer.

In person, though, he could tell right away. The glasses, the short hair. The way the kitchen looked right out of a magazine, with jars of colored pasta lined up on the shelf. A bronze casting of two men wrestling on the coffee table. He asked what his portion of the rent would be, then abruptly stated he would only be willing to pay half that amount. The

5

faggot objected, eyebrows raised, but he knew what was going on.

After the queer closed the door behind him, he turned and spit on it. Queers made him sick. He had once moved in with a man in Philadelphia who appeared straight—but two weeks into the arrangement, Carter had asked if he could join him in the shower. He was appalled that he could have been fooled so completely. It had been the only time he had used a rifle at long distance. He had wanted to surgically remove Carter Demoray from the face of the earth.

Waiting now, he began to wonder if he had lost his judgment about people. Tony had certainly been a mistake. But it was so hard to tell with just a phone call. His conversation with this one, Larry Beaugrad, had been so short, and mainly about the apartment. The only personal information he'd been able to extract was that Larry was a nonsmoker and an engineer.

He had concocted another name for himself by pulling two first names from the phone book: Brendan Kirk.

The door alarm buzzed, and he walked up to the second floor. The building had apparently been renovated recently. The gold carpeting gave off a new smell. Hearing footsteps in the apartment, he waited expectantly for the door to open, a smile practiced to look easy on his face.

Beaugrad was short and going bald. A dark, curly beard grew wild about his face, and a soft paunch bulged his checked shirt over his jeans. He grinned and put out his hand. "Hi, Larry Beaugrad here. You must be Brendan Kirk?"

He kept his hands on his hips and the smile vanished. "Sorry," he said, turned on his heel, and walked down the stairs. Beaugrad made a sound like he was punched and followed him down to the lobby.

"Hey, what's your problem? You didn't even see the place." The engineer's face was flushed, and he was breathing heavily. The man calling himself Brendan could see the surprised hurt in Beaugrad's eyes, and the easy smile came back. "Didn't need to," he said. "I saw you. And you're fat."

■ ■ ■

Alone in his room an hour later, he circled an ad, grinning to himself. "Hope you're willing to bend on that 'no weirdos,' " he said, then dialed the number.

"Boston Divers," a deep voice answered.

He almost hung up, not expecting it to be a business phone number. Then, "Is Rod there? I'm calling about the apartment."

"He's working on the boat. He'll be back in an hour or so. You want to leave your number?"

"No, I'll call back."

"It's no problem."

"I'll call."

"Your choice."

He hung up and waited for an hour and twenty minutes, lying on the bed, looking at the ceiling. The man on the phone had said, He's working on the boat. A dive shop, boats, being on the ocean. He wondered what Rod looked like.

He dialed the number again, hoping it wasn't too soon. A different man answered, younger-sounding. His heart began to pound. "I'm looking for Rod."

"You've got him."

He identified himself as Brendan Kirk and asked if the room was still available.

"Possibly," Rod said. "I'm still doing interviews."

"I liked your ad. It takes time when you don't want weirdos, doesn't it?"

"That it does." Rod described the condo and outlined the expenses. "I'll just tell you what I'm looking for. Extra money. Plain and simple. I own the place, it's a condo, so this is a good way to pick up some extra cash. There's plenty of room, over twelve hundred square feet."

"That's big. Hey, I was wondering, when I called earlier—that guy who answered said you were out on a boat?"

"Yes, I give diving lessons. Scuba diving."

"No kidding, like Cousteau? I always wanted to do that."

"Come by tomorrow night and I'll sell you some lessons."

He laughed. "But listen, I could come by tonight or tomorrow morning, if you can swing it."

"I can't do it. I'll be going out tonight. That's something else I should mention; my friend, Bette, stays over fairly often."

His hand tightened on the phone. Keeping his tone light, he said, "You've got your priorities straight. Since that probably takes care of tomorrow morning, how about we make it tomorrow evening."

"Fine." Rod gave him directions for the Green Line. Just before he hung up, Rod said, "It was a pleasure talking to you, Brendan."

"Yes," he said. "It was."

Afterward, he pulled the Yellow Pages from the lower rack of the telephone stand and looked under "Diving." In a display ad for Boston Divers he found the Beacon Street address. The store closed at six o'clock on Saturdays.

He took a quick shower and shaved. After drying off, he laid the wrinkled polyester pants and a rayon shirt on the bed and wondered if he could steal some better clothes from someone in the building. This was the type of junk Tony used to wear when he was being casual. Pretty good suits, but when he wanted to relax—trash. Showed Tony's true nature.

He put the clothes on anyhow. *Tonight's the last night*, he thought. *Be positive.*

Fifteen minutes later he was striding into Kenmore Square, enjoying the balmy summer evening. Going down into the subway station, his feet just touched the edge of the stairs. The Cleveland Circle train was about to leave, but he pushed the doors back, stepped in, and swung himself into a double seat. He crossed his legs and leaned back. *Sometimes things work the way they are supposed to.*

The train picked up speed, rocking from side to side in the narrow tunnel. It burst from the darkness into the busy late-afternoon traffic of Beacon Street. He ignored the stares of the other passengers who wanted to share his seat. Although he feigned nonchalance, his chest was tight with anticipation.

I know who's right. I make mistakes, sure. Tony was a mistake. But I don't make too many. That's what counts.

He noticed a flash of red several blocks up, in front of one of the buildings. When the train got closer, he saw it was a big red flag with a diagonal white stripe. Above it was a sign for Boston Divers. He waited two more stops and then got off. It was twenty to six.

Walking back, he chose a deli across the street from the store. He would have preferred being closer, but there was nothing to be done about it. Last thing he wanted was for Rod to see him before they met Sunday evening. Inside, he ordered a coffee and apple pie with vanilla ice cream. He poured two containers of cream and four teaspoons of sugar into the coffee. Jaw pumping steadily, he looked not at his food but at the storefront across the street. A line of melting cream stuck on his upper lip, but he didn't notice.

At five minutes before six, three men came out of the shop carrying scuba tanks and net bags. They loaded the gear into the back of a big black-and-gray pickup truck and drove off. A few minutes later, a man appeared behind the door and turned a sign in the window. CLOSED. Shoving away the half-finished plate, the man calling himself Brendan sat up straight and waited, barely breathing.

The same man came out of the store and began to pull the window gate down. Brendan's shoulders slumped. It looked as if his judgment had turned very bad. The guy looked almost forty! Standing up, looking around for the waitress, he thought, *Don't keep me waiting. I'll do something. Something worse than stiffing you on the tip.* Just as he was about to scream for her to stop talking to her girlfriend behind the counter, he looked back toward the dive shop. A girl in a green BMW had just parked in front and was getting out. She was tall, with red hair, a classic profile. Midtwenties.

She walked up to the man at the window gate and said something, a nice smile on her face. They chatted for a few moments. Then he opened the door and leaned in. A muscular man, also apparently in his midtwenties, came out. He kissed the woman, and put his arm around her. The balding man said something, and they all laughed.

Across the street, Brendan laughed also. The two girls halted their conversation briefly to roll their eyes.

39

Rod—and Brendan was certain he *was* Rod—opened the car's passenger door for the woman, then walked around and got in behind the wheel. He accelerated away from the store quickly, the BMW leaving a puff of blue smoke when he shifted into second gear. Brendan watched until it was over the hill, out of sight.

He left cash on the table and walked outside to pick up the trolley, weighing and tasting the feeling he had. A jittery feeling, one that was both attracted to the potential excitement and frightened by the possibility of more crushing loneliness.

I need to make a decision, he told himself, but he realized it had already been made.

■ ■ ■

"So," Bette said over spumoni, "how goes the roommate search?"

"This may sound simpleminded," Rod said. "But it really didn't hit me until I started interviewing people that they actually have the audacity to plan to move into my condo, use my refrigerator, my bathroom, my closets, and very likely spend some time hanging out with me. I just want the money. I don't actually want some stranger living with me."

"Mmmmm." She nodded while swallowing a mouthful of ice cream. "It does sound simpleminded."

"Thank you."

"I know it's hard to find the right person. It's like getting married."

He made a face. "Please, let's not make this out to be any more difficult than it is."

"Really," she said, leaning closer, smiling. "You've got to 'communicate' and 'work out differences' and 'trust each other.' And go with the ups and downs, like I am with Lori right now. All that good stuff."

"I can do that."

"Can you?" She smiled more broadly, and he leaned over and kissed her, thinking, *So what if it's an obnoxious thing to do in a restaurant?*

"Do you want to reconsider my offer?" he said, backing away a few inches. His palm lay against her cheek.

She looked down briefly, then met his eyes. "A rain check, please? I'm sorry, Rod, not yet."

"Fine," he said, tersely. "I'll have to go ahead and meet a guy I talked to earlier today. Seemed pretty good, but it won't be the same."

"I should hope not," she murmured.

6

ROD PUT HIS hands on his hips and gestured with his chin toward the room in general. "Well, this is the place. Living room here, kitchen right over there. The bathroom and my room are off the hallway there to the left. That closet between them, at the end of the hall, we would share for coats and stuff." He turned and pointed to the other end of the hallway. "The room for rent is down there to the right."

Brendan managed to observe Rod closely while appearing to check out the apartment. Rod wore faded jeans, a well-washed burgundy cotton shirt, and comfortable-looking boat shoes. He was a little taller than Brendan and appeared very strong.

He'd be hard to take on, if he knew it was coming, Brendan thought, both pleased and a little disconcerted. He said, "Looks like a great space."

And it did, truly. The ceilings were high, and a breeze flowed in through an open skylight. The condo was sunny even though it was late afternoon, and the linen-white walls and hardwood floors gave the place a light, clean feeling. Rod apparently wasn't fastidious—a good dusting wouldn't have hurt—but that was fine with Brendan. Fags always did too much cleaning; it was one of the things he looked out for. Nodding his head to show he was impressed, he asked, "Didn't you say you own this?"

"Yes, I was lucky. I bought this before the condo craze hit Boston full force. I was going to Boston College down the street, and I convinced my parents that it would be a good investment. So they helped me put the money down, and it has quadrupled in value since."

Brendan's smile tightened. "Your parents live nearby?"

Rod shook his head. "Try Seattle." He nodded for Brendan to follow and took a right down the hallway. "Door to your right here goes up to the roof, and here to the left is the room you'd be using."

Brendan followed him past the kitchen into a small but airy room that overlooked a tiny park. A desk stood in the corner, and beside it a bench with a set of weights. He calculated quickly that there were just over two hundred pounds on the barbell. A blue diving suit hung outside the closet door. "I didn't know these things came with feet on them," he said. "Just like little kid's pajamas."

"That's a thousand dollars' worth of state-of-the-art dry suit you're calling kiddie pajamas. A lot of our customers are into the sport just because they think it's macho. I'd appreciate it if you'd stay away from the store."

Grinning, Brendan said, "What do you expect from an English teacher?"

"That's what you do?"

"I used to."

Rod opened the closet door. A gray scuba tank stood in the back. A spear gun was propped in the corner, the triple rubber slings hanging flaccid. "All this scuba stuff and the weights would come out. I'll haul it down to the store and hope nobody sells it while I'm not looking."

"You could leave it here," Brendan said quickly. Then he realized that sounded too accommodating, so he tried to change the subject. "Do you do much spearfishing?"

"Not for some time now. I like looking more than shooting. Thing is, selling the stuff, I end up convincing myself that I need the latest and greatest of everything. That spear gun was a big deal a long time ago, but now everybody wants a compressed-air gun. So every time I sell one now, I have to remind myself that I don't really *like* putting a spear into some fish that was just minding its own business, so I don't really need another gun to sit in the closet."

"Taking pictures is your thing?"

"Sometimes. Mostly it's just a matter of being in another world. I'm plenty happy floating just over the bottom in twenty feet of water, looking at some stupid animal do its thing. Being a naturalist, without having to study."

"So you don't have to go to the Virgin Islands to have a good time?"

Rod shook his head and walked across the room to a photo. "For example," he said. The picture showed Rod in scuba gear, standing upside-down on a white ceiling, underwater. Brendan cocked his head to one side. "Ice," Rod said. "Quarry diving in the winter. It's never quite as much fun as it is work, chopping a hole in the ice and dragging on my dry suit in the van. But it's good for pictures."

"I hope they pay you enough."

"Well, I'm half owner of the shop. So paying the bills and doing my favorite sport every day is pretty good incentive. People want to go under the ice, I'm happy to show them how to do it."

"How old are you?" Brendan said, suddenly.

"Twenty-six."

"What did you take in school?"

"Business major. Why?"

Brendan's mouth went dry. He was going too fast. "I just wondered," he said, voice sounding calm. "Because you've got this great condo, own a business, and you're only a couple years older than me. I was just trying to figure out where I went wrong."

Rod looked away as he laughed, embarrassed. "Well, I was the type of business major who spent all his time screwing around on boats. I did learn how to latch onto a partner who knows a hell of a lot more than me about running a business."

"So it's working out."

"I'd say so. He'd say I still spend too much time screwing around on boats, and he'd have a point." Rod told Brendan about the race. "That's where my half of the rent comes in."

"Right. So now it's my turn—where did you go to school? You're not from around here, are you?"

Brendan's stomach clenched. This was where it could get tricky, but he was prepared. "No, upstate New York. Ithaca." He waited.

Sure enough, Rod's eyes lit with recognition, and he said, "Cornell? I had a friend transfer there during junior year."

Shaking his head, Brendan said, "Over at Ithaca College we hardly ever got together with the people from Cornell. We considered them a bunch of eggheads who didn't know how to have fun. Who knows what they thought about us."

"Well, I'll ask my friend if he calls sometime. Clear up the question for you."

They walked out of the bedroom into the kitchen.

Brendan said, "Don't go to any trouble. It probably wouldn't do my ego any good to hear. Do you keep in touch with the people you went to school with?"

Rod shook his head. "No. We all sort of drifted apart." He opened the refrigerator door and pulled out two bottles of ale. "Want a Molson's?"

"Absolutely." He actually didn't like the taste of beer, but he didn't like smoking cigarettes either, and that hadn't stopped him from learning how for Tony. So he waited, smiling appreciatively, while Rod uncapped the bottle. Then he took a long pull. It tasted bitter and gassy. "Delicious," he said. "Especially on such a hot day."

"Yeah, particularly when you've been out on the water, like I was today. Food tastes better and beer tastes so good, I begin to worry that I have alcoholic tendencies." Rod grinned. "But then I have a few more and don't worry about it."

He looked at Brendan curiously. "You asked me if I hear from many of my college friends. Are you worried I'll have a lot of parties or something? Are you up here for a job, or school? You need a lot of privacy?"

Brendan's face began to flush. "I'm just nosy. I *am* up here to study. I'll be getting my master's in education at Boston University."

"Right, you said you were a teacher. Where?"

Shaking his head as if chagrined, he said. "Ithaca High School."

"Ah, you're like me. Moved far since college."

"Exactly. That's why I decided to come to Boston. My life needs some change. And one of the few good things about being a teacher is having summers off. I don't have to start at B.U. until September, so I've got a few weeks still. It won't be that heavy a schedule; I'm here to have fun, too."

Rod sat on a stool in front of the kitchen island and waved Brendan to another. He put his ale down on the wooden countertop. "I'm working with a lot of people every day in a sort of social situation. We sometimes throw parties on the beach. You know, go diving, then eat the lobsters and crabs we caught. Bring a cooler and some charcoal. So I don't feel the need to have a whole bunch of people around at home. Do you?"

Brendan spread his hands out, palms up. "Who do I know in Boston to invite?" *All my pals are dead*, he thought.

Rod smiled. "One visitor who will be over a lot is my friend Bette."

"Have you two been going out long?"

"A year."

I wonder why she didn't move in, Brendan thought.

They discussed the neighbors, rent, and utilities while drinking another ale apiece. Then Brendan set the bottle down and said, "So what do you think? Am I a weirdo, or no?"

"Could be. But probably no worse than me. So let's give it a shot." Rod put out his hand, and Brendan shook it.

"Fooled you," he said.

HE AWOKE THE NEXT morning and immediately reached for the Yellow Pages, paper, and a pencil. He scratched down a list on the left side of a lined sheet, then, using the Yellow Pages, matched several addresses on the right side. Twenty minutes later he had shaved and showered and was walking out the door.

I know what I'm doing this time. You've got to prepare, do your work. Pay attention to the details.

First, he needed to clean out the last of the money in Tony's account. So far he had used automatic tellers in Kenmore Square, in Coolidge Corner, and on Beacon Hill. Now he went to one in the Prudential Center. He had no idea if the police could trace who used the machines. Or, for that matter, if they had the slightest reason to be looking for Tony. It was just that things were looking too good to do something stupid like use the same machine twice.

But, stupid or not, he needed money for

7

his preparations, and to pay rent. Couldn't forget rent. And Tony's card came through one more time. Altogether, he had a little over a thousand dollars bulging in his pocket when he stopped in at a Greek-American restaurant on Newbury Street and breakfasted on a stack of sopping blueberry pancakes. He was already more relaxed, and the waitress flirted and told him to have a nice day. He left a good tip and said thank you on the way out. This Rod was going to work out fine.

Back in Kenmore Square, he went into a used-clothing store and bought jeans, tan corduroys, a pair of chinos, a belt, and five cotton short-sleeved shirts in an assortment of colors: red, navy, green, pink, and white. To them he added a light, tweedy-looking jacket and several long-sleeved shirts with button-down collars. At a shoe store down the street, he bought a new pair of Docksides. He scuffed them a little on the sidewalk but decided not to worry if it was obvious they were new. Everyone buys new shoes once in a while.

He couldn't stand wearing the sticky polyester pants and shirt he had on for another minute, so he went back to the furnished room, tossed them into the trash, and pulled on the chinos, the navy shirt, and the jacket. He looked in the mirror, turned to a profile, and smiled. English teacher goes back to college. Take the jacket off and step behind the wheel of a boat.

Leaving the jacket behind because of the heat, he hurried back to Kenmore Square and bought some Boston University notebooks and a T-shirt. He bought three new course books related to education. *That's enough new stuff*, he thought, and walked down Commonwealth Avenue to the next store on his list. He found it directly across from a long, gray Boston University building.

Inside, a young man with sweaty black hair, wearing a shirt emblazoned LIBRARIANS ARE LIBIDINOUS, looked up from a box of books he was unpacking and said, "If you want an air-conditioned place to wait for the trolley, you're better off at the ice cream store down the street."

An idiotic thing to say, Brendan thought, but he smiled pleasantly and said, "No, I read the sign. I'm here for the books."

"It's just we don't get too many customers on a Monday morning in August," the clerk said ruefully. "I picked a hot day like this one to sort these books we just got in. A great idea until I started doing it, being so damn muggy and all. Being conscientious isn't all it's cracked up to be."

"I'm sure," Brendan said. "You get these books from B.U.?"

"Yeah. Students turn in last semester's books for credit on the ones coming up. Preread books we've got to call them now, instead of used." He glanced around the empty store and whispered, "It's so dumb, I tell you. Moldy oldies, I call them." He laughed through his nose, looking at Brendan with raised eyebrows.

Getting only a blank look from Brendan, the clerk shrugged his shoulders, picked up a heavy cardboard box, and set it on the table. Brendan watched him sort through the top layer of titles. Among them was a tired-looking volume of Shakespeare's complete works, paperback copies of *Candide, Gulliver's Travels, A Catcher in the Rye, Lord of the Flies, A Separate Peace,* and *Crime and Punishment.*

"I'll take the box," Brendan said.

The clerk raised his eyebrows. "You want all of them?"

Brendan put twenty-five dollars down on the table. "That enough?"

"Yeah, sure. But why these? You haven't even looked through them all."

You're lousy at what you do. "That's okay. These are what I want."

Apparently suspicious that he was letting something rare go, the young man rummaged through the box quickly. "Nothing special in there as far as issues," he said, looking to Brendan for a contradiction. He added quickly, "But they're good just for reading. What course are you taking?"

None of your frigging business. Turning away to hide the irritated look growing on his face, Brendan noticed a shelf of used typewriters in the back. Leaving the clerk unanswered, he strode over quickly and picked one with a gray plastic carrying case. The price tag said thirty dollars. He added a twenty and a ten to the cash on the table.

"Hey, those typewriters we take in for a few bucks and sell for a few bucks. If it breaks, I can't fix it, so you better run a piece of paper through it now, make sure it's the one you want."

"I know what I'm doing," Brendan snapped, and then remembered who he was now. "Sorry," he said, with a smile he thought disarming, "I don't want to be rude or anything, but I'm all set with this stuff."

The young man crossed his arms and shrugged. "Don't worry about it."

Brendan hefted the box on his shoulder, picked up the typewriter, and said, "Thanks for your help."

"That's what I'm here for," the clerk said, holding the door open. He watched Brendan stride out to the trolley tracks, carrying the heavy box and typewriter with apparent ease. "Enjoy your studies," he muttered. "You schmuck."

■ ■ ■

Later, in his room, Brendan sat on the edge of the bed and wiped the sweat from his forehead. It had been a long day. After leaving the bookstore, he'd gone to a furniture store and bought a cheap bed and dresser, leaving Rod's address for delivery. Now he wanted to skim the books he had purchased, just in case Rod asked him something that an English teacher really ought to know about the books on his own shelf. Methodically he took each book out, memorized the title and author, then raced through sections in the beginning, middle, and end.

An hour and a half later, he reached to the second layer of books and pulled out a green-and-gold-colored volume.

A sense of dread and shame swept through him.

He dropped the book and kicked it across the floor. Jerking his head first to the door and then to the window, he felt suddenly exposed, watched. *What does this mean?* he thought, angrily. *Who put this here?* For a moment, he thought of going back to the bookstore for that complaining little shit, and asking some questions in a way that would really give him something to whine about.

He inhaled deeply, then exhaled. He closed his eyes. The muscles in his jaw began to relax.

The play was standard fare for students, just like the rest of the books in the carton. God, *he* ought to know that. It made sense. Still, the damn thing sure did give him a shock, showing up at a time like this.

But after all, even then things had worked out. In a way. Wiping his mouth with the back of his hand, he considered ripping the play apart and flushing the pages down the toilet. But he didn't.

Instead, he picked up the book and began to read.

8

THE PLAY WAS *Cyrano de Bergerac*. It had been his only performance onstage, back when he was in high school in Connecticut, back when his name was, and always had been, Guy Nolan.

He was in the spring of his junior year. His hair was a little longer then, and his uniform most days was jeans, sneakers, and a cotton sweater over a short-sleeved shirt. A good day was one in which nobody noticed what he wore, said, or did. That was also a bad day, and he hadn't yet learned how to deal with the dichotomy.

The changes started in Mrs. Bennett's third-period English class when she distributed the green-and-gold copies of the script to each student. Not knowing the effect the little bundle of printed paper was going to have on his life, and those of quite a few other people, he concentrated on catching Mrs. Bennett's eye. Her attention made him feel less hollow. She was a pretty woman in her late twenties, with long, black hair and a tight figure that caused the other guys in the room to grin at each other when her back was turned. That day she wore a black pantsuit. Gold jewelry gleamed at her neck and wrists.

T.D. Weston sat two seats ahead of Guy, his big hands clasped behind his head. Massive biceps swelled inside his football jersey, and the mock ruby of his class ring glowed in a shaft of sunlight. He didn't reach out when Mrs. Bennett offered him a script, so she dropped it on his desk, her face blank.

Rude bastard, Guy thought.

She gave Andrea Sable a copy. Andrea was blond, with pale but pretty blue eyes and absolutely flawless skin. She smelled faintly of baby powder. Guy had been silently willing her to turn and talk to him since she had transferred into the school, sitting one desk diagonally across from him, two months ago. She hadn't yet, and until last week he wouldn't have known what to say.

Now, if she did, he could have asked, "Are you making it with my brother yet?"

Just as Mrs. Bennett reached Guy's desk, T.D. started to laugh. It was always disconcerting to hear his laughter. Too high-pitched for someone so big, a laugh that was always *at* somebody, and all too often at Guy. Mrs. Bennett's mouth turned up sardonically, as she dropped a copy of the play on Guy's desk and turned back to T.D. "No doubt you've seen the nose," she said.

"It's a real honker." T.D. held the cover illustration of Cyrano up to the class. "And you know what they say big noses mean."

"No, I don't, Terrence. Why don't you tell the class?"

"T.D." he corrected. "And you wouldn't like me to tell, trust me." He put his fist up to his pug nose and intoned nasally, "I mean it's a *big* honker."

She addressed the class. "You'll see when you read it, that nose has quite a lot to do with the play. You'll also see that if Cyrano were here, Terry would be dodging a sword point now." She smiled at T.D., and Guy felt a twinge of jealousy. "Cyrano knew how to handle guys like you, Terry."

Letting his wrist go limp, T.D. lisped, "Well, I sure am glad that silly Cyro isn't here then."

"Interesting," she said. "With that lisp, I guess the reverse is true of small noses."

Guy smiled broadly; the rest of the class hooted aloud. Score another one for Mrs. Bennett. T.D. glared at her, and she smiled back imperviously. Then he seemed to remember himself and shrugged his heavy shoulders.

To the class, Mrs. Bennett said, "As you may or may not know, each year I direct the school play. I do it because it is something I enjoy, and I know a little something about it—and that makes me two up on any of the other teachers in the school." She walked to the front of the class.

Guy's hands began to tremble. The everyday undercurrent of classroom noise—shuffling feet, whispers, rustling paper—all ceased. Mrs. Bennett had everyone's attention.

She laughed. "Okay! I see some scared faces out there. I hand out a script and already you're up in front of Mom and Dad and six hundred other people. And every one of those six hundred people is saying terrible things about you, and your mom and dad are covering their eyes. Am I right?"

She won't do this to me, Guy thought.

Mrs. Bennett put her hands out as if to stop a moving car. "Relax! I'll say it up front—nobody will be forced to be part of that. It's a lot of work, and I only want people who want to be up there." She sat back on the edge of the desk and crossed her arms. "But," she said, smiling, "as part of this course, I do expect everyone here to get up in front of this class within the next five weeks and take part in a scene."

The class groaned. Guy felt a cold stab in his stomach. He sat up straight. Mrs. Bennett waved down the flock of hands that flew up. "Look at all you chickens coming up with excuses already. I realize most of you would rather have your eyes jabbed out with a sharp stick than stand in front of a group. But you've got to learn to do it sometime. The very least you'll learn is that you won't actually die, no matter how much you hate it."

She walked behind her desk and opened the bottom drawer.

"You'll be surprised at how much fun it can be. There are always a few hams that emerge." She put a small cardboard box on the table.

Guy raised his hand for the first time all year. Mrs. Bennett's smile softened and she nodded to him.

"How much does this count toward the final grade?" His voice sounded rusty and harsh. T.D.'s back stiffened, and he turned around in his chair and looked directly at Guy. His small eyes glinted in his broad face, and he made his hands tremble in mock terror. From the front row, Laura Teason giggled. Andrea Sable glanced at T.D. and Guy, then looked back to the front of the room.

"It's a requirement," Mrs. Bennett said. "You won't pass without it."

Guy dropped his eyes. He could feel the rest of the class watching him.

"My advice to all of you is to study your lines," Mrs. Bennett said, passing out the envelopes she had taken from the box.

Laura waved her arm. "Mrs. Bennett, do we have to memorize the whole thing? We can't just read from the script?"

The teacher rolled her eyes. "Let's give it a try the right way first." She divided the class into five groups, by seating. T.D. was in a group up front; Guy was matched with Andrea, Bob Ernson, Jeanne Topal, and Sam Leigh. "You'll see," she said. "You'll work out different pieces within it, and just end up having to memorize a few pages. I don't expect you to remember a whole scene—unless you want to. Reach into the envelope and pick a character."

"What if I get a girl's part?" Bob said.

"Then put her back and try again. I don't expect you to be that good an actor."

"Why can't we just pick the part we want?" Laura asked. "I don't want a big one, where I have to study too much."

"Who does? This time, just take your chances. Like in the short story you read last week, 'The Lottery.' But we'll only stone you if you're *really* bad."

Guy looked up to find Andrea standing beside him, holding the open envelope. "Your turn," she said. He avoided her eyes, reached in, and picked out a folded slip of paper. "What did you get?" she asked.

Still looking down, he unfolded the yellow lined paper.

Cyrano.

■ ■ ■

Five weeks later, Guy stood in front of the green chalkboard with Andrea and performed the final scene. She had obviously worked hard preparing for her role as Roxane, and would probably have needed only occasional prompting from Mrs. Bennett had she been working with anyone else.

But with Guy, she barely stumbled at all. He made it easy for her, he was sure of that. It was as if their conversation were real, and her response to him was all that she *could* say under the circumstances. Bob, Jeanne, and Sam did a terrible job with their parts, but that didn't surprise him. Not that he hadn't been nervous earlier, too—he had vomited his breakfast in the lavatory toilet after the second period change.

Yet when he stepped in front of the class and spoke his first lines, all the numbing fear was replaced by Cyrano. The duelist was in him, moving in his body, while he went along a half-second behind, both thrilled and terrified. It was as if he had stepped through a window to a different place, and for the first time his heart beat real blood, his lungs took in real air.

And best of all, the derision on T.D.'s face meant nothing. *Try me*, Guy thought.

In the brief silence after the final line, Mrs. Bennett said quietly, "Fantastic job."

The class clapped and whistled. Bob slapped him on the back and said, "Where's the hidden mike?" Andrea grabbed his hand and squeezed, her face flushed, eyes alight. "I don't believe it!" she whispered. Guy was fiercely happy for the first time he could remember, maybe ever. He promptly walked over and asked Mrs. Bennett if he could audition for the school play.

"Of course you can, Guy. You don't have to ask; just be there and try out." She grinned. "Given the job you just did, I should be asking you. Just do that again next week, and I'm sure you'll do very well." She tapped his cheek lightly. "Hello, you ham."

■ ■ ■

That's what happened. But when he had opened the slip of paper five weeks before, he'd immediately screwed up his courage to ask Bob and Sam if either of them would switch roles with him. Both refused. Bob was the closest thing to a friend Guy had—yet he shook his head without a moment's consideration and said, "No way. You're stuck with it."

Sam said, "You've got to be shitting me. Watching you is going to be like watching a comedy act. If I didn't have to be up there at the same time, I'd bring in some popcorn and sit beside T.D." Sam cackled and slapped his desk. He yelled over Guy's head, "T.D.! He wants to switch! He's going to be the one with the schnoz."

Guy avoided looking at T.D. but could hear his affected southern drawl. "We goin' to have some fun-n, boy."

The month before, he'd been required to give a speech as part of a social studies class. He was so nervous that the paper rattled in his hands and his voice squeaked. For weeks now, T.D. had been saying to people, "You want to see my Guy Nolan imitation?" and would stutter and rattle a piece of paper in his meaty hands until it ripped apart. Guy first heard about it when Chucky came home and said, "Guy, you're famous. People are talking about you all over school." The next day he saw T.D. in the hallway with a group around him laughing. Guy ducked out the side door and walked around the building and into the main entrance.

Acting was different from making a speech, though. He was being told—forced—by Mrs. Bennett to become someone else. To put on a new personality. And he found he could do it. Cyrano was as ugly as Guy was plain, and he had raging emotions where Guy felt only a vague emptiness and dissatisfaction. At times Guy wished he had an obvious flaw, a physical deformity, to explain why he always ate lunch by himself, why people would drift away after only a few minutes of drab conversation, never to seek him out again.

Cyrano could take on a hundred men in a sword fight, compose poetry while dueling, be witty at all times. And his inner self, his vitality, was loved by a beautiful woman, though it took a lifetime for her to know him. Guy felt emotions he had always avoided in his own life as soon as he started working on the lines. And when he stepped up in front of the class, he realized he was *in control*, and for that time opposite Andrea he knew what being alive felt like. And he knew that he would do anything to feel that way again.

■ ■ ■

Andrea walked out of class with him. Her shoulder bumped against his in the crowded hallway, but she made no attempt to move away. "I loved doing that," she said. "I know it's kind of a geeky thing to do, but I loved it." She giggled quickly to herself. Turning to him, she said, "I can't believe how good we were. I mean, that sounds like, wow, what a big ego and all . . . but you know we did *really* well. Much better than I expected."

She was at that moment both beautiful and insignificant to him. He only vaguely remembered being the boy who worshipped her from his school desk. It was as if his skin were stretched by Cyrano's being. "Was it?" he said, easily. "As soon as you said the first line I knew we were going to take off. Did you work hard beforehand?"

"Every night for two weeks. That was too much. I don't *like* working that hard—but I like looking stupid even less. So I made my little brother sit on the couch and feed me lines every night. Did you study hard?"

"A few nights."

"A few nights!" She turned, amazed. "You're kidding! You led me through that whole thing."

"It came easily to me, I guess. Cyrano and I think alike."

She gave him a sidelong glance. "Your friend, Cyrano."

"It works." Casually, he added, "If you want to rehearse a little before the audition, I'll show you what I mean."

Her eyes narrowed slightly. "You know I've dated your brother?"

"I'll forgive you."

She didn't smile. "It's my business how I spend my time, but still, I'm not sure that would be the best idea."

"We're just talking about rehearsing." He stepped closer. "Andrea, I really want to do that part. I know I'll be good at it. You and I were great in front of the class, and I know we'll do the same on the stage. So never mind the rest." He looked past her shoulder and said, "Besides which, Chucky's not going to worry about you and me. Count on it."

She nodded slightly. "Yes, I guess that's true."

He felt some of his elation seep away.

Cheerful again, she said, "Yikes, listening to you, we better get started. We just might find ourselves up there. I've got study hall tomorrow, fifth period."

He did too, and had spent more than one lonely hour looking at her surreptitiously from across the cafeteria. She'd never turned from her new friends to look his way.

"Really?" he said. "I didn't know that. I'll get the hall passes from Mrs. Bennett and meet you in the cafeteria."

"Oh, Guy," she said in a rush, "if we get those parts, I don't know if I'll kiss you or kill you. Standing up there in front of all those people!" She closed her eyes and gave a small scream. Passing students looked their way and smiled.

"Well, when it gets to that point," he said, "ask me."

■ ■ ■

"Since when did you get balls?" Chucky asked that night.

They were having supper in the dining room. Guy's mother had just redecorated the room in a Revolutionary War motif. He didn't know why. But it meant they would be eating there instead of the kitchen, until the novelty wore off.

He looked up at his brother, then immediately back down at his plate. Chucky was wearing that little smile. Guy felt sick. "What do you mean?" he said.

"Dirty bird," their mother said. She reached out and flicked her finger in Chucky's hair. "Talking like that at the table."

Chucky grinned over at her. "You don't know, Ginny. I heard he's trying out for the school play. With *my* girlfriend."

She tittered. "Surely you're not worried about Guy stealing your girl, are you? Isn't she that lovely blonde I saw you with in front of the mall?"

"Yeah, that's her. Knockout, huh?"

Ginny shrugged and took a sip of her whiskey sour. "I suppose. But then all the little girls you've gone out with have been good-looking. Wouldn't you say so, Art?"

His father glanced up from his plate, cleared his throat, said, "Certainly," and continued eating. She looked at him with a weary expression and then turned back to Chucky. "She's very pretty, dear."

Meanwhile Chucky was gazing at Guy wonderingly. "No shit, you're going to stand up in front of the whole school in tights?" He made like an effeminate fencer, limp-wristed. "Forsooth, hark what I say or I'll stick you in the butt."

Ginny squealed, holding her napkin to her mouth. She looked at her husband, who paid no attention to the exchange, then back to Guy. He kept his eyes down and tried to concentrate on the food. The meat loaf had too many onions, he thought, but Chucky liked it that way.

"Oh, Chucky," she said. "It's just you and me with a couple of sticks in the mud." She took another sip of her drink and held her glass close to her face, observing Guy over the rim. Her eyes looked owlish with dark blue eye shadow.

"So what *did* get into you to decide to try out for a play?" She glanced at Chucky, then back at Guy. The corner of her mouth twitched. "I didn't think you were interested in anything besides watching TV."

Guy shrugged.

The glass clicked down hard. "What does that mean? Can't you give me a better answer than that? You'd better if you're going to talk pretty to that Andrea up onstage." She winked at Chucky.

"I've been practicing for a class," he said quietly. "I liked doing it, so I want to audition for the play."

"What?" she said, putting her hand to her ear. "You're mumbling. If you're going to talk, speak so you can be heard. Enunciate."

"Maybe they can get an interpreter for him," Chucky interjected. "You know, somebody who goes around beside Guy here onstage, tells the audience what he's supposed to have said."

She giggled. "Stop, Chucky."

"It's a good idea, Ginny, don't knock it. Thing is, Guy might get attached to him, and want him to go around, help him in class and all. Take on that nasty T.D."

"Chucky!" She covered her mouth, laughing. "No, come on."

"Problem is, then you'd just have the jerk that's following him around saying, 'Leave me alone, pretty please, I didn't do anything to you,' only louder. That gets boring after a while, right, Guy? You get tired of saying that, right? You'll have a hell of a time keeping interpreters around."

"Fuck off," Guy said.

Chucky's face emptied of expression. His gray eyes observed Guy coldly, and he said, "Looks like you and I need to have a conversation later on, little brother."

Ginny's glass slammed down on the table. "How dare you talk like that at my table!" She whirled to her husband. "Did you hear him? Are you going to just sit there?"

His father looked at him with an expression close to curiosity. He tugged at the already loose knot of his tie and said, "What's gotten into you? Apologize to Chucky and your mother."

"Chucky said 'shit.' Why doesn't he apologize to me?"

Ginny slapped her hand on the table. "I won't have it. If this is the type of thing your damn play is going to bring into the house, then maybe you had better go back to watching TV, mister. I will not listen to this childish, filthy nonsense. I try to express some interest in what you're doing, ask a few questions, and in two minutes we're down to disgusting, vulgar conversation."

"Try to express an interest?" Guy's voice began to rise. "What the hell do you think I've been doing for the past five weeks? If Chucky were trying out for this part, you'd be in his room every night, feeding him his lines. You'd be buying the goddamn material for his costume and taking snapshots for prosperity. Don't *give* me this 'express an interest' bullshit."

A knowing look crossed her face. Ginny attempted a smile, and he felt nauseated. *She's so goddamn transparent*, he thought.

"I think I see, dear. You're feeling a little jealous, and maybe that's my fault a teensy bit—"

"Don't flatter yourself," he cut in. "And I don't want to hear the latest from your analyst."

Ginny's mouth opened, then closed. She sat back in her chair and crossed her arms. Chucky rested his chin on steepled fingers, and the little smile returned to his face. His father's eyes were open wide, amazed.

When she spoke again, Ginny's voice was raspy. "You've never hurt me like that before. Get up, and get away from me. If you harbor those feelings toward me, you shouldn't eat the food I cook or live under my roof. Don't come crawling back to me later. I don't want to hear it."

He laughed shortly. "Don't wait up."

But *he* did. He stayed in his room the rest of the evening, rereading the play. Around ten-thirty he heard a quiet but heavy tread in the hallway. The doorknob began to turn. Chucky. But he had locked the door for just that reason, and his brother went away without saying a word.

Later, after midnight, he left the room quietly and stole into the den. His father kept his wallet and car keys on the desk. There were forty-nine dollars in the wallet, and he took three, plus most of the quarters on the desk. In the living room he found four dollars in his mother's pocketbook he didn't think she would miss. He added the seven dollars and change to the thirty-five already in the envelope in his nightstand and went to sleep thinking it had been a very good day.

The next morning Chucky surprised him. Guy had just come back from the bathroom and crawled into bed when Chucky pushed the door open. Guy squinted in the light from the hallway, his heart tripping. He should have relocked the door.

"Come on, Slog," Chucky said. "I'll give you a ride to school today."

"Why?"

Chucky shrugged. "Why not? Come on, hurry." He left the door open and walked down the hallway to the bathroom. In a few minutes, Guy could hear the shower running. Relieved, he lay back on the bed and thought about this morning, in light of what he had said last night. His mother wouldn't be up yet, most likely, and it didn't really matter what his father had to say. Chucky might not be a problem, after all—he could have waded right in swinging a few minutes ago if he'd wanted.

Guy decided to take the ride. He could count on one hand the times in the two years Chucky had owned the car that he'd offered a ride, and Guy was frankly curious about why he had today.

Then he remembered fifth period with Andrea and got up and raised the shade. In the morning light, the room appeared uncluttered to the point of being stark. The single bed was too short for his height, and the tangled bed sheets were the only sign of discord. Guy peered in the mirror. Good, no acne, though he needed a shave. He was up to once every three days now. Putting on a light blue robe, he walked down to the closed bathroom door. The water was still running. He knocked loudly. "Hey, Chucky, leave me some hot water." Not hearing an answer, he went in.

Steam billowed around him. Chucky looked around the shower curtain, his wet hair swept back. "What's your rush?"

Though they were close to the same height, Guy felt reedy compared with his brother. Chucky had a deep chest and heavily muscled arms. His stomach rippled from the thousands of sit-ups he'd done over the years, training for football, wrestling, and baseball teams.

When his brother stepped from the shower stall, Guy turned to the mirror and began to brush his teeth. Chucky dried himself, apparently oblivious to the fact that his nudity made Guy uncomfortable.

"This is new," Chucky said. "Seeing you in here this early. Didn't know you went in for all this hygiene stuff. You going to take a shower, too?"

Guy spit out the toothpaste and rinsed. "I shower every morning. Only I do it when there's enough hot water, after you leave. While you're out having breakfast with that asshole T.D."

Chucky grinned. "T.D. isn't so bad. He grows on you, like a fungus. He's so obnoxious you figure he can't be for real."

"Yeah, he's for real," Guy said bitterly.

"Ah, you just hold a grudge because he tried to stick your head in a toilet."

"He would've and flushed it too, if you didn't come by."

"Maybe." Chucky waved it off. "It's something that happens to you when you're a freshman, and *you* get to do it to someone when you're a sophomore."

"Never happened to you," Guy replied from old habit, and immediately kicked himself.

"Because they didn't make sophomores, juniors, or seniors big enough back then," Chucky finished, and flicked his towel at Guy on the way out. "Don't forget to shave, Guy. Better that Andrea thinks you don't have any hair than to see those scraggly things sticking out."

He's going to let it go, Guy thought, amazed. To confirm it, he said, "Chucky. Hold it a second. About what I said last night . . ."

His brother smiled and shook his head. "No big deal. We can talk about it in the car. Hurry up, I want to stop for some breakfast on the way."

Guy grinned to himself while spreading on the shaving cream. Grabbing breakfast with his brother on the way to school. Damn. He should have stood up to everybody a long time ago. Things sure were changing fast.

Chucky was putting down the top on his Camaro when Guy came out of the house. The car was white with broad orange stripes, wide

64

wheels, and chrome sidepipes. Guy sat in the black bucket seat on the passenger side and marveled at how different the car seemed when you were inside it. Chucky slid in, pumped the accelerator twice, and turned on the engine. The car idled roughly at first, then settled into a deep burble. Chucky swung away from the curb quickly, the tires sounding rough on the asphalt.

"So what's up?" Chucky asked.

Guy shrugged. "You tell me. This is about the third ride you've given me in two years."

"Then it's about time, right?" Chucky grinned, and Guy smiled back. It was hard not to, sometimes. Guy had more reason to be wary of his brother than anyone, but still, when Chucky gave that grin, eyes crinkling, it was hard not to respond. It was as if he had said, "I know you," and there was a great joke between the two of them.

The neighborhod was showing signs of the busy morning commute, and Chucky kept his foot heavy on the gas pedal, passing cars on the winding road into town. The Camaro was fast but sounded a little rough when it was being pushed. Guy pointed at the hood and frowned. Chucky nodded and said, "Yeah, it needs a tune-up. . . . So listen, I know I don't give you a ride that often, and I probably should and all, but I know you don't get along with T.D. And I like breakfast, and, you know, he and I hang out. You'll see this morning, he's not such a bad guy. None of them are."

Guy felt uneasy. He hadn't planned on them. T.D. and Jerry Palmerson and Billy Tanner. Of course, they would be at the diner too. "You want to grab some coffee there?" Guy said, pointing to a fast-food restaurant called Lucille's Spa on the corner. Chucky screwed up his face. "You've got to be kidding me. Lucille imports cockroaches for Lantern Falls. Only place you can get them in town. We'll go to The Drake's. Best hash and eggs in Connecticut. You'll like it." The grin.

Guy figured now was the best time. "Listen, Chucky, I was out of line saying what I did last night. I know you were just giving me a hard time."

"Right," Chucky said. "But the important thing in all this is what you said to Ginny. She's doing well these days with the shrink and all, and you are out of line making comments like that. No doubt about it, right?"

"Right." Guy nodded. This was going to be a lot easier than he thought.

"So you'll apologize to her tonight?"

"Sure. I mean, I would've anyway."

"Good."

They were silent for a few moments, then Guy continued. "So look, this doesn't mean anything, but Andrea and I are planning to rehearse a little beforehand. I mean, we really might have a chance at these parts. Honest, you should've seen us."

Chucky looked straight ahead and didn't say anything.

"Really, I wish you had," Guy said, his voice sounding a little desperate to himself. "It must be what it's like when you win in a wrestling meet. The feeling, I mean. I've never felt it before."

Chucky looked over now, smiling, and said, "Yeah, it's a great feeling. I never get tired of it."

"So you understand," Guy said quickly. "It's okay, me working with Andrea on this? That's all it is, you know. To get the part."

"Let's talk about it over breakfast."

Chucky swung into the small parking lot in front of the silver diner with a green neon sign at an angle over the door. The Drake's was popular with all the jocks in school. Guy had never eaten there before. From the car, Guy could see the massive form of T.D. sitting at the window in the far left corner. "All right! Corner booth!" Chucky said, raising his fist. T.D. smiled around a mouthful of food and responded by hitting the window with his fist. As they walked in, the wiry man behind the counter yelled, "T.D.! Keep your frigging hands off the window. Bad enough I got to let apes in here, they got to rattle the bars too." T.D. growled back with his mouth partially open. Guy could see food inside and felt slightly sick again. Where was he going to sit? T.D. was taking up one side of the booth now, and Jerry and Billy were crammed into the other side, their backs to Guy. T.D. frowned around his mouthful of food when it dawned on him

66

that it was Guy standing beside Chucky. *This is going to be awful,* Guy thought.

"Hey, Drake, we'll both have the hash and eggs," Chucky said. "That's what I have every day, right?"

"If you say so, Chucky," the cook said. He gestured toward Guy with his chin. "Okay?"

"Oh yeah," Guy said, distractedly, glancing back at T.D. Both Jerry and Billy were twisted around in their seats now, looking at him. *Goddamn it.* He turned his attention back to the grill. Drake used plenty of grease. A puddle of fat formed under the hash he slapped onto the plate, and he shoveled on huge helpings of fried potatoes plus toast. With a flourish, he flipped two eggs on top of the hash.

Chucky handed Guy a tray and ordered coffee, milk, and orange juice for the two of them. "Here," he said, squirting a dollop of red onto Guy's hash and home fries. "The Drake doesn't put bottles of ketchup on the tables, 'cause he's cheap. Right, Drake?"

"Right, Chucky."

"Hey," Guy said, "I'll float away—milk, coffee, orange juice."

"Don't argue, Guy. Who's the jock here, you or me? I know what's good for you." Guy felt himself grinning back at his brother. Why couldn't it always be like this?

Chucky picked up his heavily laden tray and started toward the booth in the back. Guy could see T.D.'s frown deepening as they got closer. *Where am I going to sit?* Guy thought urgently. All the booths around were taken. There were no chairs, just fixed stools around the counter, all full.

Chucky placed his tray on the table beside T.D. and said, "Oh, shit!" He looked to the right and then to the left. T.D. exchanged a grin with Billy Tanner, and his shoulders began to shake. Guy felt a sickening lurch in his stomach, and then his brother turned abruptly, looked him in the eye, and said, "I wonder what the *hell* you're going to do." And he raised his hands to his hips, elbowing Guy's tray back.

Guy screamed as the scalding coffee poured onto his chest, followed by the milk and orange juice. Chucky sidestepped away neatly. The glasses and plate crashed to the floor and shattered.

"Oh, for *Christ's* sake!" Drake yelled.

Guy started to step back but lifted his foot instinctively from the crunch of broken glass. He put his foot in the hash and slipped and fell.

T.D. was pounding the table. "Too much! Chucky, you are too goddamn much!" he howled. He leaned out of the booth and said in a falsetto, "*Fantastic job* there, Guy. But I don't know if we can *use* anybody wearing ketchup and coffee. How about if we call you?" Billy put his head back and roared. Jerry reached out and slapped T.D.'s palm.

Guy looked down at himself, smeared with food and coffee. Everybody in the restaurant was staring at him. Drake was striding around the corner now, holding a broom. "For Christ's sake, get up. Get up!"

Guy looked up at his brother and whispered hoarsely, "Chucky. You've got to take me home. I need some more clothes."

Chucky had the little smile on his face again, and his eyes were cold. "I've got to finish my breakfast and go to school."

"Chucky," Guy said desperately. "You can't leave me like this."

"Leave you? I'm not going anywhere—you are." Chucky sat down in front of his meal. "Fuck off, Guy."

EIGHT YEARS LATER, as Brendan, he moved into Rod Konrad's condominium. He carried the blue makeup case and a cheap new suitcase while the taxi driver hefted the book box and typewriter into the outer lobby. "You all set?" the driver asked.

Guy nodded and paid the fare, plus a dollar for a tip. The cabbie wiped his sweaty forehead with the bill and jammed it into the pocket of his baggy jeans. "I knew there was a reason I didn't work for Mayflower," he said, and stalked off.

Guy ignored him, pushing the button under Rod's name. The buzzer sounded, and he latched the door open. Rod met him halfway down the stairs. "You need a hand?"

"Sure."

Rod moved down the familiar steps quickly, his gray Adidas sneakers a light blur. "This is it?" he called up.

Guy balanced the case on the newel post at the top of the stairs and said, "I told you I didn't have much stuff."

9

"Yes, I know, but don't you have anything from the last apartment?" Rod carried the books and typewriter up to the landing without any visible effort.

"No, that was a furnished apartment, in a way. The guy had just been divorced recently, and there was plenty of furniture."

Rod opened the door. Guy was once again impressed by the light, airy apartment. Healthy.

"So what are you going to do for a bed and furniture?"

"All that should be delivered today. I went down to a used furniture store on Commonwealth."

Rod made a face. "A used mattress in the city of Boston?"

"That I bought new. Discount store."

"Good. The landlord bit doesn't sit easily with me, and I'd hate to start off our first day with a lecture on cockroaches."

"You've got the right," Guy said. "It's your place."

An hour later the bed and dresser arrived. Soon after, the mattress was delivered, and that driver also went away grumbling about his tip. "You're the last of the big spenders," Rod said, grinning.

"It's his job," Guy said, sharply.

Rod frowned, and Guy felt a sudden panic. "People don't give tips on your job, do they?"

"No. I was just kidding you, anyhow."

There was an embarrassed silence. Guy felt the blood pulse in his temples. *Too anxious, too anxious,* he thought. He tried a smile and said, "That's a relief. I thought for a moment I was going to have to fork over another dollar."

"Worse than that," Rod said, "how about picking us up a pizza? Bette will be coming soon."

"Great," Guy said. "Just give me time to clean up." In the bathroom, Guy locked the door quietly before looking through the medicine cabinet. Rod seemed very healthy; there wasn't even any aspirin. Just a tube of toothpaste, a toothbrush, sunscreen, a comb, razor, shaving cream, deodorant, and dental floss. Two coarse green towels hung on the door rack, and a blue terry-cloth robe on the hook. Satisfied, Guy stepped into the bathtub thinking he would buy some towels and a robe for himself that would look the same, only different.

A half hour later, when Guy stepped out of his bedroom fully dressed, Rod said, "Jesus, we look like a couple of prep school escapees." They were both wearing chinos, boat shoes, and Lacoste shirts. Rod's shirt was blue, Guy's red.

"We should wear name tags," Guy said on his way out the door. As he walked toward Beacon Street, he saw the green BMW turn onto Englewood and head toward the apartment. Bette glanced at him, and he resisted the urge to wave. *I already look the part. It wouldn't take much for me to be the one kissing her.*

■ ■ ■

"How much time do we have before your roommate comes back?" Bette murmured into Rod's ear. He hugged her tighter, her cheek smooth and warm against his. He inhaled the clean scent of her hair and said regretfully, "Five minutes at the most. Too soon."

"That *is* too soon. We *know* that." She chuckled easily.

"Is that supposed to be flattery?"

"Rod, you'll think I'm a jerk for bringing this up now, but I do wish it was me moving furniture in here."

He pushed her back slightly and frowned. "You're right, jerk. Why now?"

"I don't think we *should* yet, I'm just saying that's what I wish."

"If it's what you want, and what I want, why shouldn't we?"

She locked her hands behind his back and squeezed. He was surprised to find his breath grow short.

"Jesus, you're strong."

"Don't forget it," she said against his chest. "And I'm holding on to you. And you know my other experience with moving in with someone. We drove each other crazy and out of the apartment within two months. And you've done that—twice."

"Different people, different time, different ages."

"I know, I know." She spoke against his neck, her breath warm. "But the truth is, it scares me how much I feel for you. And we just keep going along so well the way we are right now, so I figure, why take a chance on blowing it?"

71

"That's the truth?"

She opened his shirt and kissed him. "Yes," she said.

"Well, that's a lot easier to take. But we'll have to move forward at some point."

They heard footsteps in the hallway and a key sliding into the lock. Bette grasped Rod's arm by the wrist to look at his watch. "Damn it," she whispered. "Time to clean up our act."

■ ■ ■

They broke apart as he came in. Guy felt an immediate stab of jealousy. She was even prettier close up, and now her blue eyes were shining and her face was flushed. He hadn't been able to see before how pretty her mouth was, sculpted and full. He realized he was staring as she walked forward, hand out to greet him. Put his lips against hers, taste that mouth, as Rod had undoubtedly been doing a few moments before, that was what he wanted to do. Aloud he said, "I hope you're hungry. I know I am."

She laughed and shook his hand, saying, "That's a constant state with Rod and me. I'm Bette. Since you're carrying the pizza, you must be Brendan." She took the pizza from him, put a slice onto each of three plates and the rest in the oven to keep warm. Rod poured beer while Guy laid out napkins on the kitchen bar.

"Tell us about yourself, Brendan," she said.

He took a deep breath and went through his Ithaca story. She listened carefully, giving him her full attention. She didn't seem to know anyone there or know anything about Ithaca College. Which was truly lucky, as he knew only what he'd been able to glean from a summer he'd spent subletting an apartment with a graduate student who'd never made it to the fall semester. His name then had been Don Caldwell.

About growing up, he kept as close to the truth as possible, changing the location from Lantern Falls to Ithaca. Father in insurance, older brother named Chucky, a mother he didn't say much about. Naturally, he left out what had happened during junior year. Said he became an English teacher because it gave him a professional excuse to read fiction. He had a bad moment when Bette said she loved to read, thinking she would eventually pick up that his literary knowledge was too weak for an English teacher. He resolved to downplay that aspect of his story.

She was a good listener. He paused, realizing that he had barely touched his food—he had been talking almost nonstop for twenty minutes. He abruptly began to eat, marveling that he could lose track of himself so easily. It both pleased and frightened him. This couple was the right choice; they could teach him things. But he didn't want to blow it, say something that gave him away and have to start all over.

Lost in thought, he didn't realize she had asked him a question until Rod said, "Earth to Brendan."

He looked up, blinking. "What?"

"Bette is being nosy," Rod said. "She wants to know if you have a girlfriend."

"I'm not being nosy. I just ask about the important stuff."

Guy's face began to flush. "Well, I've only been in Boston for two months. It's hard to meet people."

"It is, isn't it?"

Rod said, "I know you think you're here in this apartment having dinner with us for your own reasons. Need a place to live, go to school, whatever." Rod waved his hand disparagingly. "That's not why, though."

Guy smiled at that and said, "Oh? Why *am* I here?"

"Well with me, I see two lower units for the V-4s sitting there, drinking beer."

"So you said earlier."

"And Bette, *she* sees material for her roommate."

"Rod!"

Guy felt short of breath. Too fast, they were moving too fast. "Only if she's as pretty as you," he said to Bette. His smile felt strained.

Bette acknowledged the compliment with a smile and said, "Don't worry about Lori. She's gorgeous."

"In that case, I'll worry about me."

They all laughed. Rod drank the last of his beer and checked his watch. Turning to Bette, he said, "Are you all set?" To Guy he said, "We're going dancing now. You've got keys, right?"

Guy was stung. They were leaving him. Everything was going great, and boom, they were going off and leaving him. His face reddened. *Relax. It's always like this at first. What do you expect?* He hurried over to the kitchen sink with his own plate, keeping his face averted.

Bette glanced at him, looked back at Rod, and raised her eyebrows. He shrugged and nodded. "You're welcome to join us, you know," she said. "We're going to the Dance Factory just outside of Kenmore Square."

"Thanks, but I don't want to be a fifth wheel," Guy said. *Keep pushing*, he pleaded silently.

"You won't be," Rod joined in. "We'll make you get your own girl."

"Thanks, but no."

"Come on," Bette said, squeezing Guy's upper arm. She gave him a sidelong look, that beautiful mouth curving mischievously. "Unless you've already got a hot night lined up, Guy, you're coming with us."

■　■　■

Inside the Dance Factory, the music was loud enough for Guy to feel against his face. The walls were covered in black cloth, and on the far wall a black man with greasy, curly hair screamed about a girl you wouldn't take home to Mother. The rock video also played on television monitors hung from the ceiling. Rod towed Bette off in the direction of the bar, and she waved Guy to follow. He plunged through the crowd after them, keeping his forearms out in front, hating the touch of so many strangers. When he finally made it to the bar, Rod asked him what he wanted to drink.

"Molson's."

"Good choice." Rod bought three ales. Guy started to pour his into a glass until he noticed Rod drink from the bottle. He slid the glass back onto the bar when Rod and Bette turned to look at the dance floor. Guy stood just inches behind Bette. He could smell her perfume. The impulse to pull her back was hard to resist. She leaned into Rod, and Guy moved slightly closer.

They turned abruptly and faced him. The blood drained from his face, but he instinctively covered by moving even closer and putting his hands on their shoulders, saying loudly over the pulsing beat, "So don't hold up on the entertainment any longer. I'm ready to see some dancing."

On the floor, Bette and Rod moved well together, spinning in time with the music, clearly playing off each other. From the side, Guy could see Bette's eyes sparkling, and thought, *I could make her look that way.*

When they came back, Rod said, "Your turn." He touched Guy on the shoulder and pointed to a girl with short blond hair, who was swaying in time with the music at the end of the bar. "Why don't you ask her?"

Guy's stomach clenched.

"From what Rod tells me," Bette said, "he's got a good eye for this type of thing. She'll probably say yes."

His heart was pounding now. This was all too soon; they were pushing him too fast again. He struggled for an offhand tone. "Maybe when *he* asks, they do."

"Oh, go ahead, Brendan," Rod said. "Don't be shy."

"No." He said it with more vehemence than he intended. They stared back, surprised. Even over the pounding music, their lack of response was excruciating. Bette spoke quickly into Rod's ear. Guy looked past them to the exit, hot anger bringing tears to his eyes.

Bette stepped forward. "Tell you what. Since this is a skill Rod is not going to need anymore, we agreed he should take a shot at it for old times' sake. He'll see if she wants to come over—is that okay with you?"

No, it wasn't, but what could he say? "Sure. Thanks."

They watched Rod approach the girl. She looked up at him and stood on her toes, touching his arm for support while he spoke into her ear. "Isn't that adorable," Bette said. Rod pointed in their direction, and Guy smiled back with the most relaxed look he could muster. Bette waved and said, "Join the party."

"This hasn't turned out to be a very private evening for you, has it?" Guy asked Bette.

"Don't worry," she said, touching his arm. "I'm having fun. I'm very direct about things anyhow. If we didn't want you along, we wouldn't have asked you." The girl and Rod started back toward them. "Now *she*, on the other hand, will have to take her little paw out of Rod's pretty soon. Or else I'll have to be direct and nasty."

"Jealous already?"

"No, not really." Bette laughed. "I just like to hear myself snarl sometimes."

"She's for me, anyhow."

Bette looked at him closely. "If this is embarrassing for you, we'll back off."

"No, I would have asked somebody soon anyhow," he said and put on a smile as Rod took him by the elbow and introduced him to the blonde. Her name was Ericka. He said hi, and she nodded, expressionless. Rod stepped back with Bette, consciously avoiding the appearance of looking on. Bette turned closer into him, talking with a faint smile curling her lips.

"Would you like a drink?" Guy said.

Ericka shrugged. Her light hair framed a pretty, unlined face. She looked about twenty and had applied makeup artlessly in a way he found attractive. A little girl caught in her mother's dressing room.

"Do you live around here?" he tried again.

She nodded impatiently, and he began to feel a little desperate. "Do you work in town?" Her eyes slid past him to the video.

He glanced at Rod and Bette; they were watching him. Bette turned away immediately, and he felt all the more humiliated. Then the girl tugged on his sleeve. "Let's just dance."

He followed her onto the floor. Her back seemed rigid, but below the waist she moved seductively. With her blank stare and erotic walk, he found himself thinking of her as if she were some sort of pneumatic doll supplied by the club. He felt off balance and lumbering. She turned to face him, her expression still cool. Glancing away, he saw Rod off to his right, smiling.

She started to dance, and he did too, face hot, moving from side to side on stiff legs. The music cut into a faster beat, and Guy fought to keep up, hating the sound, hating the inevitability of making a fool of himself. And a little piece of him began to hate Rod for forcing him there. He told himself it was too soon for those thoughts and watched Ericka. She looked past him, a private smile touching her mouth.

A line of sweat formed on her upper lip, and Guy was surprised by the sudden urge to lick it off. Her upper body now matched her lower, as if tight strings loosened in her. She moved to the music as he wished he were able to. The music didn't go any deeper than his skin, but she was definitely beginning to affect him.

Her eyes focused on him, and the smile flickered. He stopped moving, ready to bolt, and then she stepped close and pulled his head down. Her lips touched his ear. "Watch the video." Taking his hands, she pulled him so he could see the wall screen, and then she started dancing again, her face turned to the television-size screen hanging over his head. It was a surrealistic adventure set in a violent future. The hero was a tall blond man wearing black leather. Silver studs winked dangerously on his arms and fists. When he danced, he fought, lashing out at circling enemies. Spinning away from his lion-maned woman, he loosed a sling, killing attackers with a flashing silver projectile.

Guy was entranced. It was like when he had just become some-body else. The danger was there, mixed in with the heady power, the *willingness* to take someone else's life and run it harder than they ever would. His dancing became more confident, looser, the tension flowing out of his arms and legs. Ericka moved closer and placed her hand on his chest. Guy smiled, catching her scent: sweet, with a hint of perspiration.

"You like watching," she said.

The muscles in his arms suddenly tightened, and he looked at her warily.

"I do, too," she shouted over the music, eyes bright and alive

77

now. She startled him further by leaning forward abruptly and kissing his chest, her lips and breath hot through the light shirt. Stepping back, she started dancing again, springing harder with the music, the muscles in her legs showing through her jeans. Her green eyes caught his frequently during the rest of the dance, and the smile he had thought vapid before took on new meaning.

The music ended, and the video flashed through a TV robot firing laser beams from its arms, a Maypo ad with a boy flexing his muscle, a scene from "I Love Lucy" with her crying, and a motorboat trying to run over a man swimming in a crowded harbor. Then another song started, showing four rock stars riding through a field on motorized tricycles. It looked as though it had been shot with a hand-held camera.

"This sucks," Ericka said. "It's an old one." She walked to the bar, and Guy followed, the moist spot on his shirt cooling. Ericka asked him to buy her a White Russian. On the way to the bar, they passed Rod and Bette. Rod had his hand underneath Bette's hair, cupping the back of her neck. "Brendan, you're looking pretty hot out there," he said.

"Thanks to you," Guy said when they were out of earshot. Ericka drank with both hands on the glass. She finished the drink in three gulps and licked the milk from her lips. Guy sipped his beer. They didn't talk, just watched the screen together until another hard-driving song pulled them back to the dance floor. For the next two hours, they danced and drank. She wouldn't or couldn't carry on a conversation with Rod and Bette. So after two feeble attempts, he and Ericka kept to themselves, except for an occasional wave across the dance floor. Guy felt both trapped and fascinated by the girl.

A little after midnight she slid the empty glass from her sixth drink onto the bar, turned, and burrowed her face against his chest. Guy stiffened as she wrapped her arms around him and hugged him close. Her breasts pressed against his belly, and the smells of alcohol, sweat, and perfume mingled. She said something he couldn't hear but could feel, a wet warmth on his chest.

"What?"

She looked up, eyes glazed. "I said, okay."

"Okay?"

She cocked her head to one side. "You know."

"I've got a roommate," he said quickly. "It would be great, but I came with those people."

"I didn't," she said, pulling the neck of his shirt open. "I came all by myself."

Guy shrugged helplessly. "We just met."

"No." She stared up at him. "No, you're not queer, are you?"

He looked around for Rod. Luckily, Rod looked up, and he caught his eye. Guy reached around her and tapped his watch, eyebrows raised. Rod nodded.

"I've got to go now," Guy said, disengaging himself, backing away. Sudden tears began to trickle down her face, and she said, "What's the matter with me? Why are you going?"

"Nothing," he said. "Nothing's the matter with you."

"Then stay with me."

He hurried through the crowd to catch up with Rod and Bette.

10

"WHAT'S THAT ON your clothes, son?" said the man who stopped for him outside The Drake's. Guy mumbled that he had spilled his breakfast. "Damn. Sit on this newspaper then," the man said. "I don't need eggs and grease on the seat." Guy slid the paper underneath himself and cranked down the window. He didn't talk for the rest of the short ride. "Better luck with the rest of your day," the man said when he got out.

Ginny's car was gone. Emergency meeting at the shrink, probably. He went into Chucky's room, took a baseball bat from the closet, and stood in front of the stereo system. His brother had done more reading in the month before he bought the stereo than he had all his life. Stereo review magazines, ads, brochures, sale flyers. He finally chose Pioneer floor speakers, a Marantz receiver with over fifty watts per channel, and a Garrard turntable with a featherweight tone arm. "Don't even consider using this," he had said to Guy the day he was hooking it up.

Guy swung the bat with all his might.

It whooshed harmlessly within an inch of the turntable. He sat on his brother's bed and leaned his forehead against the rounded end of the bat, trying to control his breathing. He told himself it would be the end of the play. He told himself getting back at Chucky wasn't worth that. He told himself Chucky might literally use the baseball bat on his knees.

He almost succeeded in avoiding thinking about the look of cold rage that would sweep over his brother's face. The look that would curdle any bravery in his own heart and leave him helpless before whatever Chucky wanted to deliver. He could never understand it. Other people could say, "Yeah, my brother pounded me." *Pounded me. That's what it feels like.* But he could no more chatter about his brother beating him than he could discuss masturbation in English class.

He put the bat into the closet, took a shower, and went into his room to study the play. Occasionally he would read the lines aloud, his voice carrying powerfully through the empty house. He would have been happy to stay there until his fifth-period meeting with Andrea, but around eleven he heard Ginny's car pull into the driveway. He hurried into the attached garage, knowing that she would not open the door. After the kitchen door slammed, he rolled his bike quietly out the side and started off for school.

■ ■ ■

Mrs. Bennett saw him in the hallway. "You're supposedly absent today, Guy. You weren't in my third period."

"Yeah, it was my mother. She's sick. I drove her to the doctor."

Mrs. Bennett frowned. "Nothing serious, I hope."

"Nothing new. Sorry about your class."

She smiled. "Don't worry, I know you're not the type to just cut."

The next period was about to start, and she glanced at her watch. He said quickly, "I was going to go looking for you."

"Oh?" She smiled at him quizzically, and he realized this was already the longest conversation the two of them had ever had.

"For hall passes," he continued. "Andrea and I want to rehearse a little before the audition, and we both have study hall next hour. I was hoping you'd give us passes, and we could go to an empty classroom."

Mrs. Bennett smiled and pulled a yellow pad from her pocketbook. "How can I say no to such initiative?" She filled out a pass in his name with quick, neat printing, ripped if off, and started on one for Andrea. She glanced up at him, and her cheek dimpled slightly. "Andrea is very pretty, isn't she?"

His throat felt constricted. He nodded.

"One thing, Guy," she said, stepping closer, her hand touching his forearm. "I just want you to remember that the primary object is to have fun with this play." He nodded again, her warm touch rendering him dumb. "Don't take it too seriously." She looked at him intently. "There are lots of reasons to be in a school play. Brings the ham out in people, as I said before, or people think it'll make them more popular. Once in a while I see someone who really wants to act, and here's their first chance—that's the best, I love to see it. I realize you might be one of those people, and I'm glad to see you're giving it a shot. But really, Guy, don't take it too much to heart. I've got over thirty people trying out, and more than two-thirds of them are there because we have that New York theater trip later in the spring." She laughed, shortly. "More like Danille Bennett spends two days keeping kids from throwing televisions out hotel windows or running off to Times Square. . . . Anyway, the point is, don't expect everyone to put as much work into this as you already have, because they're doing the play for different reasons. And don't expect them to appreciate how much *you've* done."

"I won't," he said and cleared his throat. "Has anyone said there's a problem?"

"No, no," she said, flashing a quick smile. "But I do have eyes. And you did just ask for a pass for Andrea, who is the latest pretty girl your brother has set his sights on."

Guy looked around. All the classroom doors were closed except the one to Mr. Pendergast's social studies class. Guy turned so his back was to the open doorway. "Why are you telling me this? Are you saying I don't have a chance at Cyrano?"

"No, I'm not saying any such thing. I don't know that you *will* get it either, honestly. That's why we have auditions." She cocked her head to one side. "I just wanted you to know that I realize it must be difficult having such a popular brother. Football and baseball captain. Doesn't look as if he works hard to get the good grades that he does. All that. I just want you to take our play for what it is, a school play. Relax and have fun. Don't get too competitive or worry about what people say." She squeezed his arm and started to leave. He backed in front of her, and her smile dropped a notch.

"What does Chucky have to do with the play?" Guy's heart began to hammer.

"I assumed you knew," she said, frowning now. "He picked up a script this morning."

■ ■ ■

Guy stood near the beige double doors of the cafeteria until Andrea looked his way. She was sitting near the windows with Laura Teason, Sarah Denton, and Heather Greely. She nodded to him curtly, said good-bye to the other girls, and started for the doorway. Guy watched Laura lean forward suddenly and say something to Sarah and Heather, her eyes flickering rapidly between him and Andrea. The three of them erupted into laughter but covered their mouths when Andrea looked back. Her lips whitened.

"How long is this going to take?" she said, striding past him.

His heart sank. She must have heard what Chucky did to him at The Drake's. "We just have to do one bit of the last scene for the audition," he said. "Just a page or two, and we already know it pretty well."

"So why are we doing this at all?"

"We already talked about it. You know."

She didn't answer. When he started to walk into the first open, empty classroom off the main hall, she simply shook her head and kept walking. He followed her around the corner to Room B10, near the teachers' lounge. "Trying to hide?" he joked. By her cool glance he decided it was true and stopped smiling.

"Let's get started," she said.

At first she recited from memory. Then, with an impatient shake of her head, she picked up the script and began to read in a perfunctory manner. He continued, remembering the lines easily. Her frustration broke against him like water against a rock. Now that he was in the role, her opinion—as Andrea, not Roxane—didn't matter so much. She glanced up, apparently irritated that he was able to return the lines without the script. Then she lost her place. When he patiently repeated his line, her face turned bright pink, and she slapped the script onto the table. "Maybe you have time for this, but I don't."

"It *is* a lot of work," he said. "But you're already most of the way there."

"That's not the point."

"Sure it is."

She stared at him balefully and crossed her arms. "No, it isn't. I'll tell you what the point is. I thought we were clear that the only reason I was meeting with you was to study the script."

"It is." His mouth was suddenly dry and his face began to flush.

"That's not what I hear."

"From who?"

"Everybody. I agree to study with you and next I hear you're going around telling everybody I'm your girlfriend. And the way they look at me, they think we're doing even more."

"I didn't!"

"Then where did they get it? I didn't tell anyone we were going to study together. No one."

"Then it's just the reading we did. You know we looked good up there."

"No." She shook her head. "Billy Tanner sat next to me in biology today. He said . . ." She averted her eyes and then continued. "He knew we were studying together today. But he said *studying* as if he meant something else. And I got the clear idea he heard it from you. So I'd like to know what the hell you're telling people."

"Billy Tanner does anything my brother tells him to do. This morning I told Chucky we were going to study. He must've told Billy later."

She pursed her lips and shook her head. "No. It wasn't like he was mean to you. It's just that what he was saying wasn't true." She blushed. "He said you were a good guy and he was glad things were working out for you and me. That you told him about us this morning at breakfast."

Before or after Chucky knocked me down? he thought. Aloud, he said, "That's not what happened. Chucky must have told him to say it."

"Chucky? . . . Why?" She shook her head emphatically. "Laura Teason came up to me and said she'd heard about it. Sarah and Heather knew about it before Laura even sat down with us. Everybody knows it except me!"

"Andrea, I didn't tell anyone anything like that. It's got to be Chucky having them do it."

She shook her head thoughtfully. "I can't see it. . . . I talked to him about an hour ago. Said I'd been hearing some rumors, and he said, 'About what?' I told him, and he said he knew we were going to be rehearsing together, so what was the big deal? He wasn't worried."

Guy restrained himself from answering. Apparently Chucky hadn't told her that he had a script also. Maybe he wasn't really going to try out? But if he did, Guy would be left standing onstage mouthing Cyrano's words to himself while Andrea auditioned with his golden-haired brother. He shrugged. "I don't know what to say. I told Chucky this morning you and I were going to study. That's all."

"That's all? No lie?"

"No lie." He added miserably, "Who would I be fooling?"

She looked at him for a full thirty seconds. She nodded, apparently deciding something, and he expected her to get up and walk away. Instead she said briskly, "Okay, then. I guess it's just one of those things. A rumor. Though I can't believe Chucky had anything to do with it . . . he's just not like that. Tricky and whispery. He'd come right out and say it if he had a problem." In a softer voice she added, "Like me. You know, when I'm angry I sound mean. Everybody does, I guess. It's just that I hate people talking behind my back. Really hate it. When I get embarrassed my face turns red and everybody knows they've got me. . . . Listen, what you said about not fooling anyone—it's not that no one could possibly believe that you and I would go out. Why wouldn't they? I mean, you do seem nice and all—it's just that I don't know you very well, so it drove me crazy when I thought you were spreading stories." She put her hand out, smiling cautiously. "Friends?"

He smiled back uncertainly, and her smile widened beautifully. *Now that she's dumped on me she can afford to be generous.* "Friends," he said.

Mercifully, they slipped back into Cyrano and Roxane within a few minutes.

■ ■ ■

That Saturday he took the forty-nine dollars he had accumulated over the past few weeks and borrowed his father's car to go to Bridgeport. An hour away, it was the biggest distance he had driven since he got his license.

Which meant he had to listen to his father. "Be careful. Just because everybody's insured doesn't mean you don't have to watch out for the idiots on the road. I know what the car looks like going out, I'll know if it looks different coming back."

"Okay," Guy said. "I'm running late."

His father's lips pursed. "You mean you're going to be rushing down there? Why didn't you leave more time in the first place? That's how people get hurt, property damaged."

Guy opened his mouth, then shut it. He nodded.

His father pointed his finger solemnly. "Remember that."

Father knows best, Guy thought, watching him walk up the steps, his legs spindly in Bermuda shorts, wearing the same black socks and shoes that he did at the office. No doubt the car was insured against ice floes. When he talked, his father talked insurance policies. Always about what *could* go wrong, or about what *could* happen to the foolishly underinsured—sometimes even a real-life horror story about someone incredibly stupid enough to have bought no insurance.

But never about somebody who beat the insurance and walked away rich. *Maybe it never really happens,* Guy mused. *Or maybe he's got a plan himself and he doesn't want to screw it up.* He waved to his father as he pulled away from the curb. *Anything's possible— just not likely with the old skinbag.*

Guy was indeed a few minutes late. The place was hardly what he expected. Instead of an ornate stone building with leaded-glass windows, the address torn from the Yellow Pages brought him to an old wooden building that had apparently once been a factory. He followed the point of an illustrated sword upstairs to the Rabson Fencing Academy.

A tall man with a hawkish face appeared at the top of the stairway. "You're late," he said.

Guy looked down the stairway quickly.

"Who are you looking for? I'm talking to you. Why weren't you here at the time we agreed upon?"

Guy stared back blankly.

"Well?" the man demanded.

"I got lost," Guy offered finally.

"Why? I gave you directions." Rabson put his hands on his hips. He looked about thirty and wore a burgundy warm-up suit. His black hair was swept back but not oily. Guy suddenly realized he was waiting for an answer.

"I don't know."

"Well, I do. Either you weren't listening or you listened and decided against doing what I told you. Which was it?"

"I just made a mistake. That's all."

"That's not an option."

Abruptly Guy decided he'd had enough. Chucky, his mother, now Andrea. Not this guy too. "Well, you better make it an option. Driving an hour to get an obedience lesson from somebody I planned to pay money to sounds like a mistake to me, too."

"I don't care about your money or your drive, kid."

"Fine." Guy turned down the stairway. "What you say doesn't count."

Guy heard the man take a step down behind him, and his stomach chilled. "And what's that supposed to mean?"

Surprising himself, Guy spun around and answered, "You and I made a deal, and yeah, I'm all of five minutes late. So you're telling me to go to hell, forget the lesson, forget what we said on the phone, never mind that you *said* you would teach me what you could about fencing."

"In two hours. It's almost a complete waste of time."

"I told you," Guy retorted, "it's for a play, a part in *Cyrano de Bergerac*. Anything I know about it will be that much more than the jocks who are trying out, too. It might make a difference. But you don't care about that, you don't care what you said."

Surprisingly, the man smiled, his teeth white against his tan. "Well, there is some fight in you. It's always good to know. I know you told me it was for a play, and I didn't tell you to go to hell, I *gave* you hell for being late when there's only two hours to do so much. There's a difference, you know." He put his hand out. "Joel Rabson, and you're Guy, right?"

Guy nodded and slowly reached out his hand. Rabson pumped it quickly, firmly, and then turned and walked up the stairs. "That's good," he said. "I'm glad I didn't just beat on someone who came up to use the bathroom." After a moment Guy followed him into the studio. Here it fit his image a little better. On the clean wooden floor were six strips, each about five feet wide and forty feet long, painted in yellow. Sunlight flowed through several windows on the freshly painted yellow walls. Gleaming weapons hung in racks, all looking more narrow and fragile than he'd imagined a sword would.

Rabson nodded. "Go ahead." Guy selected one from the set near the end of the row. These looked a little bigger and thicker than those on the left. "That's an épée; the others are foils," Rabson said. "You wouldn't even be touching one of these for a month if we were going to do this right. I'd have you doing leg work." The silver-colored hand guard around the grip was the only thing that made sense to Guy. The grip itself was twisted at an awkward angle. Holding it the way he would hold a hammer felt very strange.

Rabson said, "All right, that'll be our first step." With quick, sure moves, he showed Guy how to hold the épée properly. "This particular one is a competition blade, with the wiring hooked in." He showed Guy how a wire, called a body cord, could be plugged in behind the bell guard and then run up his sleeve out to a cord hooked up to a light box. "This way we electrically register the touches. I hit you, a light and buzzer go off on your side."

Rabson shook his head again. "Why are we wasting time? Cyrano doesn't care about this, does he? He's too busy making rhymes, and when he runs somebody through they know it."

"You've seen the play?" Guy said, eagerly.

"Sure." Rabson grinned. "College. Even jocks get out once in a while." He put the épée away and slid another one out of the rack. It looked at bit lighter and had a plastic tip on the end. "We'll practice with this," he said. "It isn't as stiff as the competition blade. I don't know what they'll supply you with for the play. Probably some foils, or maybe even a rubber sword, which will make the whole thing look really stupid. I'll show you what I know of theatrical fencing instead of the real thing. You make big, grand movements so everybody gets to see what you're doing, including your partner. For safety just use the flat of the blade. Without wearing a mask, these can be dangerous. You could lose an eye—one of those competition blades could go right through your temple if you're not careful."

He gave Guy a heavy cotton pad to put on his chest and a steel-mesh face mask. He himself wore a heavier leather-and-cloth vest. For the next hour he went through the basic steps and lunges with Guy and showed him a simple cutting action and a parry. The clash of steel was everything Guy expected it to be, and he absorbed Rabson's instructions with ease. "Now in the play, after making broad cuts back and forth, let the point slip underneath his blade, aim for the belly, and lunge the way I showed you." Guy stepped forward immediately, cut three times, disengaged, and lunged. The point rested firmly against Rabson's leather-covered stomach.

"That's it!" Rabson laughed, binding Guy's blade away with his own. He took his mask off and slipped it under his arm. Wiping the sweat away from his forehead, he said, "You're a good athlete, Guy. What other sports do you play?"

Guy cocked his head. "Athlete? My brother's the jock, not me."

"Sure you are. I teach people fencing for a living, remember? You're a quick study and have lots of speed and coordination."

Shaking his head firmly, Guy said, "Believe me. I don't mix with jocks."

Rabson lifted his eyebrows and said mildly, "I wasn't talking about your social skills."

Guy realized Rabson, with his fine muscles and quick movements, had probably always been good at sports and might resent Guy's attitude. Struggling to be offhand, he added with a shrug, "More like they don't mix with me unless they want a talking soccer ball." Guy felt his face go red.

"Trouble? You get pushed around at school?"

Guy started to answer, but then just nodded miserably. *My brother pounds me.*

"Why do you let them?"

Guy groaned inwardly. Not an adult lecture coming up. Putting on a quick smile, he said, "They don't exactly ask my permission."

"No, they don't. But if you don't do anything, you're giving it to them." Looking at his watch, Rabson said, "How much money did you bring today?"

Guy said cautiously, "Forty-nine. Forty-five after I pay for gas."

"Okay, give me the forty-five and put down the épée. There's another class coming in at two, and I've got another crash course to teach you. That is, if you want to learn."

"I do," Guy said quickly. "Karate?"

Rabson waved that away. "Sort of. More a matter of doing it to them before their pea brains decide to do it to you. It's technique and a . . . a *willingness* is the best I can say. I've got that willingness, I can tell you about it. Whether you've got it or not, I don't know. I'm going to show you a few things now, a few simple but painful things for the next people who want to kick you around. Whether you use it or not is all up to you. Up to that willingness."

"Thank you, Mr. Rabson," he said awkwardly. "I appreciate it, I really do."

"Joel," Rabson corrected. "Forget it. You're paying for it, remember?"

"Why are you doing this for me?"

Rabson grimaced. "Because I can, I guess. And because you need it. Now stop blabbing and pay attention."

■ ■ ■

A little under an hour later, Rabson said, "Okay, that's all I have time for. Don't go starting any fights with this stuff, but maybe you can take care of trouble when it comes. At least convince them that it hurts to pick on Guy Nolan, whether they win or not."

"Thanks, Joel."

"No problem, kid." Rabson slapped him on the shoulder and smiled his white smile. "I'm going to hit the shower before the next group comes in."

Guy sketched a wave and started to leave, then remembered, turned, and said, "Oh, Joel—is there any chance of me buying a used épée today, just to practice with?"

Rabson made a face and shook his head. "Not for today. I could put a new one together for you, but it would cost more than the four dollars in your wallet. If I sell one of the weapons I use for class, then I'll just have to replace it." He smiled. "Now if you want to sign up for a class, learn how to do the whole sport right, I'll be happy to have you. Throw in a foil at half-price."

91

Guy shook his head. "I'll be spending my time in rehearsal."

"Right," Rabson said. "Good luck, kid."

"Thanks." Guy started down the stairs. When he heard Rabson close the door to the locker room he hurried to the studio quietly, took an épée from the middle of the rack, and silently made his way out the door to his car and home.

AFTER THEY'D LIVED together for a week and a half, Guy asked Rod if he could take diving lessons.

"Your money is my money," Rod said.

They agreed he could attend all three weekly classes instead of the usual one class per week, so he could finish sooner. "After all," Guy said, "what else do I have to do with my time?"

Two weeks later, walking out of a movie theater, Bette asked Rod much the same question. "I like Brendan," she added quickly. "It's just that he's always *around*. What does he do when you're at work?"

"Comes to the store. He stops in most days, but doesn't stay long. Just talks, looks around. Always has a reason, you know, that he was walking by. Going to get groceries, going to the bookstore. He's bored waiting for school to start. Taking diving lessons is a good idea. If he passes the certification tomorrow, he can keep busy diving. Assuming he hooks up with somebody as a partner. He's friendly with me,

11

but he doesn't seem to mix with the group very much. Anyhow, once school starts, it'll probably be the last we see of him."

"What does Leo think about him being in so much?"

Rod frowned. "I don't know. He doesn't say anything about him. Brendan's friendly enough, and they say hello and all, but they don't really talk."

They walked in silence for a few minutes, lost in separate thoughts. Abruptly Bette said, "Maybe I can get Lori into flippers too."

"Still driving you crazy?"

"That's the word for it. A month since she broke up with Thomas, and she acts as if it's some world record for being alone. She wants to date someone new right now. Not tomorrow, not this weekend, right *now*."

"There's an obvious solution here."

"Tell me about it. Lori knocks on my door at midnight and asks me why I haven't introduced her to Brendan yet. Just in case I forgot the first dozen times she asked that night."

"That's why I've been seeing so much of you at my place?"

Bette elbowed him. "Yes, that's the only reason. But really, I want her to take the time to calm down. She's a charmer, and I love her, but she can be such a little heartbreaker. I told you how Thomas dropped her. I'm afraid the next guy might be shot out of his shoes if he looks at her wrong."

Rod shrugged and said, "Brendan's a big boy."

"Think so, huh?" Bette looked at her watch and said, "Let's go to my apartment tonight. Lori should be home now, and you can decide if we should introduce her to your roommate."

"I know her," he protested. "She's gorgeous and she's smart. Who wouldn't want to go out with her?"

"I know, but you haven't seen her this past week. She's nervous and prickly. And she's acting as if any man will do, but she's actually hard to please. She's getting all wound up sitting in the apartment by herself but refuses to go out to clubs without me."

"What about her other friends?"

Bette shook her head. "Lori just doesn't have that many woman friends. She's quick to see other women as competition. In my opinion, she always focused too much attention on the man in her life."

"That's possible?"

"With some exceptions," Bette said, sweetly.

"So how come you're not competition?"

Bette smiled. "It's hard to say. Probably because I liked her as soon as I met her, in spite of the way she can be. Before we moved in together, she always kept in touch, and I could tell she was making a special effort to be a good friend. You know how different we are, but sometimes we get to laughing so hard my face hurts and I can't breathe. With her, I'll do the things I'd be too much of a chicken to do on my own. And I keep her sane."

He put his arm around her shoulders. "So listen, if her sanity is slipping now, let's get Brendan and Lori together. Maybe something happens; maybe nothing happens. Maybe we get an apartment to ourselves once in a while."

"Talk to her, then decide." Bette looked up at her apartment windows. Every light was blazing. She said, "Then it'll be on your head."

. . .

The warm smell of popcorn filled the air on the second-floor landing. Bette leaned on the door and whispered, "Get set," before turning the knob and stepping into the apartment.

Lori stood before the stove in the small kitchen wearing red jogging shorts and a black tank top. Her long, curly hair was more tousled than usual. She brushed it back with her hands and said brightly, "All right, Bette! You've brought a great-looking man up to the apartment." She strode up to him quickly with the bowl of popcorn under her left arm. She grasped his chin with thumb and forefinger and pushed slightly. He responded with his best dashing grin, first right profile, then left. "Very good, Bette," she said. "I'm sure you must be pleased." Abruptly she let her brightness fade to a questioning look. "But there must be some mistake!" Pushing past Bette, who was standing with crossed arms and a rueful smile, she hurried to the door, opened it, and looked out in the hallway. "Nobody out here," they heard her voice echo down the stairs. "Looks like Bette blew it again."

"This is a little better than my normal welcome home," Bette said to Rod. "It's better because you're here. A step in the right direction. Normally she just demands instant recall on every man I talked to that day."

"Stop talking about me," Lori said, walking back in. She turned to Rod. "Do you know Bette has not been one bit helpful about introducing me to anyone new? And where have you been? I haven't seen you for weeks."

"I'm going to change now," Bette said. "You two talk."

"Oh good, I have him all to myself," Lori said.

"Keep your hands off him, Lori."

"Can I feed him?"

"If you want." Bette's door closed.

"All *right*, down to business," Lori said, standing directly in front of Rod. "Open wide," she said, raising a few kernels of popped corn to his mouth, "and don't lick my fingers. That's foreplay and Bette's too good a friend."

He laughed, and she hit his chin. The popcorn fell down his chest onto the floor. "Slob," she said, putting the bowl on the table. "Let's get to the point."

"Let's."

"I've asked my roommate, your 'significant other' as we in the know say, on several occasions to introduce me to Brendan."

"Several dozen times I hear."

Lori closed her eyes and opened them slowly. "Who *cares* how many times? The result is still the same. What's the mystery? She says he's good-looking and about my age. Does he have bad breath? Is he gay? Have herpes, AIDS, or something more exotic?"

"God, I hope not," Rod said. "All I can say for sure is no to the bad breath, and thanks for the questions to ask next time I interview a roommate."

"Rod, I'm looking for some answers here!" She stepped forward and he backed up.

"Okay, okay." He put his hand on her shoulder and said, "I think Bette was just looking out for you. Making you take the time to cool off on Thomas before going out with Brendan. Because from everything I can tell, he really does seem to be a nice guy. Kind of quiet, but definitely a nice guy."

"Quiet is no problem," Lori said. "I can do enough talking for the both of us."

"I'm sure. In any case, I'll be happy to introduce you and let the two of you look out for your own best interests."

"All right!" She stepped up on her toes and pulled his head down for a kiss on the mouth. In that brief heat, he felt a twinge of jealousy toward Brendan, which he pushed away immediately. "Bette!" Lori called, strutting down the hallway toward the living room with the popcorn, "is it okay if I kiss him?"

"No, it is not!"

"Too late!"

"So Lori," Rod called down the hall, "tomorrow night, come over with Bette and we'll have a cookout on the roof."

"All right," she said, licking butter off her fingers. "I think I can make it."

■ ■ ■

The next morning, Rod let himself out of Bette's apartment quietly, walked down to the Kenmore station, and took the T back to his apartment. The trolley was practically empty that Saturday morning, and he enjoyed the feeling of being awake while everyone else slept. It was to be a busy day: an open-water certification test in the morning, a boat dive in the afternoon, and Bette and Lori over for dinner. He didn't mind. It made up for the boring weekday mornings, sitting around waiting for customers.

Rod glanced at his watch as he trotted up the stairs to his condo. It was a quarter to eight. They had to be up on the North Shore by nine-thirty. Striding into the apartment, careless of the noise, he took a right down the hall and rapped on Guy's door twice, saying, "Time to get wet. We need to get moving right away."

Not waiting for an answer, he went into the kitchen, put bran muffins in the toaster oven, and sliced two oranges into quarters. He filled the coffee maker, checked his watch, and frowned. Back in the hallway he called in the direction of Guy's room, "Hey! How many dive instructors make you breakfast and drive you to the lesson? At least get out of bed."

Behind him, at the opposite end of the hall, the sound of the shower started. "What the hell?" he muttered as he walked back past the kitchen to the bathroom. He pushed the door open and said, "How'd you get past me?"

Guy put his head around the shower curtain, hair streaming. "What?"

"How'd you get past me without my seeing you when I was in the kitchen?"

"I don't know," Guy shrugged. "You were busy with coffee, I guess. Why?"

"Huh. And I always thought I was on top of what's going on around me." Rod noticed the time again. "We've got to roll." He closed the door, turned to go into his bedroom, and then poked his head back in. "Why a shower when you're going to be in the ocean in an hour and a half?"

"Nosy bastard, aren't you?"

Rod grinned and shut the door. In his bedroom, he pulled off his jeans and underwear and went into his dresser drawer for a bathing suit.

Something was different. Quietly, he selected the navy blue trunks from the middle of the pile and wondered what was making him so nervous. Hadn't the navy trunks been on the top of the pile before? The green ones were too loose; he always had to be careful when pulling off his wet suit not to display himself to his class. So they were almost always near the bottom of the drawer, unless the navy or the white pair was in the laundry.

Rod looked at his bed. It was neatly made, and he remembered he had taken the time the morning before. Still . . . he looked up into the dresser mirror to find Guy standing behind him, wearing his robe. *His* robe.

Who the hell do you think you are? he thought, turning. He opened his mouth and shut it. The robe was slightly darker blue than his, and had white piping.

"I thought you were in a hurry," Guy said.

Rod glanced down at his nakedness, immediately feeling embarrassed and a little angry. He stepped into his bathing suit and said, "I am. And I'm still waiting for you."

"I'll be ready." Guy left the room.

Pushing his irritation aside, Rod finished dressing and joined Guy a few minutes later for breakfast. Midway through the meal, he remembered Bette had helped him with the laundry last time, and that could very well explain the bathing suits. Though he didn't think he had washed them.

On the drive up to the cove, Rod said he had invited Lori along for dinner that night. Guy thanked Rod for making the plans, thanked him several times, in fact.

"It's not a big deal, Brendan," he answered. "Really."

As the sparkling blue ocean came into view, Rod automatically sought the familiar lift. But the euphoria wasn't there. The cheerful morning promise was sapped away by something that flickered at the edge of his peripheral vision, something that made him wish his roommate would stop talking, since his own answers sounded hollow and guarded. Briefly, he considered his reaction to Lori's kiss, but he found no real reason for guilt or concern there. The thought of Bette made him smile too easily. No, the rare moodiness had started that morning, in his own apartment.

■　■　■

Guy was certain he hadn't been caught, but he saw an opportunity to make it up to Rod an hour later when the whole wet-suit-clad group was together. Rod said, "Okay, indulge a young but senile dive instructor one more time—what is the single most important thing to remember down there?"

"Keep breathing," the class chanted back. Guy grinned and tried to catch Rod's eye.

"That's right," Rod said, not noticing. "And don't rise any faster than your bubbles. Air embolisms are bad for my business—they cut down on repeat customers."

Most people laughed. A short, chunky woman named Isabelle turned to her husband and said, "Is that supposed to be funny?" He shrugged and looked down at his gear. If Rod heard her, he didn't show it. Guy felt a protective rage surge through him. Rod was always nice to her, always said hello, always helped her although she was chronically late and always complaining: the gear was too heavy, the wet suit too tight, the water too cold, her ears hurt. Now she struggled to take off the wet-suit jacket, having forgotten to put on her hood. "It's so hot in this damn suit," she wailed.

Rod stepped behind and helped pull the jacket from her arms. "That's the incentive plan for getting you into that cold water over there." He swept his arm to indicate the beach. "Why else would you want to leave?" It was a beautiful little cove, with a sandy beach sweeping down to the water and jagged cliffs rising sharply on each side. The water's surface was giving way from the morning calm to a slight chop.

"Damned if I know," she said, leaving Rod to find a clean spot to lay her jacket while she rummaged in the net bag for her hood. Rod's smile widened slightly, as her husband and he exchanged glances.

Feeling sorry for the poor bastard, Guy thought. *Well, it's only what he deserves for letting her get away with it.* The one flaw in Rod that was beginning to irk Guy was that he was too soft on people. It wasn't weakness, Guy decided firmly. Just a misplaced sense of honor.

Last week at one of the pool lessons, Isabelle had managed to knock her own mask off, then spit out the mouthpiece in her panic. When she burst to the surface, choking, Rod came up from behind quickly and towed her to the edge. The first thing she did after recovering her breath was to turn on him, railing, "I almost drowned and it's your fault! These lessons aren't safe." Rod spoke to her in a low voice, and she answered angrily, her fat cheeks splotched with red. After a while she calmed down enough to get out of the pool and watch the rest of the lesson from the side, wrapped in a big pink blanket imprinted with a cartoon of Miss Piggy. After the lesson, Rod told Guy that he had better go ahead and take the subway home, as he wanted to stay and talk with Isabelle and her husband, Carl. Guy covered his irritation and said, "Sure, no problem," but he resented the intrusion. He had counted on stopping off, having a beer somewhere, and watching Rod meet people, as he did so easily. When Rod came home later that night Guy asked, "Did you make her quit?"

"That's up to her," Rod said, and went off to bed.

Now she was back, whining and jabbing again. Guy wasn't going to take it, even if Rod did.

He had to hurry. Stepping a few feet away from the group, he was immediately hidden in the dense brush. Angling along the water's edge, he remained hunched over until he reached a huge boulder, which stopped just above the slapping waves. Once in the crevice behind the boulder, he climbed all the way up to the parking lot out of sight of the other divers. He had pushed the hood of his suit back to hear better. Sweat poured down his face onto the shoulders and chest of his wet suit.

Isabelle's car was a white Honda Civic. She drove; her husband sat in the passenger seat and listened as her mouth moved. At least that was the way it had looked when they'd shown up late that morning, and he had no doubt that was the way it was every morning. Guy stuck his dive knife into her front left tire. Stale air hissed out against his face, and the car sagged toward him. Still kneeling, he smashed the window with the butt of his knife, unlocked the door, and went to work on the inside of the car. He slashed the seats, ripping out hunks of foam, and jabbed the gauges and the radio into plastic shards. Sweat rained off him onto the ruined seats. His bladder suddenly felt very full, and he started to take off his wet suit to leave a real present for Isabelle when he caught a glimpse of himself in the mirror. His hair was hanging in wet strands, and his eyes bulged as he gasped for breath.

Out of control, he thought, and stopped. Looking around, he wondered if any cars had passed by that he hadn't seen. For that

101

matter, he might not have noticed if a diver had walked up from the beach. He slicked his hair back and took a deep breath. The car was in shambles, and he had already been gone over five minutes. They would notice him missing if they took a head count now.

He started to put the knife back in his leg sheath when he noticed the little stuffed pig clinging to the gearshift stick. He took it off with trembling hands, swept the foam rubber from the seat, and put the little doll on its side. He sliced the head off and jammed it between the pig's spring-clip rear legs. "Eat your bacon, Isabelle," he said, and hurried down the hill.

"Wouldn't you know I had to take a leak *after* I got the suit on," Guy said to Frank, a muscular man of about twenty-five who had been his partner at a few of the pool lessons. "Have they assigned people to instructors yet?" he added casually.

Frank shook his head and helped Guy on with his gear.

"Let's go talk with Rod. Maybe we can get hooked up with him."

Frank shrugged and smoothed his mustache. "Okay. Why not?"

Rod looked up from his clipboard as they picked their way along the rocky beach. He was wearing his wet suit with the hood pushed back. His tank and vest lay at his feet, with the regulator hoses hooked neatly away from the sand. When they stood before him, he automatically started checking their equipment, making sure their weight belts weren't covered by any other straps, they had enough air, and their carbon dioxide cartridges were properly screwed into the vests.

"Looks all right."

"We were wondering who you were taking down yourself," Guy said.

"I'll take a couple who need the most attention, and a couple who are all right." He grinned. "I'll let you two decide which category you fall into." Stepping back, he called the group together and introduced the other instructors who were to help with the certification: Shelley, a 250-pound walruslike man with a bald head and curly beard; Clark, a divinity student with a shy smile; Miguel, a whippet-thin diver who needed a dry suit even on the warmest of New England summer days; and Jason, a Boston University junior who spent too many hours hanging around the dive shop not to be put to work.

As Rod ran through the people assigned to each instructor, Guy felt both pleased, that he wasn't assigned to someone other than Rod, and left out, as if he were the last person waiting to be picked for basketball in gym class. Finally only he, Frank, Isabelle, and Carl were left. "Come on, you four," Rod said. "Looks like nobody else will play with you."

After checking everyone's buoyancy, Rod led his small group on the surface to the center of the cove, trailing the red-and-white dive flag on a float. The other groups were spaced out similarly, some along the walls of the cove, others farther in toward the beach. Rod kicked along at an easy pace, using the snorkel. Periodically, he gave each person the thumb and forefinger okay sign and waited for the response. Guy signaled back, then jerked his thumb at Isabelle, chugging along beside him. He shook his head in broad derision.

Rod didn't get it. He spun around quickly and was beside Isabelle with a few powerful kicks. She stopped and treaded water. Rod looked at her and then back at Guy. Even through the faceplate, Guy could read the perplexity on Rod's face. He stared back, trying to think of an explanation.

Luckily, Isabelle pulled the snorkel from her mouth to complain. Rod treaded water with easy strokes and took his mouthpiece out. Guy let himself drift closer. Carl kept his head down, looking at the bottom twenty feet away. *Enjoying the quiet,* Guy thought disgustedly. *If he had the balls to keep her in line, he could just tell her to shut up when he wanted quiet.*

Isabelle put the oral inflator valve from the vest into her mouth and blew until the skin around her face mask turned bright red. Rod laid his head back and moved his fins in long, easy strokes. "That's not necessary," he said.

She glared at him through the faceplate and inhaled dramatically. When she had exhaled enough to make the vest balloon tight, she rested, hanging exhausted in the water, with her arms stuck out to the side, her legs slack.

"This stuff is so heavy to push through the water," she said.

"You've got me worn out, and I haven't even started the test. Why'd you have to bring us so far out?" With the mask over her nose, Isabelle's voice sounded particularly petulant.

"I don't know why you want to work so hard," Rod said. "You're going around with your vest three-quarters inflated. I told you in the shallows that you were buoyant enough with just a few breaths in there. The easy part is being underwater. Supporting all this junk on the surface is about as much fun as going jogging while holding barbells over your head."

"I hate this." Her lower lip trembled under the mask. "I wish to God I were in my car on the way home now."

Guy let himself sink so they couldn't see him laugh. He put the regulator mouthpiece in and joined Frank a few feet below the surface. Carl swam over to Rod and Isabelle. Guy watched the three sets of legs. After a few minutes of consultation, Rod gave the thumbs-down sign, and they all settled to the bottom in twenty feet of water. *Wonder what it took to get her down this time*, Guy thought.

His buoyancy was comfortably negative, and he sank to his knees in the sand. The water was colder here than on the surface, and it took a moment for him to adjust to the difference, but he was basically quite comfortable. The visibility was good for about fifteen feet, although there was little to see right where they were. Rod had said the more interesting spots were along the wall. Guy didn't care. Just being there and showing Rod what he could do were his only concerns.

Rod had them form a semicircle, and he motioned to Isabelle to start the drills: clearing the mask, buddy breathing, taking off and then donning the tank. She hesitated, and Rod put his hand on her shoulder. He touched her mask and then demonstrated clearing his own. Even from a distance, Guy could see her fat chin thrust out as she started.

A few minutes later, when she had finished, Rod clapped his gloved hands, cheering. Guy shook his head slightly. He wondered again what Rod had said to convince Isabelle to go down. It would have been fun to knock her mask off and watch her scramble for the surface. But there was no way he could get away with it, so he would have to settle for her expression when she saw her car.

He knew just the right way to handle it with Rod later. Start off solemn, saying vandalism was awful and all that nonsense. But then look sideward with a hint of a grin and say, "But if it had to happen to anyone . . . how much did you pay them, Rod?"

Rod would crack up, for sure.

Maybe he wouldn't say anything in the car but wait instead for dinner. In front of Lori and Bette, start it off with something like that, then let Rod tell them what a pain Isabelle had been for the past few weeks . . .

Rod tapped his faceplate.

Startled, Guy jerked his head back.

Rod flashed the "okay" signal. Guy returned it and confidently pulled the mask back to let the water gush in. He then tipped the lower part of the mask from his face and exhaled from his nose. He could see again, although an annoying trickle of water streamed near his right eye. He cleared it again. Rod waited. Guy's heart beat faster. He cleared the mask one more time, snorting hard through his nostrils. Still it trickled. He signaled to Rod he was all set. *Screw it, I'll fix it later*, he thought.

But it got worse. During buddy breathing, Rod seemed to hold on to the regulator too long, although by the bubbles it was obvious he was taking only the agreed-upon breaths. At the end of the exercise, Guy was hard-pressed to see more than a few feet away, and Rod had to tug at his hand to get him to release Rod's tank strap. He tried to clear the mask again. Rod gave him the "okay" sign, inquiring.

No, I'm not goddamn all right, Guy thought, but he returned the signal. He reluctantly began to take off his tank.

He could not see, the water was over his nose now, and he forgot that the mouthpiece would twist in his mouth when he pulled the tank off. Simple physics. But he almost panicked when he sucked down a little water. There on his knees, almost blind, with water trying to find its way into his mouth and nose, he was half a beat from bugging out for the surface. Rod watched, his arms crossed.

Isabelle made it, Guy told himself and somehow managed to fumble the tank back on. He bit into the mouthpiece.

Rod tapped him on the chest and pointed toward the surface. He started up gratefully until Rod grasped his arm. He shook his head and touched Guy's mouthpiece. Guy's heart began to hammer—he had forgotten the emergency ascent.

He took three deep breaths, pulled out the mouthpiece, and started for the surface. *Do it.* Kicking, he let out his breath slowly, silver pearls floating to the surface. Rod swam up with him, still breathing out of *his* regulator. Guy's every fiber wanted to pump his way to the top faster, shove past Rod and get to some fresh air. But he kept at Rod's pace. Just before the surface, he thought, *If I can do this, there's nothing this jock can do that I can't.*

■ ■ ■

He made the mistake of trying to breathe. When his head broke into air and sunshine, he opened his mouth to suck down a deep first breath and swallowed a mouthful of a passing wave. He was vaguely aware of his left hand pushing on Rod's shoulder, but mainly a panicky babble filled his head: *Get me up, get me on top of something, something solid, something to stand on—*

He vaguely realized that Rod's head was in the crook of his arm and that he should stop, but his body had different plans. He pushed Rod farther down.

Through his choking, he heard a hissing sound and felt pressure at his neck and chest. His vest was inflated. Rod spun him around, twisted his own head away, and pushed off. Guy labored in a breath, coughed, and then vomited a mouthful of seawater. He hung limp in the vest. The awareness of his failure seeped in to replace the fear.

I panicked and tried to climb on top of Rod, he thought dully.

Rod's mask was askew and full of water. He pulled it off completely, took out the mouthpiece, and said, "You all right now?"

Guy nodded.

"Good. Guess you'll remember to turn your back to the waves next time you come up, right?"

"Yeah. I'm sorry, Rod." His voice was barely audible.

"It's okay. Maybe I brought you along too fast with the classes one right after the other. These other people have had a few more weeks to absorb it all. Anyway, it's no big deal. Maybe another pool lesson, and I'll take you out again next week. You pass that and you'll still be certified before you start school."

"You're not going to pass me?" Guy's voice rose in spite of himseslf. "I just got a mouthful of water."

"Brendan. It wasn't just that. You were having a hell of a time with your mask, and I thought you were going to shoot for the surface when you were taking off the tank. Then when you *did* just get a mouthful of water, which happens to everyone once in a while, you forgot about your vest and tried to climb your way out. On me. What if you were with a partner with less experience? I've seen it before, so I just kept breathing my air and pulled the emergency inflator on your vest. Somebody else might've panicked too."

Guy winced at the word.

"It's not a big deal here in the lessons. I just want to make sure you're all set before I let you go. Really comfortable in the water."

"Are all of them passing?" Guy pointed downward.

"Never mind what they're doing."

Guy stared back at him.

Rod shook his head. "Look. Don't worry about what they think. They're not going to know anyhow, unless you tell them." He glanced at his dive watch. "I've kept them waiting too long." He slipped on his mask, jackknifed neatly, and was gone.

"You bastard," Guy said.

■ ■ ■

Isabelle and Rod popped to the surface a few minutes later. She turned away just as a wave broke and laughed aloud as it slapped the back of her head. "That was *great!*" she said to Rod. "It was so much easier than I thought. You really do have enough air if you just relax, don't you?" She inflated her vest.

Rod took his mouthpiece out and grinned. "Still want your money back?"

"Are you kidding?"

"That's what I like to hear. I'll be back with Carl in a minute." He dropped down again.

She spun around, splashing with her arms until she saw Guy. "Wasn't that wonderful! I was so scared at first, were you? Then I got mad at Rod, but I figured, what the hell, give it a shot. I'm always like that, mad one minute, laughing the next. Crazy me. Guess it's because I'm scared. That Rod's a good guy, though, am I right? He made me give it a try, and after I got over wanting to wet my pants, I loved it. How about you?" She rolled awkwardly toward him.

She passed and I didn't, Guy thought, and put the regulator back in his mouth.

"Hey, I was wondering, what took you guys so long? I was staring up at you. It looked from there like you two were having a wrestling match."

Guy took a quick compass reading to the shore, deflated his vest, and sank below the surface. The bottled air howled through the regulator. He could see the orange of Rod's and Carl's vests as they started up. For a moment, he seriously considered waiting for them with his knife drawn. *It's only a matter of time, you sanctimonious bastard,* he thought.

And that realization suddenly made it easier. Just a matter of time. Sure, he would take the extra two lessons. That was why he was with Rod, for lessons. That was the point. What shame were two more lessons, when the end was going to be the same?

He swam underwater to the beach until it was too shallow; then he got out and waited for his teacher.

■　■　■

"You shouldn't have left the group," Rod said.

"Sorry. Isabelle's blabbing was getting to me. She must be driving you nuts, huh?"

Rod shrugged. "She was just scared." He pulled his clipboard out of a red poplin bag and began to call names, checking people off as they came out of the water. Guy moved away and sat on a boulder near the water's edge.

What was that "She's just scared" comment supposed to mean? he raged. *Was that some sort of jab at him?* Guy tugged off his hood and quickly stripped off his gear. He filled the orange net bag, keeping his eyes averted from Rod until he was able to control his expression.

He began to brighten when he remembered Isabelle. She waited impatiently to talk to Rod. A blond woman named Jill and her boyfriend were talking to him, and for once Isabelle couldn't get a word in edgewise.

Finally, Isabelle surprised Guy by just calling out cheerfully to Rod, "I'll see you at the store sometime—for air. Thanks a lot, you did a great job!" She started up the hill to the parking lot. Guy stood up.

Rod answered, "Hey, you did the hard stuff, I just talked!"

She turned back, smiling, just as Carl appeared at the top of the hill.

"You better come on up here, Belle," Carl said. "Somebody trashed our car." The disgust in his voice carried all the way down the hill. Carl held out his hand, and Isabelle took it. She bit at the knuckle of her left hand, and Guy heard her say in a small voice, "What for?" Rod stiffened, excused himself from Jill and her friend, and hurried up to the parking lot. Guy caught up and asked, "What's going on?"

"You didn't hear him?" Rod said tightly.

"Hear who?"

Rod looked at him oddly, and then they were at the parking lot. The little car really did look savaged, with its flat tire and broken windows. Tears ran down Isabelle's face and Carl's hands were on his hips. Guy felt a grin coming on and rubbed his jaw to cover. Glancing slantwise at Rod, he sobered immediately.

A vein throbbed visibly in Rod's forehead, and his face grew rigid. In a clipped tone he asked Carl if he needed a hand with the tire.

"Sure."

They worked silently, and Rod had a sheen of sweat on his

forehead when they let the car settle onto the spare ten minutes later. Guy considered offering to help, but he didn't want to disturb Rod when he was acting that way.

Rod turned to Isabelle. "I don't know what to say, Isabelle. One of the reasons I chose this dive site is that in a good town like this, you don't figure on this type of thing happening. I guess they picked on your car because it was closest to the trees, and harder to see from the road. Can you think of any other reason someone might do this to you?"

"No." She shook her head firmly. "I can't."

"Well, send the bill for the deductible on your insurance to us at the dive shop. I feel wrong letting you go with all this damage." He smiled for the first time since coming up to the parking lot. "Especially since you worked so hard to pass the certification."

She smiled back weakly. "I did, you know."

"I *do* know."

Her smile widened, and even Guy recognized a girlish prettiness inside the normally petulant face. "That's nice of you." Carl put his arm around her and said, "Come on, Belle. Maybe if we're lucky, the insurance company will total the car and I can buy you a new one."

She snorted. "Big spender." When she opened the door, her face wrinkled in distaste. She picked up the little pig doll and handed it to Rod. "Little coward," she said, shaking her head. "What I wouldn't give to have him in front of me now."

"I'd love to teach him some manners," Rod said. "With a sledge-hammer."

"Give him one for me," she said, flicking the stuffed pig from Rod's hand, down the cliff. "The punk."

■ ■ ■

Rod told Guy during the ride to the marina that he was welcome to come along on the boat but he couldn't go diving. "I need to stay in the boat, and you're not certified. I can't send you down as a partner with some customer I've never met. You understand, right? It wouldn't be safe for either of you."

"Sure," Guy said. His chest felt constricted.

"Look, my choice of words—talking about you panicking—that could've been better. But you'll see, after a few more lessons you'll be more comfortable in the water and you'll learn automatically how to use your gear. A little water down the windpipe will still be lousy, but you'll remember how to stay afloat while coughing and gagging. And if you don't want to talk about this in front of Lori and Bette, I don't have any reason."

"That's good," Guy said. "Because I'd kill you if you did."

Rod laughed. "I'm shaking."

Afterward they bought four good-sized lobsters from the divers. "Some people like the catching more than the eating," Rod explained to Guy. On the way home, they stopped at an open-air market for corn and salad makings, at the liquor store for beer and wine, and, finally, at the butcher's for fresh sausage.

At the apartment, Rod carried the charcoal up to the roof and lit a fire in the Weber grill. Deciding to wait until the flames burned down before showering, he stretched out on a chaise lounge, closed his eyes, and instantly realized two things: one, he was comfortably tired and would love a beer; two, he was comfortably tired and did not want to walk downstairs to get one. But the skylight was open, so he found the energy to pad across the hot tar roof and yell down in the direction of Guy's room. "Brendan! You've got a man dying of thirst . . ."

There was a crash from the direction of his own room. Guy stumbled into his line of vision, head turning right, left. Rod's grin evaporated. "What *are* you doing?" he said, quietly.

"What are *you* doing?" Guy retorted. "Are you spying on me or what?"

Rod cocked his head. "What is it with you? I was just asking for a beer."

"Oh." Guy's forehead cleared. He laughed, a short bark. "I must be a little nervous. I was just looking in the closet for a tablecloth."

Rod swung the skylight open farther. "Just relax and hand me a beer. You'll do fine."

"Sure thing." Guy hurried to the kitchen and came back with a bottle of ale. He handed it up to Rod.

"That's not a twist-off. Can you open it?"

Guy grimaced and rushed back to the kitchen. Rod could hear him rattling through the drawers. Finally, he returned with the opened bottle. "At long last," he said.

"Sorry to put you through all that."

"It's nothing." Guy's smile was a nervous twitch.

"And, Brendan?"

"Yeah?"

"I've got a tablecloth, and I'll take care of the lobster and the table and everything else. You cook the sausage. We'll have a good time tonight. Lori's a lot of fun, once you get used to her."

"Okay." Guy nodded. "Yeah, I know, I'll be fine."

"That's the attitude." Rod went back to his chaise lounge and sipped his beer. He tried closing his eyes, but the sleepy feeling was gone. After catching himself checking his watch for the fifth time in as many minutes, he swore softly under his breath and went downstairs.

■ ■ ■

Twenty minutes later, Guy let Lori and Bette in. Rod was still dressing, so Bette made the introductions and then drifted off toward his room. She was wearing a lavender summer dress; her hair was loosely tied. Lori wore a white miniskirt, a red cotton blouse, and reflective sunglasses. Guy found it disconcerting to look at her directly.

Then she took the sunglasses off, saying, "Jesus, I thought I was going blind there. You must have felt you were about to get a speeding ticket. You know. State cops always wear these reflector things so you can't see where they're looking."

"And that's why you wear them too, I suppose."

"You've got it." She handed him a white cake box, which was cool to the touch. "Ice-cream cake. Refrigerator."

She followed him to the kitchen. Guy looked around the apartment: the framed Sierra Club posters, open skylight, the clean, sunny kitchen with the butcher-block island. He was comfortable here, and knew without looking where the pots and pans were kept, what he would find for food behind the green refrigerator door. He thought of Rod's promise not to mention the certification dive. Rod could be trusted, at least as far as talking about it at the table. He'd probably tell Bette, though, and she'd tell Lori.

"Nice place," she said. "I haven't been here for months. I think Bette and Rod use it as a vacation place from me when I get nutsy."

He exchanged the cake for a plate of raw Italian sausages and a bottle of white wine. He poured a glass for her and said, "Now they have me to face."

Lori smiled behind her wineglass and leaned against the counter, legs crossed. "I guarantee I'm worse."

Guy noticed the smooth, muscular definition of her thighs and calves. He liked her size; her forehead was about chin height to him. She smiled. "Looks like you could use a pair of those sunglasses yourself." Then, before he could answer, "What did Rod tell you about me?"

"He said, 'Lori's fun once you get to know her.' "

"Sounds like him." She laughed, considering. "Sounds like me too."

"What did he tell you about me?"

She pursed her lips. "I'm not telling you. I'm working on being more subtle myself. See what it's like, you know. So I'm not going to blab everything I hear."

He smiled slowly. "That's not fair."

"You're learning." She laughed easily, her teeth white and even. "But I'll give you a break. What he said was good, and I already think he was right."

The lump that had been building in his chest all day melted down into a more pleasant kind of tension. He picked up the plate of sausage and nodded at the stairway, saying, "Let's go to the roof."

She took the bottle and led the way. Guy had been hoping beforehand that Rod and Bette would be around all evening to keep the conversation rolling, but now he realized that was simply stage fright. As soon as he'd opened his mouth, he'd known the evening was going to be fine. Rod was just what he had been looking for all these years. Talking to this girl was so easy. He was already semierect. Before, he wouldn't have been able to look at her directly, never mind flirt. She was two steps above him now, and the sudden urge to run his hands up her legs underneath her skirt was almost over-powering. The sun was just beginning to set when they reached the roof deck.

"This is beautiful," she said. "The sky, the wine, and a good-looking man who's about to feed me."

Guy laughed. "The little things in life, huh?" He raked the coals smooth.

Her lips twitched, but she didn't answer. She settled back into a lounge chair. He glanced up her skirt as she crossed her legs. Hard to tell if she was wearing panties, but trying was the fun, he told himself. He looked down. The bulge in his pants was noticeable, but not to the point of being embarrassing. Perfect.

The aroma of the cooking sausage filled the air. He rolled the other lounge chair over beside hers, so they faced the grill in a **V**. "More wine?" he asked.

She held up her empty glass. While pouring, he glanced to the other rooftops. No one else was out, no one to see them. He was slightly disappointed. Anyone looking at them would assume they were lovers already, he was certain.

"So tell me about your dive today," she said.

"Why?" He poured carefully, not wanting her to notice that his hand had started to tremble.

"Why not?"

"Just not much to tell." He sat on the lounge chair. "Really."

She shrugged. "Okay. Don't tell me. Shoot down my conversation like that, I'll make you do all the talking." She crossed her arms and set a wide, false smile on her face.

"That would be cruel. Bette must've told you, I'm too shy to do all the talking."

She put her sunglasses back on. He could see himself reflected in her twin lenses, foolishly grinning as she kept her gaze and expression unmoving, like a mannequin. He knew she thought she was being funny, a good ha-ha, but if she didn't stop it soon he was going to wipe those sunglasses off with the back of his hand.

"All right," he said. "I went on a dive class, learned some stuff, and then went out in the afternoon on the boat. Helped the paying divers with their gear."

"That's more like it. Don't ever try to outbrat me. I've had years of practice."

"Got it."

"So are you all done now? Do you get a license or something?"

"Certified," he said quickly. "We've got a couple more lessons to go." Guy stood abruptly and walked back to the stairwell for the kerosene lantern Rod kept on a shelf. He had learned long ago, the best way to change a conversation is to interrupt it entirely. Leading it away leaves too many strings. He watched Lori while lighting the lantern. She kicked off her sandals and stretched. Her plump breasts pushed the red blouse tight against her nipples, and her skirt hitched up a little higher. She rolled her head toward him languorously and patted his lounge chair. "Lie down. It feels so nice out here tonight, doesn't it?"

"It does. Having this roof deck makes the Boston skyline seem like a part of the property." He poured more wine for both of them. The bottle was beaded with condensation. She touched the back of his hand when her glass was half full. Her fingers were amazingly warm.

"That's enough for now, Brendan. I'd like to get drunk nice and slow tonight."

The glow of the lantern threw Lori's face into shadows. Her lips curved into a smile when he lay back down. He took a deep breath, inhaling a mixture of her perfume, the scent of cooking sausage, charcoal and the summer smell of nearby trees, and a hint of freshly mowed grass three stories below. He exhaled and took a sip of the wine, marveling at the changes in his life in the past month.

115

"I think we've lost Bette and Rod," she said.

Guy frowned and looked at his watch. "Yeah. What's keeping them?"

She giggled. "Come on, Brendan. What do you think? They're lovers who haven't seen each other since this morning."

The challenge in her tone made Guy wilt. He suddenly felt naive. Then angry. Goddamn Rod. Here he was feeling so proud of himself for just carrying on a conversation with a woman, while a floor below them, Rod was fucking.

The wine tasted sour. Standing, he began jabbing the sausages onto the plate.

"Brendan, are you okay?"

Don't ask me that! Guy almost threw the heavy barbecue fork at her. Instead, he breathed deeply and answered cheerfully, "Of course I'm okay. All the more food for you and me. It just occurred to me that he probably didn't put the lobsters in, though. Let's go down before the water boils out of the pot."

"If the lobsters aren't cooked, *I'm* not going to be all right," she said. "I'm starving."

But when they got downstairs, Bette was setting the table and Rod was peering into the pot. Guy could see the bright red of the lobsters before Rod put the lid back on.

"We're all set here," Rod said.

Bette looked up from the silverware and said, "Are you two having fun?" Hair cascaded over her shoulders. Her feet were bare.

"Of course," Lori said. She squeezed Rod's arm and teased. "But not as much as you two, I'll bet."

After dinner, Rod and Bette retired to Rod's room. It was time for Guy to kiss Lori, and he had lost his ability to talk. During dinner, conversation had centered on Rod, as he talked about his family life in Seattle. Guy was both curious about Rod's difficult relationship with his father and irritated that Lori's attention was directed away from himself. His confidence, already shaken before he came down from the roof, had seeped away altogether. She sat on the sofa beside him, her arms crossed loosely in her lap. Giving him a sidelong look, she asked, "Something the matter?"

"Like what?"

She shrugged. "Whatever."

"No."

"Oh, I thought there might be. Because we were all chattering away at dinner, and now the two of us seem to have dropped into a black hole."

"I guess I'm just a little tired, you know. Long day with the diving and all."

"I get it," she said, with forced gaiety. "I'm boring you!"

"Don't be ridiculous." As soon as he said it, he realized his tone was too curt. He was blowing not only the evening but the whole damn *thing*. He stood abruptly. "I'll be right back."

Her expression cooled a few degrees more. "Going to the little boy's room?"

"You've figured me out."

"Not yet."

He smiled quickly and went around the corner into the hallway, purposely treading heavily. In the bathroom he snapped on the light and turned on the water faucet. Backing quietly into the hall, he shut the bathroom door loudly. Looking toward the living room, he couldn't hear or see any sign that Lori was moving from the couch. He put his ear to Rod's door. He could hear Bette's voice and the deeper sound of Rod's answer but couldn't understand what they were saying. His heart began to pound faster, and the tension in his belly and chest spread throughout his body. It was a tension more compelling than frightening. He looked down the hall and checked his watch once again. He couldn't stay for more than a minute.

He stepped into the closet. The door opened and closed silently thanks to the oil he had applied on the hinges earlier in the week. Once inside the pitch-dark space, he closed his eyes and felt for the spike. He had spent an hour one morning while Rod was at work, carefully figuring the right angle, drilling the hole, filing the sharp end of the spike, and painting it, so when all was done he could pull the greased steel out silently and look into Rod's bed. When the spike slid back into place, the flat end stopped exactly flush, safely out of casual view behind the ornate frame of Rod's Winslow Homer print.

Guy had considered the risk. If Rod looked closely inside the curlicues of his frame, sure, he might notice a smudge of grease, a slight unevenness in the wall. For that reason, Guy had been very careful, had always cleaned up afterward, always made sure the spike was sufficiently lubricated beforehand. Rod had almost caught him greasing it earlier, when he'd yelled down from the roof for a beer. But Guy was sure he had gotten away with it. He knew what he was doing.

Also, he thought, putting his eye to the peephole, *Rod's got his mind on other things.*

He drew his breath in sharply. It was a hot night, and their blanket lay tangled on the floor. They had left the light on. He could not have directed them better himself. Bette was underneath, her legs wrapped around Rod. He moved in her slowly, the muscles of his back and arms rippling under a sheen of sweat. Her face was flushed, and she bit gently at Rod's shoulder. Rod pressed her head harder against himself and then slid his hand down to her rosy-capped breast, squeezing and holding.

From his vantage, Guy began to breathe more quickly. It was as if *he* could feel her soft mouth at his neck, taste her salt, feel her breast in his hand. He was as rigid as the spike he was holding in his hand.

They began to move faster. Rod moved his hands back to cup her buttocks, and she locked her hands around his back. Bette began to cry out, and just before he heard the sounds of the two of them climaxing, Guy slid the spike back into the hole and left the closet.

In the bathroom mirror, he saw that his face was flushed. He unzipped his fly and pulled down his pants. His cock stood immediately with an enormous erection. Rubbing the head with a little of the clear fluid that had trickled out while he'd been watching them, he imagined how it would feel to do that to Lori, to quell her dark-haired challenge, to answer all the heat that came off her. To wake in the morning with someone *real,* someone who people—Rod and Bette—would be impressed to see him with. He stuffed his penis back into his pants and flushed the toilet. By the time he had finished combing his hair, the bulge in his pants had subsided, but he decided it was still something that Lori could see, if she were looking.

He hurried back to her.

"I almost went after you," she said. "You've been gone for a while."

"I can't go into details."

"I could if I were you. I'll talk about anything. I'll embarrass the hell out of you if you stick around."

"That sounds like a good offer," he said, putting his arm around her. "I probably need to break some of my polite ways."

"You do. *Some* of them."

He kissed her. She was surprised and backed away a little. "Are these the manners you're breaking?" she asked, but with a smile. He nodded and kissed her lips again.

"Hmmm. Well, I guess it's probably my influence . . ."

"All your influence . . ." He pulled her tight against his chest, enjoying the warmth of her breasts against him. She was so much smaller than he was, he was certain he could pick her up and carry her into his room.

"Well, then," she said, pushing back to look at him eye to eye, "if it's my influence, I'll just have to pay the consequences." She kissed him back harder, running her fingers into his hair. Their teeth clicked when she opened her mouth, and she laughed, pulling her head back briefly. She said in a deep voice, "Excuse me, sir, but do you have clumsy kissing insurance?" and then she was at his mouth again. He could taste the garlic in her mouth from the salad, and he realized his mouth probably tasted the same.

He suddenly became aware of his awkwardness, straining against her on the couch, and told himself it was time to stop, anyway. He sat back, and she opened her eyes. "Who turned on the lights?" she asked.

"Can I see you again?" he asked.

"You're not seeing me now?" She smiled, a little perplexed.

"Sure. I mean, I was hoping that maybe next Saturday night we could get together."

"Next Saturday. A week away." She nodded. "Sure. That would be nice. In fact, this week—"

"Good," he said, standing. "Next Saturday it is."

"Fine," she said, smoothing her skirt. "I'll see you in a week."

Guy's stomach clenched. "Oh. Did you and Bette come in separate cars?"

"Yes, we did, Brendan. We knew Bette would be staying the night." She glanced up at him from under her dark lashes.

"Okay, fine," he said. "I'll walk you down."

At her car, she stood on tiptoe and gave him a brief but warm kiss. When she got in the car and started the engine, he felt a sudden pang of sadness, of disappointment that things—that he wasn't a simpler man who could take her back upstairs right now and do what they both wanted to do. He rapped on the window, and she rolled it down. "We'll have a great time next Saturday, Lori," he said. "That's a promise."

"Good," she said, smiling brilliantly. "I'll hold you to it."

He stood until she was around the corner; then he hurried upstairs, turned on the shower, slipped back into the closet, and pulled out the spike. And watched.

GUY LEARNED SOMETHING about him-
self and Cyrano de Bergerac when his brother
and T.D. interrupted the audition while he
and Andrea were on the stage. It was more
than his stomach remaining calm as the two
of them slammed through the double doors,
Chucky grinning to the group of thirty or so
students and calling hello to Mrs. Bennett.
More than ignoring T.D.'s cackling as he
jerked his thumb to clear two seats in the front
row. More than being able to return Andrea's
stricken gaze without concern.

12

It was that he was dangerous.

He let them interrupt thoroughly, Chucky
loudly apologizing to Mrs. Bennett for being
late. "Good crowd," T.D. said to Chucky,
as he appraised the group of students in the
orange-and-blue auditorium. Guy heard a
few snickers, but mostly people smiled nervously in T.D.'s direction or pretended not to
notice him. "God, I love this theater stuff,"
T.D. said. He glanced at Mrs. Bennett and
then stared directly at Guy. "I'm like that

guy on TV, Gene Shalit. A critic. My favorite movie was *Texas Chainsaw Massacre*." He lunged toward the stage, holding an imaginary chain saw. "RRRRrrrrr, you stink!"

Laura Teason collapsed back in her seat giggling; Chucky grinned and said, "What a nut."

"Guy, I hate this," Andrea whispered.

"Be quiet, T.D.!" Mrs. Bennett called.

"Hey, T.D.," Chucky said, in a loud whisper. "When it's my turn up there, pul-lease don't saw me up!" He made his voice high-pitched and wrung his hands. "I can't stand it when people *criticize* me!"

"Oh, damn it!" Andrea said, quietly. Her face began to turn red. "Why's he doing this?"

"Don't worry," T.D. said. He gestured up toward Guy. "I'll put your little brother in charge when it's your turn." He stood up, trembling his body and arms. "Oooh, it vibrates! I'm scared to hold it!"

Guy walked to the edge of the stage and said calmly. "You finished?"

T.D. frowned. A wrinkle appeared in his broad forehead, then he snarled loudly. "Mind your own fucking business. I wasn't talking to you."

"T.D.," Chucky said in a warning tone.

"What did you say?" Mrs. Bennett said, sharply.

"That's okay, I'm talking to you." Guy locked eyes with T.D. "And if you're done making an idiot of yourself, it's time for Andrea and me to finish our turn, and then let other people up. That's what we're all here for."

T.D.'s face flushed red and his voice rose. "What the *fuck* did I tell you?"

"Who cares?"

"Get away from me before I rip your head off and shove it up your ass!"

"All right, T.D., that's it!" Mrs. Bennett's high heels clicked down the cement steps. "Out of here. I don't need that mouth around when these people are here to work!"

"He was asking for it—" T.D. began, but she waved him off.

"Don't be ridiculous. He did nothing of the sort. You two were looking for trouble the minute you walked in."

"Not me, Mrs. Bennett," Chucky said from his seat. He held open a script. "I'm here for a part. I know some people have studied a lot in advance, but I guess for the school play you give everybody a chance, right, Mrs. Bennett? I mean, you don't have to be in one of your English classes, already studying and doing scenes and all, to get a part in the school play, do you?"

"That's got nothing to do with being rude," she said, evenly.

His gray eyes clear and innocent, Chucky said, "Honest, I was just saying hello and all. Kidding around a little."

T.D. said, "Let's get out of here, Chuck." He looked back at Guy. "Leave the faggots behind."

"That's it, T.D." Mrs. Bennett pointed to the door. "Get out."

"Come on, Chuck," T.D. repeated.

"I'm staying."

T.D. fixed him with a hard glare.

"Move, T.D.," Mrs. Bennett said.

"You coming or what?" T.D.'s face turned bright red.

Chucky shook his head. "What did I just say?"

T.D. switched his gaze to Guy. Hoarsely, he said, "I know what you did. And I'm going to nail your ass."

"Any time except for now." Guy turned his back on him and faced Andrea.

T.D. grunted and started for Guy. But Mrs. Bennett moved in front of him, with her arms crossed. "You push by me, and you're on a month's suspension. Or you can leave now. What's it going to be?"

She escorted him out of the auditorium.

■ ■ ■

Afterward, she sat in T.D.'s former chair and said, "I've got zero patience for you, Chucky. I should have walked you out the door too, so don't push your luck any further with me." Her voice rose to in-

123

clude Guy. "That goes for the both of you. Keep the drama onstage."

Guy nodded.

"No problem here," Chucky said.

"Oh, be quiet." Mrs. Bennett looked at her watch. "Guy and Andrea, go ahead with the scene."

Guy said softly to Andrea, "Are you ready?"

"No, damn it," she whispered. "Why did they have to come in like that? I was nervous enough as it was."

"That's exactly why. They wanted to make me look stupid, and you just happened to be standing beside me."

"What did I do to him?"

"Nothing. I told you, he's just after me."

"I'm going to get Chucky for this," she hissed.

"Start now. Make them all look like idiots. Sit down and start reading your lines as soon as I get backstage."

"I know, I know. Hurry."

"Today," Mrs. Bennett said.

Guy ignored her. He locked eyes with Andrea. "You know the lines. If you mess up, just read from the script. We're still ten steps ahead of everyone else."

"Okay," she said in a small voice.

"But Andrea?"

"What?"

"You *are* Roxane." He hurried backstage. Andrea started her lines, faltering a little at first; then her voice grew steadier. She began her imaginary sewing, sitting on the edge of her chair, knees primly together. From behind the curtains, Guy watched.

In his eyes, her jeans and robin's-egg blue sweater began to fade and be replaced by the black of the widow's mourning gown. They had again chosen a portion of the fifth act, where Cyrano, noble but physically ugly, reveals to Roxane that he was the one who wrote the letters, who whispered to her in the darkened courtyard, the one who loved her all his life—it was he, instead of her husband, Christian. She loved his soul in return, never knowing that the handsome but inarticulate Christian had joined with Cyrano in a pact to make for her one perfect lover. After Christian died on the battlefield, Cyrano visited her in the convent as a friend only, every week for fourteen years, never revealing the truth. When she discovers the truth as he lies near death, she cries, "I never loved but one man in my life, and I have lost him—twice. . . ."

Once when he'd been reading the play alone in his room, Guy found suddenly that he couldn't see well and a tear plopped onto the page. That hadn't happened in as long as his memory could stretch, maybe never. Now, stepping out onto the stage, Guy found his chest too tight, as if a live animal were trying to burst from him to envelop Roxane in a loving embrace. He used an oak cane he had picked up in a secondhand store, leaning heavily. He wished he had brought the épée. His decision that it was too early to show up with it didn't change, but as Cyrano grew within him, Cyrano's desires became his own—and the duelist hated being without his sword.

She turned to him and said, "After fourteen years, late—for the first time." As the audience's whispering and fidgeting settled into quiet attentiveness, Cyrano became more tangible to him than ever before. Roxane was sitting in front of him, sewing, and she was happy to see him. Her smile almost made up for the pounding ache in his head from the assassin's blow. He wanted to keep his wound from her, though he knew he would soon be dead, never to see her again. The real pain was in his heart, jagged-edged—not even slightly dulled by time—the knowledge that even now she did not know he loved her. And that if he told her, her face might wrinkle in disgust; or worse, she might laugh.

And the layer of fear beyond that—that maybe he had just been a fool, that had he spoken sooner, like a normal man, he wouldn't have thrown both their lives away. Guy knew those thoughts, knew them to be real, whether they were in the script or not. The words came to him without an effort of memory; he simply said what he felt to Roxane and the lines of the play came out.

■　■　■

"When do I get my turn?" Chucky said loudly, as Guy and Andrea were leaving the stage.

125

Guy strained to hear.

Mrs. Bennett was clapping along with the students, and she didn't answer Chucky immediately. *"Excellent,* Guy and Andrea. That was really exceptional. I can tell how hard you've worked."

"Mrs. Bennett?" Chucky said.

"Sometime tomorrow evening," Mrs. Bennett said. "There are quite a few ahead of you, and I'm sure many of them will be auditioning for the top roles. I assume you want one of those?"

Guy watched Chucky turn from the teacher and look up into the auditorium. Laura Teason was talking with Bob Ernson, urgently. Guy could feel the chill of his brother's gray-eyed stare thirdhand. Bob colored.

Chucky turned back to Mrs. Bennett. Loudly, he said, "Of course. I want Cyrano."

Mrs. Bennett stared at him. "Against your brother? Oh God, that's just great."

Mrs. Bennett was surprised a few minutes later when Bob said he had decided to try out for the part of Ragueneau instead of Cyrano. "It's the funny part," he said. "I don't know. I just figured I'd try it." He didn't look directly at her.

"I don't understand, Bob. I was certain you wanted to try out for Cyrano."

He shook his head.

"That means I can try out for Cyrano right now," Chucky said. "I'd love to do it, especially this section. It's funny, you know, how he talks about sitting on an iron plate and throwing a magnet into the air and the plate follows . . ."

"Did you say something to Bob?"

"How? I've been right here beside you."

"How about it, Bob?" she asked, sharply.

"No."

Mrs. Bennett stood up. "Okay, who's next for Cyrano?"

Nobody answered.

Guy didn't bother to look over his shoulder. Nobody was going up against his brother after he had stated his case.

"Come on," Mrs. Bennett said. "Nobody else wants to try out for Cyrano?" She surveyed the mute group of students, all the males looking studiously elsewhere. She checked her watch and said tiredly, "I don't have all day to fight the pecking order around here. Go ahead, Chucky, read the part. You've got ten minutes."

Chucky made good use of the time. Jealousy pumped ice water into Guy's stomach as Chucky cleverly read the lines and even acted out some of the pieces. People laughed aloud when he straddled a huge imaginary locust and reached back to insert the "villainous saltpeter" which was to drive it to the moon. Maybe the others were surprised, but not Guy. He had been reminded afresh in the restaurant how adept at lying his brother was. *That's all acting is for him. Lying. As different from me as possible. Big jock working hard at the lines.*

Guy felt a little sick as a smile formed on Mrs. Bennett's lips.

When Chucky finished, she said, "You surprised me, Chucky."

"I surprised myself," he said. "Can I have the part?"

"Friday, Chucky, Friday. There are a few people waiting to audition, if you haven't noticed, and some are going to have to go on tomorrow night. So Friday morning I'll put out a list, just like the football team."

"That's okay. If it's like football, then my name will be at the top of the list."

"We'll see. There's still tomorrow, and I have already seen some very strong competition." Probably not even realizing it, she glanced at Guy.

Guy felt the warmth of Andrea's hand and smelled her scent before she spoke. Close to his ear, she whispered, "We still have a good chance, Guy. You're much better than he is."

Chucky stared past Mrs. Bennett at them, his lips a thin horizontal line.

Guy grinned back and then turned a warmer version of the grin to Andrea. "*We're* much better than he is," he said, squeezing her hand.

She stared at Chucky and murmured, "We are."

Guy walked Andrea home, wheeling his bicycle alongside.

She sprang along quickly, radiating enthusiasm and a touch of anger. "Really, Guy, you'll see," she said. "Those parts are ours. You saw the way Mrs. Bennett looked at us."

"I saw." He also saw Chucky maneuvering. "We've got it made," he lied.

"Chucky thinks he's such a big man," she said. "Like the way he and T.D. tried to embarrass us. I never saw that side of him. But he couldn't touch you, acting. You were so *real*."

Guy looked at her. "You felt that?"

"Absolutely." When they reached her house, a nice-looking colonial on an elm-lined street, she turned to him and said in a quieter voice, "Thanks for walking me home tonight, Guy. Even if we *don't* get the parts, I've had fun working on it, and all. You know, with you."

Guy didn't know what to say. All that evening, talking with her had been easy. He'd had no doubts before the audition, or while he was onstage, that Cyrano would be his. Even when Mrs. Bennett had told him in the hallway that Chucky was trying out, he hadn't been overconcerned.

Now that he had seen his brother onstage, been reminded again how he could manipulate a roomful of people, including Mrs. Bennett, Guy wasn't so sure that Chucky might not just strut off with the part too. "Yeah." His eyes faltered away from Andrea's. "I know what you mean."

Andrea crossed her arms. "It kind of gives me goose bumps when we're up there. Doesn't it with you? I mean, at first I was really thinking, 'Oh my God, I'm in front of all these people,' but then that starts to go away. And we're just doing it. Think what it'll be like when we're wearing costumes!"

"It's all I think about."

"All?" She gave him a sidelong look.

He started to answer her and stopped.

She said, "Let me ask you something, Guy."

"Sure."

"You know when we were rehearsing that time and I got really snippy?"

"I remember."

"Well, I apologized, kind of. But tonight, looking at the way Chucky embarrassed me right along with you, I figure he could have done the same type of thing then."

Guy nodded.

"So what I'm saying is, I'm really sorry I acted like such a brat."

"It's okay," Guy said seriously.

"Jerk!" She tapped her forefinger against his chest. "You could disagree with me, say I wasn't a brat at all, you know." She was only a foot away from him, standing in front of the door. He knew he should touch her, but he didn't know how. He tried desperately to think of what Cyrano would say, knowing she wanted the words, to hear about his feelings. . . . But Cyrano might not be his.

"Well," she said, and paused. When he didn't answer, she said, a touch abruptly, "I guess I'll go in."

"Okay."

"Good night." She touched his shoulder with a little pat, opened the door, and stepped in.

"Andrea!"

"What?" she held the door open, waiting.

"We'll see what Friday brings," he said. "You're a beautiful Roxane. Really beautiful. You're sure to get the role. I can't wait to see you in costume—I just hope I get to see it standing beside you, instead of from the audience."

"I sounded all right?" she asked. "Nobody laughed at me, did they?"

He shook his head emphatically. "No one would. Nobody laughs at a girl like you."

She cocked her head slightly and laughed. "Listen to this! Cyrano really has affected you, hasn't he?"

"You have."

She laughed merrily as she closed the door saying, "I like it."
From behind the closed door, he heard her say, "I like it a *lot*."

He went home to wait for Friday.

■ ■ ■

From the front steps of his house, Guy could hear his mother laughing in the kitchen. The Camaro was parked in the driveway. *Three guesses who's making her laugh*, Guy thought. He hesitated before opening the door.

His initial elation with Andrea's attention had begun to twist on itself before he was four blocks from her house. Guy was almost angry with her. It wasn't the right time; it was too much. Guy felt as if his insides were made of glass, and all it would take would be a little push, a little more pressure, for him to collapse onto the razor-edged shards.

Now he had to contend with Chucky being home first, entertaining Ginny.

She stopped laughing when Guy stepped into the living room. He could see her through the kitchen door. Taking a sip from her highball, she waggled her fingers at him and then looked in the direction of the kitchen table, beyond Guy's view. From the way her face softened, Guy was certain she was looking at his brother. She never looked at Guy or her husband that way. "What were you saying, dear?" she asked. She put her hand to her mouth, holding back another giggle. "I wish I had some film," she said.

"What do you mean, what was I *thaying*? Weren't you *lith*ening?" Guy started for his room, but his brother beat him to the hallway.

Chucky was holding a huge carrot to his nose and was wearing a wide-brimmed felt hat that must have been one of Ginny's. "Hold it, sailor," he said, leaning forward, so Guy had to back up. "I got a question for you. Who would be the fairest Cyrano? You or me? Fairest now, not *fairy-est*—I know you've got that sewed up."

Ginny started to laugh again. She leaned against the doorway and said, "Chucky, you're too much!"

When Chucky turned to grin at her, Guy walked away.

His brother clutched at his sleeve, suddenly angry. "Goddamn it, I'm talking to you. What took you so long tonight?"

Guy didn't answer.

"Oh, Chucky, what *could* you be worried about? You *know* you'll get the part if you want it—" his mother started.

Something hard hit Guy on the back of his head. The carrot bounced onto the floor. It was surprising how much his head hurt; the sudden jarring made him dizzy. But he kept his hands by his sides, not willing to clutch his head in front of his brother. "What's your problem?" he said.

Chucky was holding the hat crushed in one hand, his back to Ginny. "You listen, Guy, you shut your mouth and listen to what I'm telling you. You stay away from her. And you stay away from me."

"Chucky!" Ginny said.

"You heard me, Guy."

Guy closed the door behind him and locked it.

■ ■ ■

He went to the bulletin board outside the teachers' lounge Friday morning. He was a half hour late, and everyone else was in class. From across the hallway, he could see in inch-high Magic Marker letters, CAST LIST. He hesitated beside the lockers in the doorway, looking right and then left down the empty hall.

His eyes were still smarting from being out in the daylight. He had not gone to school on Thursday. His mother had yelled to him from outside his door, but he'd just told her he was sick and would be staying in bed. He had closed the curtains and pushed the dresser up against the door. She'd left him alone, as he'd known she would. She really just didn't care. After there was absolutely no sound in the house, he used the bathroom. In the kitchen, he drank three glasses of water and tore the drumsticks off the turkey in the refrigerator. He spent the rest of the day and another night in his room.

Now he licked his lips and stared across at the piece of white on the bulletin board. Did Mrs. Bennett know the power she held?

Probably. Probably laughed in bed with her husband about what she put her silly students through.

Guy heard the click of heels down the hallway and stepped back farther in the doorway. Laura Teason strode down the hall and stopped in front of the bulletin board. She was wearing tight jeans, midcalf black boots, and a pink sweater. He saw her start as if goosed. She looked up and down the hallway but apparently saw no one to share what she saw. He walked across the hall and said, "How does it look?" the first words he had ever said to her in three years in the same school.

"Oh," she said, startled.

He looked over her shoulder.

He was to be Cyrano.

Chucky was to be Christian.

Andrea was to be Roxane.

"I don't believe it," Laura breathed. "I'm supposed to be Lise? Opposite Bob Ernson?"

"Thanks, Mrs. Bennett," Guy said. He took a deep breath, turned to Laura, and squeezed her shoulder. "Don't feel bad. You get to tell Ragueneau off and have an affair with one of the Musketeers. There are worse parts." She looked pointedly at his hand, but he couldn't care less. He spun away, the adrenaline pumping through his veins, and set off looking for Andrea. Laura was beside his elbow.

"Your brother's going to be furious."

"Think so?" Guy said. "He got a good part too."

"You know so!"

"I suppose."

"It's not fair," she said, darkly.

He turned and faced her, laughing easily, feeling it right from his stomach. Cupping her right hand in both of his, he said, "Oh, come *on*, Laura, if it's anything, it's *fair*. You know that because you did everything you could to help Chucky get an *unfair* advantage."

"Let go of my hand."

"Sure." He squeezed it a little but let her pull away. She backed off a step, looking a bit frightened. "Listen," he said, "you and I get to have some nasty words onstage, when I tell you to stop messing around with the Musketeer. It's a good part for you, really it is. Calls for some flirting, someone who's pretty."

Her eyes narrowed, and she said, "Bull. It calls for a bitch."

"Yeah," Guy said. "Mrs. Bennett is a casting genius." He spun on his heel and started for the double doors.

"I'm going to tell your brother what you called me," she yelled.

"I'm going to tell your brother," he mimicked.

"And T.D.!"

"Please do."

"He'll smack that look off your face! Who the hell do you think you are?"

"That's the question, isn't it?" he said, and pushed through the doors.

■ ■ ■

Guy's mood only improved after he saw Andrea in the hallway. She kissed him. Right in the hallway, in front of everyone. And she promised to meet him just outside the cafeteria at noon, and they were going to walk in together, go through the line, and sit down and have lunch, in sight of all.

He stopped in the lavatory just before twelve and used the last stall on the end. No one else was in the black-and-white tiled bathroom. After a minute he heard the door open and close and the quiet tread of someone walking in. He could hear whoever it was walking along the stall doors, pushing them in. With a tickle of apprehension, he looked under the gray partition and saw the heavy black engineer boots that he recognized from Mrs. Bennett's class.

T.D. was looking for him.

Guy pulled up his pants and buckled his belt. The boots stopped right in front of his door. Guy imagined T.D. figured that he was cowering inside—"Oh please don't hurt me, T.D., oh please"—as he might have been, if the list had read differently that morning. Guy opened the door.

T.D. stared at him for a moment, hard. T.D. outweighed him

by fifty pounds. Some of it was fat, but his arm and chest muscles swelled under his football jersey. The boots were steel-toed. Guy knew he should be frightened.

"Knew I saw you running in here to hide," T.D. said.

"Uh-huh." Guy gestured to the toilet bowl. "Guess you really had me scared."

"Don't bother to flush, because I'm going to wash your mouth out in your own piss."

"And here I thought you were just going to stare me to death."

T.D.'s face went slack, and he cocked his head to one side. "How stupid are you? You eat your Wheaties or something, decide you're ready to take me on? I got enough on you already to send you down the Puerto Rican Whirlpool, the way you talked to me in front of everybody. Then you call Laura a bitch, and now you're wising off to me again." T.D. shook his head, and when he opened his mouth again, Guy hit him.

Guy planted his legs the way Rabson had shown him. He turned his fist slightly and connected solidly with T.D.'s mouth. He got a left into T.D.'s cheek before the bigger boy responded.

T.D.'s first punch glanced off Guy's head, and Guy fell back over the toilet, his back against the cool cinder-block wall. He grabbed the sides of the stall and buried his foot in T.D.'s stomach. T.D. expelled a gust of air, then covered his belly with his left arm. He drew back his right, and Guy kicked him in the face.

It was a good kick. Guy was braced tightly against the wall, and his left heel was hooked against the lip of the toilet bowl. Something gave in T.D.'s face. T.D. put his hands to his nose and backed out, muffling a scream. Blood streamed from between his fingers. "Hold it, man," T.D. moaned. "Stop." He turned to the mirror and took his trembling hands down. Guy followed him out of the stall. T.D.'s nose was crooked, and the blood poured down into his mouth. "You little bastard," he exclaimed, wincing. He peered into the mirror at Guy and said, "You broke my goddamn nose."

"Yeah?" Guy said, and slammed the heel of his hand into the back of T.D.'s head.

T.D.'s face made a wet sound against the mirror, and then he shoved himself off the sink, roaring. When he turned, Guy kicked him in the testicles. "No!" T.D. cried.

Guy went for the knee. Rabson had said you could cripple somebody for life with a good kick to the knee. The blood was pumping in Guy's arms and legs, and he was willing to poke T.D.'s eyes out.

But T.D. turned his leg just in time, and caught the blow on his muscular thigh. T.D. launched himself up at Guy, swinging. Guy danced away, then stepped in fast for one straight jab at the nose again. He almost laughed aloud when it connected, but T.D. just grunted, lowered his shoulders, and hooked toward Guy's belly. Guy twisted away, but the blow hit his left bicep with enough power to send him stumbling through the bathroom door into the hallway. His left arm was numb. Guy's mouth suddenly felt dry; things were moving very fast.

T.D. came charging out, the blood streaming from his nose onto his heaving chest. "You could have stopped it," T.D. rasped. "Now I'm going to pound your face into the pavement." Guy circled away. T.D. was crouched over, obviously still hurting from the kick to the groin, still trying to catch his breath. Guy swung his left arm, trying to get the feeling back into it.

"Guy!" He jerked his head left for a quick look. It was Andrea, her yellow hair flowing as she ran from the cafeteria entrance. "T.D., stop it, leave him *alone!*"

"It's okay, Andrea," Guy said. His breath was rushing in and out, and he could smell T.D.'s sweat.

A crowd of other students began to gather. "Knock him on his ass, T.D.," a voice called. T.D. was blowing hard. *Too many cigarettes after practice.*

"Look at T.D.'s face!" a girl's voice said. T.D. glanced toward her, and Guy stepped in for another shot at his nose. But T.D. pulled his head back fast and jarred Guy's vision with a left jab. Guy backed off and tasted salt in his mouth. "Come on, you faggot," T.D. ground out. "You wanted to dance."

"Both of you stop it!" Andrea said.

"Mind your own business," another girl's voice said, and then both Guy and T.D. looked to see Laura Teason standing on the

135

sidelines, her eyes narrowed. She flicked her red-tipped index finger at Guy. "Give it to him, T.D."

T.D. charged. He put his head down and drove at Guy full force. Guy backed up several steps toward the lockers, moving fast, and when T.D. was almost on him, he lunged off to the left, leaving his right leg behind. T.D. tripped over his foot.

The football player didn't get his arms up in time. His broken nose hit the lockers first. He made a high-pitched scream that sent a chill down Guy's back.

But the feeling translated quickly into a sudden exhilaration. Guy looked around at the circle of other students. Laura looked shocked and disgusted. Andrea's expression was much the same . . . plus something else. Maybe fear.

Guy looked at the blood on the back of his hands and felt the soreness in his shoulder. It all felt wonderful. He leaned over and rapped his knuckles against T.D.'s forehead.

"No more," T.D. moaned, covering his face.

"So this is what it's like, huh?" Guy whispered.

GUY WAITED OUTSIDE the Dance Factory for three nights before seeing Ericka. It was a Thursday night, and the crowd was heavy as he followed her in. The music was driving hard, and his nose wrinkled at the smell and touch of so many people.

She went directly to the bar and ordered what appeared to be a White Russian. Guy leaned against a cloth-covered post and watched her watch the video. She wore red pants with tight cuffs and a pair of white, two-inch heels. He noticed the glint of an anklet. Her tank top was stretched tight, outlining her breasts snugly. Guy was struck again with how pretty her face was, in a blank sort of way. He thought of Rod picking her up the first time, took a deep breath, and strode up to her.

"Remember me, Ericka?"

She sipped the milky drink, holding the glass with two hands. "What do you want?"

Guy bent down to hear her over the music. "To apologize. I hated running out on you

13

like that, but my friend's girlfriend was getting sick. We came in the same car."

"She didn't look sick to me." Ericka looked past him, at the video. "You looked like you wanted to be with *her,* anyhow."

Guy was surprised. He didn't think she had been paying that much attention. Or that he was so obvious about Bette. "No," he said. "You've got it wrong. She did get sick, we had to stop the car. Too much to drink. Besides, I came back here to see you, didn't I?"

She shrugged. "I guess so. I saw you watching me over there." She gestured toward the pole. "Are you going to run tonight, too?" She drained her glass.

"No." Guy nodded toward the dance floor. "Want to?"

She shook her head. "Buy me another one of these and we'll go. That's what you came for, anyhow."

■ ■ ■

They walked past the big green wall of Fenway Park and took a right into Kenmore Square. Halfway there she put her hand in his, again surprising Guy with her humid touch. He tried to make conversation.

"Do you go to school around here? Boston University?"

"Supposed to," she said, looking straight ahead. "It's what the Dads is paying rent for."

"But you don't go."

She looked at him.

"So what do you do?"

"You'll see." She giggled.

He almost jumped. The feeling must have transmitted to her, because she hugged his arm against her breasts, her features suddenly animated. "You're going to be so glad you came with me. I'm good at this."

Guy's mouth was dry. They were walking past the subway entrance, and he resisted an urge to run down the stairs. He imagined the train down below. The only thing between being humiliated and not was to push this girl away, put a token into the turnstile, and let the Green Line take him back to Rod's apartment. Her fingers tightened on his arm.

"I'm good enough for the both of us," she said. "You've never had anyone like me, because this is all I like to do, all I'm good at. You don't worry about a thing."

"Not a thing, huh?" He tried to say it lightly, but he heard his voice quaver.

"Not a thing." She smiled for the first time, looking beautiful to him in that moment. She continued holding his arm to her, as if he were saving her from falling off a cliff. Tugging him toward a huge stone apartment building, she pulled keys from her shoulder bag and let them into the lobby. The floors looked like real marble. The elevator was modern. She pushed the button at the top, fourteenth floor.

The apartment was a small one-bedroom with wood wainscoting and a view of the Charles River. Guy could see the lights of Cambridge. He stood in the living room and looked for a place to sit. Against one wall there was a leather couch, but there were no chairs. The floor was covered with a thick Oriental rug. The opposite wall was dominated by a huge television, VCR, and stereo.

"My parents picked the apartment, gave me the sofa and the rug. I picked out the stereo and all, and the bed, courtesy of Mr. American Express." She pulled him to the sofa, and he sat down. "Now I'm going to make you feel good. You'll see."

His heart was pounding as he watched her go into the bedroom. Closing his eyes, he thought of the night before. After giving up waiting for Ericka to show at the Dance Factory, he had gone home. Hearing Bette's voice inside Rod's bedroom, he had slipped into the closet and watched. Now, with the scene of Rod moving faster and harder into Bette in his mind, he began to relax. He could deal with this Ericka. And if she laughed . . . she would only do it once.

"You're not falling asleep on me, are you?"

Guy opened his eyes. Ericka was wearing only a long T-shirt. Her bare legs were firm and very white. When she walked over to the VCR to push in a cassette, he saw she wasn't wearing any panties.

The TV screen was gray snow while the tape hissed. She dimmed the overhead lights, stepped into the kitchen quickly, and came back carrying a ceramic plate with a small mound of cocaine, a short, red-striped straw, and a razor blade.

"Part one of making Brendan feel great," she said.

"Why are you doing this?"

"Why not?" She held the straw out. "Come on. You'll like it."

"I've never done it."

"All the better."

She chopped the coke and made four lines, then snorted two, one in each nostril. Then she handed him the straw. He stuck the straw in his nose and inhaled. Tears sprang to his eyes. It was like breathing water.

"You won't feel like crying soon."

Guy looked at her sharply. He could read no insult in her face, but he was still cautious. He did the other line and palmed the razor blade.

She kissed his cheek, her lips soft. He moved to put his arms around her, but she pushed him back gently. "You lie back. Watch the TV. Let me have the fun, let me play with you."

Guy began to feel very, very good. All was right with him. And if things started to go wrong, there was always the razor. The edges of it bit slightly into his hand now, but the small pain was an anchor to his control. He suddenly saw the mistakes he had made, the people he had killed unnecessarily. But it was all right. He knew what to do now, because he was so strong. He could walk through the wall if he wanted to. Guy laughed aloud and stroked Ericka's fine, silky hair. If she didn't behave, he could cut it all off. She unbuttoned his shirt, then his belt buckle.

"That feels good," she said and then pouted. "But remember, you lay there and take what I'm giving. That's my fun."

"Sounds good to me, good to me." Guy laughed aloud at his redundancy. He looked at the television and realized Ericka had put on a porno tape. Enthralled, he watched a scene similar to his reality, a girl kneeling in front of a naked man. He closed his eyes and leaned back farther into the couch. The naked man became Rod, and the woman Bette. And then he became Rod, and Ericka became Bette.

And a little while later, when he screamed aloud with pleasure, holding her head in his lap, Guy Nolan knew that once again he was complete.

■ ■ ■

Two hours later he rolled out of her bed and began to pull on his pants. The shades were open, and he could see cars and people moving down on the street. A small crowd began to pour out of a nightclub with a red neon disk for a sign.

"You're going?" Her voice was sleep muffled, petulant.

"Got to. Subway will close soon." Guy wondered if Rod was still up. It would be perfect, Rod saying, "Where have you been?" And he would tell him. Rod would say something for sure about him not waiting for Lori on Saturday night, and then they both would laugh.

"You can stay the night."

Guy strode quickly into the bathroom and turned on the light. The girl's stockings hung from the shower rod, looking small and misshapen. He repeatedly splashed his face with cool water, pushed back his hair, and dried off with her towel. It didn't smell clean. He considered using her toothbrush but decided against it. *Diseases.* He went back into the bedroom.

"You're not staying." She hugged the sheet to her breasts. "It's not like I'm asking you to get married or something. I don't like being alone. You know?"

He sat on the edge of the bed and put on his shoes. "You'll be all right." He started to get up, but she grabbed his arm, pulling him back down. Her breath was faintly sour. Thinking what she had done for him, he turned his face away, nose wrinkling. Her kiss landed on his ear.

His body remained stiff in her arms.

Suddenly angry, she pushed him away. "I treated you great, I made you happy. You were shaking like a leaf! I bet you never did

141

it before." Ericka swung at him ineffectively, her fingers brushing the top of his head.

He slapped her backhanded. She collapsed on the bed and curled over, sobbing. He started for the razor blade in the other room, but as fast as the thought came the rage left.

What she said didn't change what they had done earlier.

Guy stood over her, his hands clenched. "What did you expect? I'm not going to spend my night with a nympho whore. Who knows what kinds of bugs are crawling around in you?"

She curled tighter, her sobs coming out in long hiccups. He left the apartment and pushed the button for the elevator. By the time he reached the lobby, Guy was smiling. *So what if it got a little rough toward the end?* She'd done it to him the way any man would like it done. And he hadn't had to kill her. Or Rod. And there was still Saturday night.

■ ■ ■

Guy was beginning to get angry at Rod. First off, he hadn't asked where Guy had been that Thursday. The secret about Ericka was bursting inside him, but he just couldn't blurt it out at dinner. Instead, Rod had asked about the date he'd planned with Lori, giving advice like he was such a pro. Said that Lori was "rubbed raw," that she could be more difficult than she appeared at first, that he should take it easy with her.

On top of that, Saturday night he told Guy, just as he was walking out to meet Lori, that Bette would be spending the night at the condo. Two messages—Lori's difficult, but stay with her so I can have the place to myself.

Guy hesitated, slapped his back pocket, and went back into his room. He stood before the closet, thinking.

Rod was pushing him too fast. Too goddamn fast.

He opened the closet door and pulled down the blue makeup case. From it, he took all the cash and the little packet of fake I.D.'s he had accumulated in his travels.

He slammed the front door on the way out.

. . .

"Something doesn't fit about you," Lori said. They were at dinner, and she had been asking probing questions for the past hour: How can you afford to pay rent and go to school without working? What kind of house did you own? What color was it? Tell me about your major in school. What kind of kid was your favorite student?

He began to search for a waiter. "How's that?"

She toyed with her wineglass. "I don't know. I mean you're quiet and all. Nice, maybe kind of tense in some ways. But then I'll see you looking at me, or at Rod or Bette, and . . . I don't know, I see something *different*. Something a little more wild than an English teacher from upstate New York with a green ranch house."

He said, "Well, I really am just an English teacher who paid his mortgage like a diligent worker ant, and when I sold it, I made enough to give me the luxury of a year off. But if you see something more exciting than that, then I'm happy to hear it."

She cocked her head. "Exciting . . . well, yes, there is that too. I'll get you to tell me all about it, you know."

"We'll see," he said. "In the meantime, let's not starve." They ordered chicken wings, mooshu pork, and shrimp noodles and had another two rounds of drinks. Lori's fortune cookie told her patience is a virtue, and she burned the little slip of paper in the candle lantern and laughed. Guy followed suit.

"You even seem a bit different than the Brendan I met last week," Lori said.

"How so?"

"I don't know. More confident, I guess." Her lips curved into a mischievous smile. "What've you been doing, you're feeling so smug about?"

There was a hint of jealousy in her question, and laughter rushed up from his belly. He practically shouted.

"That good?"

"Very."

"Ready to tell me your secret yet?"

"Maybe you'll get lucky and I won't have to."

"Sounds ominous," she said, and changed the subject.

After dinner, they went to Quincy Market, and drifted among the bars for two hours until Lori stretched languorously and said, "Let's catch a cab." When it arrived at her apartment building, she looked up at her window and said, "No lights. Looks like Bette isn't home."

She turned to him and grinned. "I guess we knew that, didn't we?"

Already? he thought. The confidence he had been feeling flowed out his arms and legs and lay on the floor of the cab. Guy could hear his heart. It was as if it were on a circuit of its own, pounding a fearful beat. He squeezed his hand into a fist, angry at himself, at her. The cabbie glanced back at him, and Guy realized suddenly that both of them were waiting for an answer.

He clutched at the memory of Ericka, momentarily retrieving the feeling of warmth pouring out of him into her. Guy took Lori's hand in his and put his lips close to her scented hair. "Knew it? I arranged it."

"That's funny," Lori said aloud. "I thought I did." She nodded toward the driver. "So pay the man and let's go."

Guy followed her up the stairs, his mouth dry, his body feeling awkward. All the food and drink lay heavily in his belly. How about the shrimp? Seafood was supposed to be an aphrodisiac. He chewed at the inside of his mouth. Rod didn't have to count on what he had for dinner making him a good lover.

Why was she making him follow her up the stairs? She wasn't acting at all like Ericka. He struggled mentally for the girl kneeling before him, the video, and the lines of coke. But already his image of Ericka was flickering out. He looked down at his clothes, the boat shoes, the chinos. Diving, the scuba lessons . . .

". . . you panicked . . ."

Rod and Bette would believe anything Lori told them. Guy's mind raced. How did he get into this, going to the apartment of a girl who would talk, a girl who knew people he knew?

144

Lori glanced over her shoulder as she unlocked the door and let him in. She frowned, "Are you all right Brendan?"

"Nothing's the matter with me."

She laughed and put her palm against his cheek. "Well, good. You just looked for a minute there like I was about to skewer you." She closed the door behind him.

14

ANDREA WOULD NOT talk to Guy. She turned away from him when the shop teacher, Mr. Santelli, grabbed his arm and started to hustle him and T.D. off to the vice principal's office. He almost called out to her but didn't.

Mr. Terault sent T.D. to the nurse's office. He was a short man with graying hair and hard little eyes. This was the first time he and Guy had ever spoken to each other, and he looked repeatedly in Guy's file as if to find an explanation. "I've never seen you in for anything like this, . . . Guy." He took his glasses off. "You know that T.D. is going to have to go to the hospital. If you were an adult, this would be a police matter."

"He started it," Guy said. "And he's a lot bigger than I am."

"That's not an excuse, that's bragging," Mr. Terault snapped. He turned a page in the file and looked up. "Is your brother Chucky Nolan?"

Guy nodded.

"It seems I was seeing your brother in here

every week when he was a freshman. But then he settled right down. Are you trying to follow in his footsteps in your"—he consulted the folder—"junior year?"

"T.D. and I were just kidding around," Guy said. "It just went too far."

"It certainly did." Mr. Terault put the folder aside and stared hard at Guy. "I kept wondering why I've heard about you recently, and it just came to me. Mrs. Bennett said this morning that both you and your brother are in the play. Isn't that right?"

"Yes."

"Which part do you have?"

"Cyrano."

"You like being in the play, do you?"

Guy paused. Then he shrugged and said, "I love it."

"Well then, you better listen to what I'm saying. I don't want to hear about a lot of catch-up going on between you and T.D. I don't want you being the fastest gun who's trying everyone out. Because if I do, you'll be lucky if you can get a seat in the back row of the auditorium, never mind playing the lead role. Got it?"

Guy licked his lips. "It wasn't my fault."

Mr. Terault waved that away. "I don't want to hear it. It takes two, and T.D.'s face is proof you weren't some victim. The only reason I'm not kicking you out of school for a few weeks is that your record shows nothing like this, and I've had T.D. in here all too many times." He nodded to the door. "So get out and make this your one and only visit."

As Guy put his hand on the knob, Mr. Terault said, "I know who you are now, Guy. And I'll be watching."

■ ■ ■

"I hate violence," Andrea said. "I can't stand it when guys try to show off." They were in the room next to the teachers' lounge again.

"So I should have let T.D. push my face in so I wouldn't be showing off?"

"I didn't say that."

147

Guy looked around the room. "I figured I was in for a lecture, given the location."

Her chin lifted. "What's wrong with the room?"

"Look, Andrea, what was I supposed to do?"

"Couldn't you have talked to him first?"

Her expression was earnest. *She's really not too bright*, he realized. Guy shook his head and said, "Not without blowing bubbles. He came into the bathroom to shove my face in the toilet."

She jerked back. "Gross!"

"That was my opinion."

"What a pig! Who does he think he is!" Andrea's face flushed angrily. "What makes him think he can get away with stuff like that?"

"Because he has," Guy said, and quickly added, "but not with me. Not like that."

Andrea bit her lip and met his eyes for the first time that afternoon. "A lot of people saw you hurt him," she said. "I bet they were awfully surprised."

"I'm sure they were." Guy sat down on the teacher's desk and said levelly, "Especially that I was the one to do it."

"Yes," she said. "I thought I knew you. And I was shocked."

"Is that good?"

She looked out the window a moment and then turned back to him. "I don't know. Honest to God, I don't."

■ ■ ■

Three weeks later, Laura Teason sat down beside the two of them in the cafeteria and told them she was having a party the Friday before the Saturday opening of the play. Neither answered right away, and she ran her fingers back through her hair and said, "Well? You need it in an envelope with an RSVP card?"

Guy looked at Andrea and then nodded to Laura. "Thanks. We'll be there."

"Okay, then. We could use some more pot, but if you don't have the connections, bring beer. Maybe Chucky can loan you an I.D., Guy. Plan on heading over to my house right after rehearsal."

"Do you know how to get there?" Guy asked Andrea.

"Don't worry about it," Laura interrupted. "Just follow Chucky's car. He knows the way."

• • •

But on Friday, Chucky didn't arrive until later. The party had started off better than Guy had expected. Andrea, who was wearing tight black jeans and a white cashmere sweater, held his arm lightly as they walked in. He found it easy to talk with the other cast members and saw acceptance and interest in their eyes.

Until his brother walked in the door. Guy could feel the others fall back from him, as if blown away by a cold wind. Chucky walked up to the two of them and said, "Well, Guy, you're making so much progress, it makes me proud. You took on T.D., and now you're standing here at a party without stuttering and spraying beer all around. It does an older brother's heart good."

"Why don't you get lost, Chucky?" Andrea said.

Laura came up to them. "Did you say Guy stutters? I hope he doesn't do it onstage."

Andrea turned to him. "Come on, we can leave."

"It's not a problem," he said.

"It is to me." She walked away.

Chucky watched Andrea, and Laura watched him. When his gaze swung back to Guy, his face was a little flushed, his eyes hard. Something flickered behind his expression, and he smiled. "So what's different, Guy? Why shouldn't I just shake this beer up and spray you with foam, for old times' sake? What's different?"

Guy tested the weight of the near full can in his palm. *Shove that full force in his face, I'll have time to do some real damage.*

"Uh-uh," Chucky said, standing straight. "Don't do it."

"Do what?" Laura said.

"Who knows?" Chucky said, grinning. "Isn't that right, Guy? You don't know and neither do I."

"Not again," Laura said. "This is supposed to be a party."

"I've been doing this for years," Chucky said, kissing her on the

149

ear. "The stories I could tell, the things I've done to him. Right, Guy?" He winked. "Remember Teri? She left last year? You remember, Laura, big bazoombies, all us guys were going nuts."

"Yeah, I remember," Laura said.

"Well, I told Guy here she called. Said she called, asked for him, wouldn't talk to me, just wanted *him*. I acted jealous, pissed off all day. Guy's choking and swallowing, trying to work up his nerve to call her. Finally sits down in the living room, writes out some of the witty things he wants to remember to say on a piece of *paper*, and then he calls." Chucky stood straight, popped his eyes wide open, and spoke into an imaginary phone. "Hi, Teri, it's me, Guy. . . . Guy Nolan . . . I'm returning your call . . . yes you did! . . . *You did!*"

Chucky slapped his leg. "Goddamn, he loses it totally, top of his lungs, tears going down his face, telling her she better stop fooling around with him. Me, I'm dying in the kitchen, dying. He hears me, slams the phone down, and runs off to his room. Didn't see you for two days after that, did we, Guy?"

"About that," Guy said cheerfully.

Chucky's grin faltered. Then he continued. "Yeah, that was my brother, hurrying down the hallway, looking at his shoes, hoping nobody would notice him. Put your fist out, he'd smash it with his face. But now I've got to think twice, don't I?"

Guy just grinned at him. Laura said, "What's going on with you two?"

Chucky ignored her. "Well, just you remember. T.D.'s a walking lard bucket compared to me. And I won't stop because I'm feeling sorry for you anymore."

"Yeah, that's good," Guy said, nodding. "I'll have to think up a good excuse, too."

■ ■ ■

"What's Chucky doing in your dad's car?" Andrea asked. They were on the way out of the house when Chucky got out of the car on the driver's side and slammed the door shut. He started up the walk toward them. "Well, if it isn't the handsome couple after a fine night of partying," he said. "Leaving us already?"

"What were you doing in there?" Guy said.

"Checking the mileage," he said, grinning. "Forty-two thousand, two hundred and fifty. As the older brother, I have obligations. If it's off by the distance from here to Andrea's house to home—six point two miles—then we'll have some interesting conversation tomorrow."

"Oh, for God's sake!" Andrea said. "Why are you doing this?"

Guy could see it coming. He could read his brother so much better these days, after having learned how to slip into a part himself. His brother let his dazzling grin fade. He looked directly at Andrea and let an embarrassed expression move across his face. "I think you know why, Andrea," he said, quietly.

Guy clapped slowly—one, two, three.

Andrea touched his arm and said, "No, don't."

"Mind your own business, Guy," Chucky said, harshly.

Andrea turned to Guy, saying, "Please go on to the car, okay?"

He looked back at her silently for a moment and then said, "You're not falling for this, are you?"

"I want to talk with Chucky alone!" Andrea tossed her hair impatiently. "Trust me!"

He turned his back to her and strode off to the car. Once behind the wheel, he looked back at the two of them, seething. It was all he could do to keep from turning the ignition on and running over the both of them with the family sedan. After a time, it appeared as if Andrea were almost entreating Chucky. But she came toward the car soon after Laura walked out of the house. In the moonlight, Laura's face showed bitter jealousy. Andrea's was unreadable.

Andrea slammed the car door. "Let's go," she said.

They didn't talk for the first few minutes. Guy kept his attention straight ahead, and Andrea looked out the passenger side window. Finally she turned to him and said, "I actually *like* you a lot more than him. I really do. That's why I agreed to do the play with you.

And just to show everyone that I do what I want, not what they expect. So I can't tell you why I sent you off to the car and acted like a bitch."

He nodded. "All right."

They rode on in silence for another minute, then she stamped her foot and said, "Damn it! It is *not* all right! I shouldn't have done that to you, and you shouldn't have let me. You should be angry at me. You should be furious."

"I am, but not at you. I know how good Chucky's act is, how good he is at talking. What did he say?"

She looked shamefaced. "It doesn't matter."

Guy waited.

She said, "I guess I expected some big romance from him, but all he was trying to do was get me to leave and go parking. Right then. He was very insulting about you. It was like he was just trying to beat you. I didn't matter. And then he backed right off when Laura showed up."

"Would you have gone if she hadn't?"

"No!" She looked at him quickly. In the dim light of the passing cars, Guy had to look at her several times before he realized she was crying.

"Hey, you don't need to do that."

"Yeah, well it stinks being me sometimes."

"Why? You've got everything." He took her hand.

"Like what?" she said, snatching it back. "Because I'm pretty? Because I'm *popular*? So what, I listened to Chucky mostly because I knew how *good* we looked as a couple, and that's a stupid reason to be with somebody. Really stupid."

"So you might've gone with him," Guy said dully.

"No." Then she said, softly, "I don't know, maybe."

He swallowed that and said, "You know how many times he's fooled me? You caught on to him right away, compared to me." Guy almost asked her the question that was always at the back of his mind: Have you ever slept with Chucky? Instead, he said, "I never imagined you crying about something like this."

She sniffed. "What did you think I would cry about?"

Beyond his control, his lips twisted into a smile. "Like if you had a party and none of the right people showed up."

"Stupid." She began to go through her purse. "I'd cry about that too. So what?" He gave her the box of Kleenex that his father always kept in the car.

"If I had a party, I'd be glad if *anyone* showed up," he said.

"I know. Believe me, I know that." She blew her nose and dried her tears. "But that's already changing. You saw the way everybody was looking at you tonight. All the guys thinking about that fight you had with T.D. and all the girls wondering what they missed."

They rode in silence for a few minutes. Finally she sat up straight, put on a smile, and said, "There. Now you've seen me cry and know that I've got feelings. What else do you want to do tonight? Stick each other with some pins?" She peered out the window. "Where are we?"

Without giving it a lot of thought, he had turned down River Road. It was a narrow road that was only infrequently used since the old mill closed down. Except to go parking. There were a number of places where cars had pushed through the underbrush to avoid the view of passing drivers. Cheap privacy on the water.

"By the river."

"Oh." She stared at him and then said, "So, my crying made you want to go parking with me? I don't know if I like that."

Guy took a deep breath and pulled the car over. He slid the gearshift into park and faced her. He said, "No. You being pretty and fun and smart makes me want to take you parking. The crying kept me from being afraid to ask."

She didn't answer at first. His mouth was dry, and his heartbeat quickened. "Well," she said, finally. "That sounds like the truth."

He nodded.

"You don't tell the truth very often do you, Guy?"

He shook his head. "Hardly ever."

"Me either," she said. "I just don't worry about it as much as you do."

He grinned. "That's the secret?"

"You bet," she said, softly. "Now let's find a place where nobody can see us."

. . .

Finding the right spot took awhile. He first nosed the car down what appeared to be a path, but it ended abruptly in an oak tree. "I don't think this will work, with half the car still on the street," she said.

He tried several spots farther down the road, growing more uncomfortable all the while, until Andrea said, "That looks good." She pointed to a shadowy area near the apex of a sharp curve. He looked at her in the faint lights from the dashboard, but she didn't notice, leaning forward, staring off into the darkness. The path was deeply rutted, and he had to be careful not to bottom out. They continued for several car lengths under the bower of trees, until they reached a small clearing overlooking the shimmering river. They were bathed in cold moonlight. "Good choice," he said.

"Watch it," she said. "If you ask me if I come here often, I'll smack you."

"I'm not that brave."

She patted the seat beside her. "How brave are you?"

He shifted to be beside her. A little bell went off in his head. Should he have pulled her close instead of moving toward her? He pushed the thought aside, thinking instead of Cyrano sweeping his hat off and bending down to kiss Roxane—something, he remembered abruptly, that never happened in the play.

Her mouth was firm against his. She kissed him back, and he moved down across her cheek to her neck. Her skin was incredibly soft and smooth, and the feel of her cheek against his was all he had imagined. He groaned aloud, inhaling her perfume. She was so good to him, so delicious. He nipped at her neck.

"Ow!" Andrea pushed him back and rubbed her neck. "Are you trying to mark me?"

Guy's throat was tight. "Sorry."

She flipped down the passenger side visor. "Doesn't this car have a mirror?" She turned the rearview mirror to look at herself. He turned on the light. "Sorry," he repeated.

She shrugged. "Just take it easy, all right? And turn out the light." She snuggled back in his arms. "Am I bossy, Guy?"

He thought for a moment, then said, "Not really."

"You're lying again," she teased.

"That's true."

"So if I am, I am. I'm worth it. Don't you want to kiss me again?"

He put his arms around her again. She put her hand to his chin. "Slow now. It's gross when guys stick their tongues in your mouth right away."

He winced. His sense of Cyrano faltered. He became more aware of the car, sitting in the little clearing. Looking over her shoulder, he could see in the moonlight an old striped mattress near the underbrush. With a sudden clarity he saw it in bright daylight, sodden, and surrounded with a litter of used condoms.

Guy closed his eyes, leaned forward, and kissed her, gently, firmly. She sighed a little and pushed back harder, and their teeth clicked. "Oh, yes," she murmured and kissed him back harder, opening her mouth slightly.

He decided to touch her breasts. She stiffened when his hand touched the bare skin of her belly, but she didn't stop him. Nor did she stop him when he slid his hand underneath her bra and massaged her breasts, squeezing her nipples. She didn't object when he unsnapped her jeans.

By then he was terrified.

It didn't look like she was going to stop him, and he wasn't hard anymore. He had deflated like a pinpricked balloon when she'd complained about the hickey. She was half on top of him now, kissing him back, her nipples little rocks against the palms of his hands. His mind filled with the knowledge of how far he had come, to have a girl like her in the car with him, half-naked and wanting him, moaning for him. How any other male in the school would kill to be in his place. How *he* had dreamed of being here. . . . What was *wrong* with him now?

"Take off your shirt," she said, and started with his buttons. He helped her, latching onto the glimmering hope that when he was naked, against her body, he would warm up. He hit his knee on the steering wheel taking off his pants. He considered stepping out of the car to take his clothes off, but quickly discarded that idea as ridiculous. She giggled. "Oh boy, oh boy, it's getting cold," she said. "This is going to feel good. Let's get in the back."

She opened the door and stepped out, automatically covering her breasts. He admired her naked body in an excruciatingly detached way—she was more beautiful than he had imagined, with firm breasts, a flat stomach, and high, rounded buttocks. . . . And his body was asleep from the waist down. The door slammed behind him. "I'm ready," she whispered. "Hurry back here, before I freeze to death."

He looked down at his penis, frozen to a smaller size than he had ever seen it.

"Come *on!*"

He stepped out into the cold and opened the back door.

■　■　■

She said, "Has this happened to you before?"

"Never," he said.

They were sitting up now in the backseat. Andrea had reached into the front seat and had pulled on her sweater immediately after it became apparent he wasn't able to enter her.

She made an exasperated sound. "Guy, stop lying. You never tried to make love to anyone else before, did you?"

He lay his head in a corner of the seat, not touching her. This was the family car. He had ridden in the backseat hundreds of times, thinking only that his life was inordinately dull. "No," he said. "You're right."

She bit at her lower lip and then reached forward and got her panties and jeans. She dressed quickly.

"Here." She draped his pants over his knee, her eyes averted.

He dragged his clothes on, probing himself, trying to judge how much he was hurt. He wanted to ask her to help but couldn't imagine how she possibly could. There was only a dead, grainy feeling that hinted the damage was too substantial to face at once. He felt like a piece of wood. Andrea got in the front seat and looked straight ahead.

"How about you?" he asked.

"No." She shook her head. "Not the first."

He stared at her, wondering who it could be. He couldn't help himself. "Did this ever happen before?"

"Of course not!" She stared at him. "This is not me, Guy. This is your problem. It's not my job to . . . to rejuvenate you! This is the type of thing you read about happening to men in their forties, it shouldn't be happening to us."

"Andrea, what are you saying? That I'm sick? I'm crazy or something?"

She shrugged. "Maybe you're just different. You know, some men are like that. They don't like women."

His voice was hoarse. "No, don't say that. I'm not queer."

"I don't know, Guy. All I know is that it's not my fault you can't get hard. It's not my fault."

15

"MY NEXT BOYFRIEND isn't going to run off to play with the fishies every Sunday morning," Bette said.

Rod buttoned a light-blue denim shirt and tucked it into his jeans. "My next girlfriend won't make idle threats in the morning. She'll make me breakfast." He rolled up his sleeves and put on his dive watch.

"She sounds like a fool." This said while she was yawning, Bette bunched the pillow under her head and observed him. "I wish we could spend the day together."

"I know you do." He sat on the edge of the bed and kissed her lightly. "I do, too."

"It's not fair, you know. I don't think Brendan came back last night. I didn't hear him anyhow, and he always makes so much noise banging around in the bathroom."

"So what's not fair?"

"Well, we introduce them, and they get to have Sunday mornings together and we don't." She grabbed the front of his shirt and tugged. "What's fair about that? Huh?" He kissed her again, lingering.

"You're right, it's not fair. Assuming he's not here."

Bette threw off the covers and headed toward the hallway wearing only a pair of lime-colored panties. Her light skin had turned summer ruddy; smooth muscles rippled in her legs. At the doorway, she covered her breasts with her hands and yelled down the hall, "Brendan! Are you here?"

No answer.

She dropped her hands and grinned back at Rod, saying in a fair imitation of a baritone, "Looks like he got lucky last night."

"Not as lucky as me." Rod looked at his watch. "Thing is, though, he's supposed to get certified today, and I was going to give him a ride. I'll call him."

Bette put her hands on her hips. "You will *not* call him. If he needed a ride, he would've called you. There are more important things than a scuba certification, Rod Konrad."

"Like what?" He put his hand on her waist.

She grinned. "You need a description?"

"An explicit one."

She grasped his wrist and pulled it up against her breast and looked down. "Ah, what a shame. No time."

"I can be a little late." His voice was hoarse.

"We get started, you'll be a *lot* late. You know it."

"I don't care."

She laughed. "Not now you don't. But you'll do a hundred in your van making up for lost time. No, I'd feel guilty, I couldn't enjoy myself."

"Hah."

"Not as much," she amended.

"Tonight, then."

"Tonight."

"In the meantime, why don't you follow me to the beach in your car? At least I can look at you some more."

"Okay. I'll be sure to pout whenever you look my way. And when you take out the dive boat this afternoon, I'll have some lunch, take

159

some photos, do some shopping, and you can meet me at my apartment afterward. What time do you think?"

"About six."

"You're on."

■ ■ ■

Bette walked up the stairs to her apartment a little after five-thirty, wishing she had put on more sun block. She'd fallen asleep on the beach after Rod left for the boat dive. Afterward, in addition to buying a new summer dress, she'd picked up a frame for a photo she had taken, with the timer, of her, Rod, and Lori on the couch. Her forehead was hot; the skin over her cheeks felt tight and shiny. More freckles on the way for sure. A cool bath, along with a tall lemonade beside the tub, if Lori had left any, would start the evening off right. She marveled that Rod was able to keep up such a pace during the day and still be fun at night. She smiled to herself and hoped that Brendan and Lori had had as good a time last night.

He was sitting at the kitchen table when she walked in. "Hey, Bette. How's my girl?"

She wrinkled her brow faintly. "Fine thanks. Where's Lori?"

"She's gone."

"Gone?" Bette put down her shopping bag and opened the refrigerator door. "Ah, plenty of lemonade! Lori normally goes through this stuff like she was plugged into an IV." She turned back to him and felt a tickle of apprehension in her belly. He was leaning back in the chair in a way that didn't look too comfortable. As if he was trying to appear relaxed but wasn't. He hadn't shaved, and his hair was uncombed and sweaty looking. "So did Lori go out to the store?"

"That's what the girl did, she went to the store."

Bette sipped the lemonade and then ran her tongue along her lips.

"Everything okay, Brendan?"

"Everything's okay, Bette."

Her stomach chilled. He had never been rude in any way before.

Something must have gone wrong with him and Lori. Bette didn't want to have to deal with one of Lori's scenes now.

"Good!" she said. "I'm going to take a bath now and try and forget about that sun our friend Rod likes to stay under so much."

She strode out of the kitchen toward her bedroom. Along the way she noticed the hall telephone line was pulled into Lori's room. The door was closed. She hesitated before her roommate's door and then reflexively looked over her shoulder. Guy was standing in the kitchen doorway, watching. Bette continued on to her own room.

Why should I care if he sees me? she thought. After all, I could be just going to take the phone. Thinking that troubled her all the more. Why should she care *what* he thought? She looked at her watch. Rod would be along soon. *I should tell Brendan that.* She pursed her lips. *Why should I? So he's had an argument with Lori. He wouldn't be the first guy. Why get yourself in an uproar, scaredy-cat?*

In her room Bette stepped out of her shorts and halter and put on a blue silk robe that felt cool to her skin. She went back into the hallway. He was still standing in the kitchen door. She ignored him, though her breathing quickened as she stepped into the bathroom and turned on the water. She snapped the door lock and didn't care if he could hear it.

When the tub was full, she slipped out of the robe and stepped into the lukewarm water. A cold bath always sounded better than the reality. Leaning back, she closed her eyes and tried to relax. She felt as if she had just drunk three cups of coffee. She bent forward, turned on the cold water, and rinsed her face, then turned the flow off. After soaping up, she splashed water on herself, trying to ignore the goose bumps that were forming on her arms and legs.

Outside the bathroom door the floor creaked.

She went rigid. "Brendan! The bathroom's occupied."

The knob turned slightly. Bette's heart began to pound.

"Brendan!"

He kicked the door in. It smashed against the tub. Bette tried to stand, but he shoved her shoulder with the heel of his hand, and she

161

slipped and fell back into the the tub. Water sloshed onto the floor and against his legs. "Stay there," he said.

"Get out!" Her voice was savage with fear. "What are you doing?" *God, this isn't happening*, she thought. *Not here, not in my own place. It's always in the news; you always read that it's somebody you know.* She pulled the shower curtain just under her chin.

He ran his fingers through his hair, then rubbed the side of his face, not quite looking at her at first. The day's growth of whiskers rasped. "Shut up," he said, taking a step closer. He turned his eyes to hers now, and she couldn't help but cringe. His eyes were red-rimmed, feverish.

"I don't have any clothes on, get the hell out of here!"

He swung his arm back and tore away the shower curtain. "Shut up, I said. Stop yammering at me."

Bette sank deeper into the water and brought her knees up to her chest. She felt a tear slip down her cheek, and she brushed it away quickly. *Don't show him that*, she thought.

"I've listened to *enough* orders. *Enough* advice. *Enough* of people telling me how to act, of me *worrying* what they think."

"I don't know what you're talking about, Brendan. Please just leave."

"No." He shook his head. "No. I'm not. What are you going to do?"

She paused. Then, quietly, "Just get out."

"Or what?"

"I'll scream."

He grinned and knelt beside the tub suddenly. "You go ahead." His right hand flashed out and he had her by the neck, his forearm straight. He slammed into her, forcing her head into the corner.

Bette couldn't breathe. Her hands were slippery with soap. She dug her fingernails into his sleeve and pulled. The button snapped off, revealing angry scratches up to his elbow.

Her scream was a gag. She tried to push him away with her leg. He leaned closer and shoved her head underwater. *It's not fair, I couldn't get a breath, it's not fair.* . . . She reached up, trying for his eyes. All she felt was his hair.

She was pulled free from the water. He raised his head and said calmly, "You just nod your head when you want me to stop."

She jabbed two fingers at his eyes.

He ducked and caught her right hand with his left. Grasping her thumb, he wrenched it backward. Excruciating pain raced up her arm. He stretched his arms wide, pitting his muscles against hers, stretching apart her arm and neck. *He's going to hurt me,* she thought with surprising detachment. *It's my body, but he's going to damage me.*

She made herself go limp. She nodded.

His eyes narrowed, and he squeezed her throat even tighter. He twisted her thumb viciously. "It's up to me, right, Bette? It's up to me. Nod your head."

She nodded again.

He let go of her hand. She forced herself to fold her hands in her lap, even though she could barely breathe. He relaxed the grip on her throat. "Do we understand each other? Say yes."

She coughed.

"Say yes," he hissed.

She did, her voice croaking.

He sat back on his heels, both hands on the edge of the tub. "You did the smart thing, Bette. Because you're right, you could scream. And someone might even hear you and figure they should come down and check it out. But by the time they decide to break the door in, you'll just be a pretty girl for the guys at the morgue."

She had been keeping her head down since he released her throat and suddenly realized she was trying to keep from being able to identify him. As if he were a gunman robbing a bank.

She looked up. "Why are you doing this, Brendan? I never did anything to you." It was painful for her to talk. She touched her throat lightly.

"I never gave you the opportunity." He chucked her under the chin. "But I might."

"Where's Lori?"

"Gone. I told you."

"Where?"

He hit her with two stiff fingers across the cheek. It didn't actually hurt, just jarred her. "Drop it about her. She's not worth worrying about. She's a bitch. You're a lot nicer."

Bette's eyes brimmed with tears, but she fought to keep her voice steady. "She's my best friend. Where is she? What did you do to her?"

Blood rushed to his face, and his hand balled into a fist. When she cringed back against the tile, his face relaxed suddenly, and he snorted, shaking his head. "Jesus, you don't listen." Cupping water in his left hand, he rinsed away the residue of soap on her knee. "Forget her, I said. She was just a substitute."

She drew her knees back.

He smiled, being reasonable. "I know it will take a little getting used to. I'm going to be patient. God knows, that hasn't been one of my virtues, but it's going to be."

Bette kept her voice even. "Rod wouldn't like you in here with me. He's going to be along any minute, and he'll be very angry with you. Don't make it any worse, Brendan."

He made a face. "Rod's never on time, you know that. Besides, I'm tired of doing this shit. My name isn't Brendan, it's Guy. All these lies, I don't need anymore. *I* wasn't letting me down, it was all those substitutes, people like Lori, like Rod."

"He'll be here any—"

Guy slapped a sheet of water in her face. "Oh, Bette, you know he won't," he said, shaking his head. "Rod Konrad. I'm supposed to worry about him, huh?" Bending so his face was only inches from hers, he said, "Why? He's going to beat me up?"

"He'll kill you."

He laughed soundlessly, his breath hot on her face. "You think so? I don't. I should know. I've killed more people than I have fingers. I've strangled, I've stabbed, I've even run people over with a car. Makes a bump, then a crunch, then you check the rearview mirror to see if they need another pass. See if the arms are moving,

164

if they're trying to sit up and look at their legs, six feet away. You know.

"Rod's going to be mad at me, huh? I'm mad at him, always telling me what to do, as if he knows everything. I think he better be afraid of me, but that's the secret. You don't give them enough time to worry about you—you just do it to them first."

Bette crossed her arms over her breasts. "What do you want, Brendan?"

Sitting back, he said, mildly, "Guy. The name is Guy. Start using it. What do I want?" He shrugged. "You'd be surprised. Really, I want the same as everybody else." He ran more water over her leg, just touching her with the edge of his hand. "I want to be loved. Have a wife. Not be laughed at. Not have to take any more shit from anybody. I just don't have a tolerance for it, which is kind of the understatement of the century."

"I never laughed at you. Neither has Rod or Lori."

He shrugged. "Not yet. You would've. Lori would've talked."

"About what?"

He hit her with the two fingers again. "Wrong question. Questions are wrong altogether, get it?"

She nodded, but her blue eyes narrowed coldly. There were red marks on her cheek from his fingers.

He grinned. "You are a toughie, aren't you? Okay. Stand up."

"Can I put some clothes on now?"

He winked at her. "I don't see why you'll need clothes, but you can get out of the tub."

"So you can stare at me?"

"Do you want to stay in there?"

She shook her head. He stood up and put out his hand. She ignored it, braced herself on the edge of the tub, and stood. She wrapped herself in a towel from the rack. Her back was to the open door. He nodded. "See, I'm reasonable." She started to turn around, but he put his hands on her shoulders. "Did I tell you about this too?" he said, glancing down.

Her face turned scarlet. She looked directly into his eyes. "Don't do this, Brendan."

165

"I *told* you, it's Guy." He took her head in his hands and forced her to look down. "That's all Guy you're seeing there. That's what you do to me."

The phone rang. When Bette felt the pressure on her head relax momentarily, she kneed him in the groin.

He doubled over, and she was in the hallway. *He probably locked the door,* she thought, and hesitated. He lunged out of the doorway and grabbed her ankle.

"Let go!" she screamed. "Let me go!" Bette clasped her hands together and hit him between the shoulder blades. It made a dull thudding sound. He tugged her foot to his chest, and she fell against Lori's door and grabbed the doorknob to keep her balance.

"You shouldn't have done that, Bette. I was going to be good to you. Now I'm going to have to do you, too." He looked up at her, gasping for breath. Behind her, the phone continued its insistent ring. Bette yanked her leg free and kicked him in the face, jamming her heel against the bridge of his nose. Howling, he released her and covered his face. She twisted the knob, spun into Lori's room, and turned the lock on the heavy wooden door. Then she snatched the phone off the dresser.

"He's going to kill me," she cried.

■ ■ ■

"What? Who is this?" Rod said.

"Rod, it's me, it's me! Brendan—he's trying to rape me, or kill me. I don't know."

"Brendan?" Rod said, amazed.

"Do something! I'm locked in Lori's room."

"Hang up," he said. "I'll call the police."

"Don't hang up on me," she screamed. Just then there was a loud crash against the heavy wood door. It made a cracking noise but didn't give. "He's breaking down the door."

"I've got to. Smash the window, yell to the neighbors. Tell him the police are on the way. Tell him I am too." Rod hung up.

. . .

Rod dialed 911. "Somebody's trying to kill my girlfriend. Eighty-five Bay State Road, apartment five." He slammed the phone down and ran out of the little Newbury Street grocery store to his van.

He was doing fifty by the end of the block. With the emergency flashers going, he laid on the horn and weaved among the cars double-parked on both sides of the street. He kept the gas pedal to the floor and sped past the stop sign at the second intersection. A brown-and-white taxi squealed to a stop just in time, and the driver flipped his middle finger at Rod. At the last block before Massachusetts Avenue, Rod turned right down Hereford Street. The rear of the van was heavy with scuba tanks, and it swung wide, the tires protesting in a high-pitched squeal.

"Slow down!" A bearded man yelled from the sidewalk, pulling a blond-haired little boy closer. Rod floored it at the yellow lights crossing Commonwealth Avenue and continued on two blocks to take a left onto Beacon Street. The next two lights were green, and he worked the van up to eighty miles an hour. He shot underneath the entrance ramp to Storrow Drive and began to veer to the right for Bay State Road.

A blue Volare pulled out of the exit ramp, and Rod stood on the brake. "Damn it!" He spun the wheel to the left and slid sideways. The driver of the car suddenly recognized his plight and stopped. The rear of the van crumpled the car's left fender, and Rod stomped back on the gas pedal, straightened out, and continued down to Bette's apartment building. The car's horn sounded plaintively behind him.

Rod jumped out and looked up at the front window, but that was Bette's bedroom. He ran into the lobby. No key. He pushed the buttons to all the apartments with both hands. "Come on, goddamn it!" He pounded on the glass door. Nobody buzzed him in. Running back outside, he took one of the fist-size white rocks lining the walkway, went back in, and smashed the glass door. He reached inside, twisted the handle, and charged up the stairs. When he reached Bette's floor, her apartment door was slightly ajar. Then the screaming started.

• • •

After Rod had hung up on her, Guy had crashed against the door again, and it had cracked more loudly. "Damn you, Brendan!" she shouted. "Leave me alone! The police are coming. They'll shoot you!" He hit it again. "Rod's calling them now. He's furious with you. He'll be here any minute."

For a moment there was silence. Then he attacked the door with increased frenzy. Bette looked around the room wildly. She took a jar of pennies from Lori's dresser and smashed the window. It looked out onto a side street. "Somebody help me, he's trying to kill me," she screamed. Two college-aged girls looked up at her curiously but kept walking. Then the door cracked more loudly, and the wood around the lock started splintering. She stared at it, transfixed, and he hit it again.

She backed into Lori's closet, pushing against the clothes. Hanging on the inside knob was a jump rope. She quickly wound two loops around the doorknob and slammed the door shut. In the sudden darkness she fumbled, whimpering to herself as she struggled to reach the thick wooden rod overhead. She flipped one of the rope handles over it and finished tying the two ends together just as she heard him break through the bedroom door. She could hear his labored breathing.

Bette clapped a hand over her own mouth. Her heart pounded so loudly she was sure he could hear it, and the air whistled through her nostrils.

He punched the closet door.

Bette stifled a scream, backing farther into the closet. The coat hangers jingled. She grabbed one and pulled the hook straight, so when she made a fist, about two inches of the sharp end stuck out between her forefinger and middle finger.

Suddenly the rope over her head jerked tight, and light shone in from the edge of the door. The rod creaked and began to bend. She pulled back on the knob with her left hand. "I know you're there," he rasped. She saw his fingers grasp the door at eye level. She yanked back on the knob with all her strength, pinning his hand. She raked the point of the coat hanger across his knuckles.

He cursed and snatched his hand back. She slammed the door. Dropping the coat hanger, she twisted the doorknob shut with both hands, prepared to use all her strength to keep him from turning it open again.

He hit the door viciously. "That's the biggest mistake you ever made. You stupid, stupid girl." Bette bit her lip to keep from screaming. "Pull the light cord if you want a little preview of what I'm going to do to you."

Then he was gone. She heard him walk out of the room and down the hall. The apartment door slammed. Bette began to cry and reached up and pulled the light cord. Then she began to scream. And scream.

Lori was in the closet, too.

16

GUY ALMOST DIDN'T show up for opening night after the disaster with Andrea. The numb feeling had slowly peeled away to a black despair that kept him awake, staring at the ceiling all night long. When morning came, his lethargy was so profound he stayed in bed. Eventually, toward late morning, he drifted off into nightmarish black-and-white dreams. No one tried to wake him.

When he awoke around four, he considered not doing the play at all. The thought of standing before a crowd, of people looking at *him*, focusing on every word, made his heart trip too fast. Almost as badly as it did at the thought of facing Andrea. Packing a bag and sticking his thumb out for a ride was the most attractive idea, but it seemed to require more energy than he had. Instead, he dragged on some clothes and went into the kitchen to make a sandwich. He should be hungry, he realized, having skipped breakfast and lunch. He mixed together tuna and mayonnaise and put bread in the toaster.

Would she tell anyone? He thought of her the first time they were to rehearse, when he'd come to pick her up in the auditorium. Whispering, her head in close with Heather, Sarah, and Laura, whispering, whispering. Girls were like that, always talking to each other, trading secrets like currency.

Dozens could know by the time he stepped up onstage, if she had picked up the phone. And by Monday his humiliation could be a common commodity for the whole school. The staring eyes, the snickering. The comments in the hallway.

Chucky strode into the kitchen. "Make me one too, Slog," he said, punching Guy's shoulder lightly. "I'll give you a ride, and this time, I promise we won't stop off at The Drake's." He laughed as if they'd shared a good night of drinking there. "Bet I'd need a machine gun to get you through those doors again." Chucky had his costume in a big athletic bag. He put the hat on and jabbed the cupboard beside Guy's head with one of the foils Mrs. Bennett had handed out. "You're not going to be using that rusty thing you picked up at the fencing school, are you?"

Guy shook his head.

"Good. I wouldn't want you to get too jealous of Christian and really run me through to prove it." He touched Guy with the point.

Guy couldn't help but respond to his brother's warmth, even though he knew it was false. "Face it now, Chucky."

"What's that?"

"Christian dies first."

. . .

The first scenes were the hardest. When the curtain lifted, he was thankful that for a moment his role called for him to sit inconspicuously in a crowd, waiting for the start of the play within the play— when Cyrano chases Montfleury offstage for the way he "heaves up his lines like a hod-carrier." In the rehearsals, he'd always enjoyed this scene. Now, as he waited for plump Tommy Collins to come out and prattle the lines, he thought how cruel it was of Cyrano to do that.

171

Cyrano's cape was wrapped around his shoulders, his hat brim pulled low. He peered out at the audience. His mother was wearing a hat too, mindless of the parents behind her. She twisted the program while keeping her eyes on Chucky. His father was looking at his hands.

Following his mother's gaze, Guy watched Chucky. Admittedly, Chucky was the person to watch, so far. As Christian, he chafed under Roxane's gaze, desperate to be with her—but he lacked the wit, the confidence, to engage her in conversation.

Every girl's dream come true, Guy thought sardonically. Chucky in love, but shy.

No wonder his mother was sitting bolt straight, her eyes bright. So were Sarah, Heather, and the others, all watching tongue-tied Christian. Watching him gaze at Andrea as Roxane, unable to answer the invitation in her eyes.

Andrea wouldn't talk to Guy during the brief rehearsal before the play, except to recite her lines. Mrs. Bennett cautioned her to show more emotion, and she flickered a glance at Guy and nodded.

Now, Guy set his jaw and lowered his head. The black brim of his hat closed out the scaffolding, her balcony. The rubber nose was not as ridiculously long as Mrs. Bennett had originally intended. Nevertheless it trembled near the edge of the hat. He expected a laugh when he first showed his face. That was as it should be. But the audience should be *with* him afterward. He'd been sure before that he could pull it off . . . but now the sick feeling in his heart was appallingly close to the way he'd felt in the car the night before.

The taped music heralding the entrance of Montfleury began to play. He fumbled mentally for the first lines, panicking until they came, then arranged himself so he could stand up quickly. He replayed in his mind the scene that was about to unfold: Jerry Lassiter, playing Valvert, makes the mistake of insulting Cyrano's nose. In the duel that follows, Cyrano composes a poem while fencing with Valvert and runs him through on the last line. It was one of Guy's favorite scenes.

And, Guy thought grimly, *it'll blow Chucky right off the stage.*

He tuned in to Tommy Collins again. ". . . zephyrs fan his burning cheeks—"

He stood up. "Wretch!" he bellowed. "Have I not forbade you these three weeks?"

. . .

Cyrano was with him instantly. Guy felt his body swell inside the costume. The cold, trickling feeling was replaced by a contemptuous amusement at the buffoon on the stage with a garland of flowers about his head.

The audience laughed at the nose. But, except for Valvert, the other characters onstage did *not*. They knew it was worth their lives. Cyrano sent Montfleury scurrying away, and Guy could feel Cyrano's immediate satisfaction.

. . .

A few minutes later, the audience laughed again: Valvert said, "Dolt, bumpkin, fool, insolent puppy, jobbernowl!"

And he removed his hat, bowed and said, "Ah, yes? And I— Cyrano-Savinien-Hercule de Bergerac!"

Valvert's voice was squeaking. His chest rose in and out rapidly. Faintly, inside the character, Guy recognized Jerry Lassiter had a bad case of stage fright. But it was only a faint understanding, overwhelmed by Cyrano's contempt for a man who dared to insult him without the skill to back it up.

It took a great mental effort from Guy to land the foil blade flat against Jerry's side, so it looked in profile as if he had been run through. Cyrano wanted to go for the throat.

. . .

In the following acts, Guy remained a half-beat behind Cyrano, amazed by the things his mouth said, the fluidity with which his body moved. The pain of watching Chucky court Andrea was intense—but even that was beyond any emotion in his life, and the sympathy of the audience was tangible.

The only frustration was the stilted movements of the other characters. Jerry Lassiter was just the first. The others—Bob Ernson, Toni Larkin—all showed signs of stage fright. Laura Teason did a good job in her small part, perhaps because it was so close to her real personality, and she just had to remember a few lines. And, of course, Chucky was enjoying himself. Except for the shyness, his clean-cut hero role wasn't too different from the one he chose for himself on a daily basis.

In the second act Christian and Cyrano were supposed to embrace. As Guy moved forward with his arms spread wide, Chucky reached out for a handshake. The audience tittered.

Guy was jolted but recovered quickly by grasping Chucky's hand and pulling him off balance. He squeezed his brother's shoulders and shoved him back in what appeared to be a rough soldier's embarrassment. Chucky's eyes glittered, but he finished the act correctly.

Andrea's coldness was jarring. Roxane wasn't supposed to be like that to Cyrano, ever. After her lines in the pastry shop, Guy could see Mrs. Bennett in the wings talking urgently to her. But during his impassioned speech in the third act, when he spoke up to her under the balcony, he could feel her resistance begin to melt. Whether it was the urgency in his voice or the words alone, he did not know.

But he did know that the white-hot pain in his heart when Chucky climbed the balcony for her kiss was only partially Cyrano's.

She kissed *him* during the scene change after the fourth act. "Guy, it's just like we rehearsed it," she said, holding on to his arm. The taste of her lips was still on his. "Listen to them clapping. The next act is going to be even better."

"Andrea"—he felt as if he were speaking from a great distance—"we should talk about last night."

She made a face and looked around to see if anyone could have overheard. "Shush. Later." She gave him a peck on the cheek and hurried off to change.

Guy felt a sudden lightness that had everything and nothing to do with Cyrano. He hurried back to the dressing room and changed into the threadbare old-man clothes, more anxious than ever to be back onstage. Back alone with his Roxane.

■ ■ ■

Guy picked up the cane and adjusted his hat when Toni Larkin stepped up beside him. She was dressed as a nun. Smiling nervously, she stepped out onto the stage and announced to Roxane that Monsieur de Bergerac had arrived. The volume on the background organ music Mrs. Bennett had insisted on including grew louder, almost intrusive.

As he left the sanctuary of the backstage, Guy glanced to Kyle Tandee, who was running the lights and sound. His head was down. Guy saw his brother standing across the stage in the wings. He was smiling in a hard, tight way. Then Guy noticed that T.D. was sitting in the front row, near the auditorium's double doors. Guy was certain he hadn't been in the audience before.

T.D. was sitting back, his hands clasped behind his head. Apparently the kids on either side and behind him weren't going to complain. There was a smug look on his face that Guy hadn't seen since before their fight.

Guy felt a crawling apprehension. His brother behind him, and T.D. before him. He put his hand on the hilt of Cyrano's sword and the strength flowed into his arm, though tainted by age and pain. He locked his eyes on T.D.'s briefly. The bigger boy grinned openly.

Slightly shaken, Guy turned his attention to Andrea and pushed thoughts of T.D. and Chucky away. It was the same as the first time they'd auditioned, only stronger. After a brief exchange with one of the nuns, it was just the two of them, for a time, Cyrano and Roxane. She was wearing widow's black, and in his eyes Andrea herself was as far away as Chucky, T.D., and the rest of them. His head ached from the assassin's blow, and he could feel Cyrano's life seep away.

I must tell her, he thought. *I must tell her before I die.*

"After fourteen years—late for the first time," she said.

175

He sat beside her, and they talked. The loneliness of the tiny room that Cyrano occupied haunted Guy far more than was emphasized in the play. Cyrano looked forward to these weekly visits with Roxane, lived for them. And now he was dying and had to recognize that it wasn't just his promise to Christian that had kept him from telling her the truth for so long. It was fear, too. What if she didn't really mean it when she said she would have loved Christian *even if he were ugly?*

He said, "His letter! . . . Did you not promise me that some-day . . . that someday . . . you would let me read it?"

She handed it to him. Her fingers paused on his hand, and then she resumed her sewing.

A tear blurred his vision momentarily as he unfolded the letter. He began from memory, "Farewell, Roxane, because today I die . . ."

. . .

The tape sputtered. There was a rasping noise over the speakers, then muted voices. Guy was jarred out of his role. *Something is wrong!* Andrea's face whitened. He half-heard the voices as he continued to recite the letter.

". . . So heavy with love, I have not told . . .

. . . *this is your problem. It's not my job . . .*

"And I shall die without telling you! No more shall I . . .

. . . *men in their forties . . .*

"Shall my eyes drink the sight of you like wine . . .

. . . *it shouldn't be happening to us . . ."*

Suddenly he recognized the voices over the speakers. And what they were saying. The glass lining his insides shattered, and he saw himself sitting there in front of his parents and a hundred and fifty other people, wearing a silly costume and a long rubber nose. T.D. was laughing aloud now, pointing at him, the corners of his small eyes crinkled with vindictive glee. His mother talking urgently to his father. Heather's and Sarah's heads were close together, their eyes on him.

Andrea stared at him, hotly. Over her shoulder, Guy could see Mrs. Bennett starting toward Kyle Tandee. *Hurry!* he thought. *Move!*

He forgot his lines.

Andrea mouthed the word "How?" The taped voices were all the clearer in the silence:

Andrea, what are you saying? That I'm sick? I'm crazy or something?

Maybe you're just different. You know, some men are like that. They don't like women.

No, don't say that. I'm not queer.

I don't know, Guy. All I know is that it's not my fault you can't get hard. It's not my fault.

The sound snapped off abruptly. A girl's laugh, high and musical, drifted from the back of the auditorium, and then both Sarah and Heather started giggling. Guy looked at them, the nose projecting into his line of vision. Sarah noticed him staring at her and clapped red-tipped fingers over her mouth. His parents were pushing their way out to the aisle, his mother's lips compressed in a tight line, her face red. His father hurried behind quickly, apologizing to the people she pushed.

Andrea fled from the stage.

Guy fumbled for his lines. *It doesn't matter,* a voice in his head said. *Roxane's gone.* But still he tried. "Never more, with a look that is a kiss . . ."

Mr. Terault stood up and clapped his hands. "That's it tonight, the show is over. File out to your right, please. Go on."

He turned and walked to the edge of the stage and said, "Go in the back, Guy." When Guy just stared at him blankly, he slapped the stage with his palm and called off to the wings, "Mrs. Bennett! Come get him out of here!"

His parents had already left the auditorium.

He felt a hand on his shoulder, shaking him. He didn't move. They all filed past him, staring at him, not ten feet away. Most of the parents were red-faced, hustling along the kids he went to school with every day. They stared at him directly, with knowing eyes. Some even laughed aloud. Billy Tanner licked his lips and said, "You get stuck again with her, give me a call."

T.D. hadn't moved. He lounged back, cackling that high laugh of his.

Freak show. The freak kept them entertained tonight.

"Move it!" Mr. Terault was saying angrily now, his hard little eyes snapping. A trace of saliva was in the corner of his mouth. "Get him up, Bennett. He's made enough of a spectacle already."

The fingers on his shoulder tightened. "Come on, Guy." He looked up at her. Her lower lip trembled, and he thought she was going to cry. *You?* he thought, standing abruptly. He said, "So I ruined your opening night. What do you think this does to me?"

"Oh Guy, I—" she started to say, but he was already past her. Backstage everyone gave way to him as if he were a leper. Toni Larkin in her nun's habit rolled her eyes as he strode past. "Where's Andrea?" he asked Bob Ernson, but Bob just put both palms out and said, "Got me." The back door slammed shut as several other actors hurried out.

It's ruined. Cyrano de Bergerac *is ruined.*

Guy sought the rage that should have been coursing through his veins, but found only a shrinking emptiness. He had to urinate but didn't want to go to the men's room in front of everyone. He knew Chucky and T.D. had to be behind this—Chucky hadn't just been checking the mileage in the car the night before. He was vaguely aware that Mrs. Bennett and Mr. Terault might believe him. That it might even mean some trouble for Chucky. But Chucky had still won. Just another prank, maybe a little worse than the others.

Unless Andrea stuck with Guy. If she stayed with him, that would make all the difference. Guy pulled off the nose. He heard laughter behind him and turned to see Laura Teason watching him in the mirror. "Aren't you *glad* you got that part now, Guy?" she said, wiping the rouge off her cheeks with a tissue. "You were *such* a big man for a while."

"Why aren't you running out the back door, too?"

"Should I? No one is laughing at *me*."

"Where's Andrea?"

Laura's mouth made an O. She turned from the mirror and looked at him directly. "You are *crazy* if you think she wants to see you. Her parents just met her at the back door. She practically went out with a bag over her head."

He hurried out the back hall to the parking lot. Chucky's Camaro thundered by. Guy's patent leather shoes clattered on the asphalt. Someone in a blue Chevrolet whistled and called, "Nice legs." Heavy laughter erupted from the car behind. Guy almost turned back then, overwhelmed by how he must look, still wearing the costume tights, makeup streaked down his face. But he saw Andrea's blond hair gleaming under the parking-lot light, just as she got into the back of her father's green Jaguar.

By the time he reached the car, the lights were on; they were just pulling out. He stood in front of the car and waved his arms. "Andrea!"

The horn blew. Andrea's father was just a dark shape behind the steering wheel. The front passenger window rolled down. A blond woman who looked like a forty-year-old Andrea looked out at him with icy blue eyes. "You've got a lot of brass standing in front of our car. If I'd been behind the wheel, I might've run you down, I'm so angry. Now get away. You've put Andrea in enough of a spot already."

"Please," he said, putting his hands on the car door, trying to see past her to the backseat. Andrea kept her head down.

Mrs. Sable's lips compressed, and she pushed his hand off the door. "Damn it, what did I say? You little idiot! Bad enough you take her parking, but you have to get her wrapped up in some ridiculous joke. One of your friends' idea of fun? Do you know what you've done to her?"

"Done to *her*?" He couldn't control his voice. The stupid woman. "What the hell do you think happened to *me*?" He hit the roof of the car with his fist. "You think *I* arranged that?"

Mrs. Sable blanched and said, quickly, "Lock the doors, Roy."

"Wait. I just want to *talk* to Andrea." He hurried to the back door and hit the window with the palm of his hand. Andrea was seated behind her father. She looked away from Guy, out the window

179

beside her. He slapped the window again, and she jerked but still wouldn't look at him. That infuriated him all the more. "Look at me, goddamn it."

He hurried around to her side just as Mr. Sable got out of the car. Andrea's father was a tall man with heavy shoulders and sandy hair. He looked as if he spent lots of time at the health club—tight, clear skin, firm jaw. Guy reached for Andrea's door, but Mr. Sable reached him first. "It's locked, kid," he said. He drew Guy close by the shirtfront. He smelled of cigarettes and after-shave lotion. His breathing was hard, but Guy's struggles to pull away were ineffective. "Listen," Mr. Sable said. "The door's locked, and it's going to stay locked to you."

"I didn't do anything. It's not my fault." Guy put his hand on Andrea's father's shoulder and pushed.

"Shut up!" Mr. Sable said, shaking him. "You're not her type. You're a loser. A whiner. She wasted her time on you, and it slapped her right back in the face. Well, okay, she's learned her lesson maybe, but she doesn't have to keep learning it over and over. Get it?"

Guy didn't answer. Mr. Sable shoved him over the trunk, knocking the breath out of him.

"Get it? You try to make it with my daughter, get her tied up in a humiliating thing like that—in front of *everybody*—and then pound on my car to get at her? You must be crazy."

"Daddy!" Andrea opened the back door. "Stop it, please. Just go away, Guy! I don't want to talk to you, I don't have anything to say. Just leave me alone."

"Shut the door, Andrea!" her father snapped.

"Roy, get in the car," her mother called, sharply. "There are people watching."

Guy fought to fill his lungs. Pale blue eyes bored into his.

"Want to take a swing at me, kid? There's nothing I'd love more, so come on."

Guy shook his head. Mr. Sable grunted disgustedly. "I didn't think so," he said. "Don't come crying around Andrea again. She's a beautiful girl, and she's going to do a whole lot better than you.

So go home, crawl off, go see a doctor. I don't care. But don't ever come around us again."

He yanked Guy from the car, slipped behind the wheel, and drove off. Andrea kept her head down all the way out of the parking lot.

■ ■ ■

Ginny was waiting for him in the kitchen when he got home. "You are hopeless, Guy," she said, quietly. She was leaning against the counter, holding a highball. Her pose belied her tightly coiled tension. "Absolutely hopeless. You finally do something besides sit in front of the television. Get the lead in the play. Even looked like you got yourself a girlfriend. Then this."

"It wasn't my fault!"

The ice clinked in her glass, and she downed half of the drink. "You ought to wear that on your forehead. 'It wasn't my fault.' " She shook her head. "You and your father. He's handling it the usual way, down in the basement filing coins. The two of you are a couple of winners. Nothing's your fault, but nothing seems to go right around you either, does it, Guy?"

"Do you think I would have done this to myself?"

"I don't know," she said, pushing away from the counter. "I really just don't know. You'd do a lot to embarrass me. It's always the parents who look like monsters, the ones people point to, saying, 'What did they do to them?' "

He stared at her incredulously. Blood pumped into his chest and arms; his breathing grew short. "Goddamn it, everything doesn't come back to you!"

"Don't you raise your voice to me."

"I *will* raise my voice, damn it! That was *me* up there. I was the one they were laughing at, not you."

"Shut up!"

"You know who set this up as well as I do."

"I do not!" she said, vehemently. "I most certainly do not, and I don't want to hear any more about it."

181

"Well you're going to," he said, slamming his fist down on the kitchen table. "You're damn well going to."

She threw the drink in his face. "Go away," she screamed. "Get away from me and leave me alone!"

He almost hit her.

Instead, he walked slowly over to the refrigerator and used the cloth hanging off the door to wipe his face. "You know he did it," he said, quietly. "He was in the car before we left the party."

Her voice was shaking. "I don't know what you're talking about." She brought an edge to her voice. "It's your problem, not his. If you drag your brother into this with the school, then you can just find another place to live, Guy. I won't have him mixed up in your mess. You're not going to drag him down with you."

"He dragged *me* down, he—"

"You're lying!" Her face was bright red now, and tears coursed down her cheeks. "You have no *right*. No *right*, you lying little bastard! I don't know where you came from. I don't know you! Nothing like this ever happened to me when I was your age, everything was fine. I was popular, I was like Chucky, people liked me." She threw her glass across the room, and it smashed against the basement door. "You're your father's son, all right, you're his. You're nothing, you're stupid, people laugh at you! Well that little blondie, Andrea, she got a taste of what I live with every day, and she's luckier than I am. She found out early!"

His mother stormed out of the kitchen and pounded up the stairs.

■ ■ ■

Guy went into Chucky's room without knocking. Rock blared out of the stereo speakers. Chucky sat back in his easy chair. Posters of Mick Jagger and Robert Plant flanked him on each side. A foldout from *Penthouse* was taped over his bed.

"What do you want?" he said.

"I know what you did." Guy had to yell over the music.

Chucky turned down the volume. "So what? I know what you *didn't* do. *Couldn't* do. So does the rest of the school." He grinned wolfishly. "Don't feel bad, Guy. You get some fat chick who smells bad, you'll probably do fine. Andrea's just too much for you."

Guy stepped closer. The cold glitter in Chucky's eyes was back, but he didn't care. "They'll believe me, Chucky," he said. "Mrs. Bennett, Mr. Terault. They'll believe me when I tell them you were in the front seat of the car after the party. That you could have put your tape recorder under the seat, then retaped it here over the background music."

Chucky tapped his forehead. "Always thinking, Guy. They might just believe it."

"Why, Chucky? You had to know that bad how far I was getting with her?"

Chucky laughed through his nose. "No, Slog. I had faith. Faith you'd blow it somehow. This was even better than I expected, though. When I first heard it in the garage, it was all I could do not to run into your room and replay it. I'd already made a copy of the background tape, so it was a simple swap when Tandee wasn't looking. I even timed it so it'd be just the two of you onstage and upped the recording volume so nobody could miss it."

The dark mantle fell even heavier on Guy's shoulders. It was worse knowing the details. "I'll still tell them," he said, finally.

From the chair, Chucky kicked him in the stomach. He hooked Guy's heel with his toe, tripping him. Guy fell on his back, flashing suddenly to Mr. Sable, rich man, driving the green Jaguar. Then Chucky was on top of him, his knee planted in Guy's chest. "Pretty goddamn hard to breathe, huh, Guy?" Chucky grabbed a handful of his hair and slammed his head against the floor. "I think you know by now, Ginny and Art aren't coming to the rescue. So you just listen here."

He yanked Guy's head forward and back. "That's right, nod your head, you're going to listen. Yeah, you can tell everybody, and some of them will believe you. I might get some time on suspension, no big deal. But I'm not even going to do that. Because you're not going to tell." He slammed Guy's head again.

In a falsetto copying Mrs. Bennett, he asked, "Do you know who planted this tape, Guy? Did Chucky have anything to do with it?"

183

Then in his normal tone, he jarred Guy's vision with each word, asking, "What's—your—answer?"

"No," Guy moaned.

"What's that?" Chucky cupped his ear. "Say again?"

"No. Chucky didn't have anything to do with it." His brother's face was only about a foot from his. The thought of fighting back, of digging his hands into Chucky's eyes, flickered and then went. His arms remained paralyzed by his sides.

My brother pounds me, he despaired.

Chucky pinched his cheek hard and twisted. Tears welled in Guy's eyes. "Poor Slog the Blob," Chucky crooned. He pushed himself up off Guy's chest and nudged him with his toe. "Get out of here. Let another five or six years pass before you think of coming into my room again."

After gasping in a few breaths of air, Guy stood and started slowly for the door.

"Hey, Slog," Chucky said, casually. "How the hell did you ever take on T.D.?" He was back in the chair, his legs crossed on the footstool now. His eyes were frank, interested. His color was almost back to normal.

Guy didn't answer.

"Ah, get out of here." Chucky picked up a magazine. "Even if you were tough for a little while there, you're not anymore."

THE TWO POLICEMEN who burst into the apartment kept their guns on Rod until they saw his identification and listened to Bette's story. The guns went back into their holsters, but the taller one, a huge guy with a blond crew cut, sat beside Rod and Bette on the living room couch until a detective showed up. "Hey, Lieutenant Rabinovitz," he said, standing.

"In a minute." The detective went into the bedroom.

When he came out he said to Rod, "Pull up your sleeves and push back the hair from your face."

"Why?"

"Just do it," Rabinovitz snapped.

Rod glanced at Bette and unbuttoned his sleeves. Rabinovitz took the palm of Rod's hand between thumb and forefinger and twisted his arm slightly, looking on each side. He did the same with the other arm. He pushed back Rod's forelock, and the hair

17

around his temples. Rod jerked his head away. "What's with you?"

"He's looking for the scratches," Bette said, dully.

Rabinovitz looked at her intently. "Tell me about them."

"On his wrists," she said, in the same monotone. "You were right. He kept his sleeves buttoned; I didn't notice at first. She had sharp nails, Lori did, she should've put out his eyes. I tried, but he was quick. He knew what he was doing."

Rod began to stand up. The blond patrolman moved closer, and Rabinovitz waved for Rod to sit back. "Relax, there are two of you here and one dead girl. I've got to check."

"How did you know he was scratched?"

"Blood under her nails."

Rod's heart was still thumping. "Well, not mine, damn it." He jerked his thumb at the blond policeman. "We told him who did it. My roommate, Brendan."

"He said his name was Guy," Bette interrupted. "He told me to call him Guy."

"No last name?"

"No."

Rabinovitz scratched an entry in his notebook. A small man with a potbelly and bad teeth, he chewed on a toothpick while listening to them describe what had happened. After a few minutes, he interrupted Rod and said to the blond officer, "Dontano, call in. I want a car over at Konrad's apartment *now*. This Guy or Brendan—whatever he wants to call himself—is probably not stupid enough to go back there, but sometimes Christmas hits a couple times a year."

Rabinovitz bent down and looked more closely at Bette. Then he said, over his shoulder, "Where the hell is the medical examiner? Have him take a scraping under Miss Sayers's nails too, then get her over to the hospital. Have a policewoman meet you over there, and then bring her back to the station. Konrad and I'll head over to his apartment."

"Why do you need to do that?" Bette said.

"He still doesn't believe us," Rod said.

"Sure I do," Rabinovitz said. "Just tying it up. Let's go, Mr. Konrad."

Rod turned to Bette. "I won't go if you need me."

"You find him." Bette drew away, her blue eyes hard. "That's what I need."

■   ■   ■

On the ride over, Rabinovitz unwrapped a mint and said, "You have any idea if he has a gun?"

"What?"

"A gun—you know, I want to know what we're going in against."

"No." Rod rolled down the window and inhaled deeply.

"That's a help," Rabinovitz stuck the candy in his mouth. "If it's right."

"I mean, no, I've got no idea, all right?" Rod knew his voice was shaky, but he couldn't help himself. "I mean, I'm the last person you should ask. I just lived with the guy. And introduced him to Bette and Lori. I thought I knew him, but for all I know he might have a machine gun and hand genades in there."

Rabinovitz crunched audibly on the mint. "That's a point."

They met two other patrolmen on the landing outside the condominium, a black man about Rod's size and a smaller officer with a handlebar mustache. The black policeman whispered, "If anybody's in there, he's quiet." They drew their guns. Rabinovitz took Rod's key and motioned for him to stand back in the hallway. He knelt beside the door, quietly twisted the key in the lock, and turned the knob. The black patrolman kicked the door open and hurried in against the right wall, his gun extended. The other two followed.

Guy wasn't there.

They found the blue case in his closet. Rabinovitz took a light pair of cotton gloves from his inside pocket and pulled them on. "What we have here," he said, taking it down, "is a goddamn clue, just like the movies." He opened the case and started as the lights around the mirror winked on. "Cute," he said. The detective stared across the open lid at Rod. "Did you know your roommate wore makeup?"

Rod shook his head.

■ ■ ■

Rod's memory of Brendan—he found it impossible to think of him as Guy—was as elusive as picking up a little ball of mercury off the floor while wearing gloves. Guy's face came to him only in snatches, as he thought about specific times together: diving, eating pizza, going out to the Dance Factory.

"You lived with him, for Christ's sake," Rabinovitz said. "Don't you know anything about where he came from? Who he lived with before? Didn't you check any references?"

Rod told the detective about what Brendan had said about his previous roommate, his family in Ithaca.

"Shit, anything he's told you is probably going to be useless. I want stuff you figured out on your own, little facts that we can use to tag him. Like if anybody called. Or if he called anybody."

Rod's eyes lit up. He went into the kitchen, went through the mail, and pulled out the phone bill. It showed only Rod's calls. "Damn it!"

"Come on," Rabinovitz said. "I'll have a team going over this room. Let's go see if your girl knows any more." After stopping at Bette's apartment for Rabinovitz to talk with the medical examiner, they drove to the police station. Rod gave a description of Brendan to a detective using an Identikit. The rendering was as accurate as Rod could give, but he was still dissatisfied. So was Rabinovitz. "Jesus. That could be a couple of thousand people. Particularly in a college city. Doesn't anything stand out about him?"

He set Rod down in front of a stack of mug books.

About an hour later, just as they were going back to Rabinovitz's little office, a dour policewoman with frizzy red hair brought Bette into the station. Bette looked young and wan. Her head was bowed, and her arms were crossed against her chest. Rod put his arms around her, but she didn't relax her pose. Gone was the warmth, the soft-hard of her body. Now Rod felt only the bones in her arms, her forehead against his face. He whispered, "Are you okay?"

She twisted away from him and said quietly, "That's a stupid question."

The policewoman jerked her head at Rod and said to Rabinovitz, "He's the guy who made the introductions, right?"

Rabinovitz picked at his teeth, idly, then said, "Are you done here?"

The policewoman rolled her eyes and turned. She patted Bette on the shoulder and said, "You'll be all right, sweetie."

Rod looked at her departing back and then hugged Bette tighter. She didn't pull away or move closer. "What happened at the hospital?"

She shook her head slightly. "Nothing."

"Don't tell me 'nothing.' Talk to me."

"Later."

"Miss?" Rabinovitz held the door of his office open for her. When Rod started to follow her in, the detective said, "Not just now. I'd like to talk to her alone first."

Rod took her elbow. "Will you be all right?"

Bette laughed.

Her hand flew to her mouth instantly, and she blanched. "I'm sorry," she said to the detective. "It was just that question again."

The door to the detective's office closed behind her. Rod walked over to a long bench against the wall and sat back stiffly. He was absolutely still for a moment and then slammed his elbow against the plaster behind him. "Damn it!"

"Hey!" the fat desk sergeant said. "I'll do that to your head, you keep it up."

"Shove it!"

The sergeant stared at him, then said, "You part of the investigation on that murder on Bay State Road?"

"That's right."

"Well, just sit and calm down. Don't tell anybody else around here wearing a blue suit to shove it."

Rod looked at the detective's closed door. In a quieter voice he asked, "Can I make a phone call?"

"Sure." The sergeant jerked his thumb toward a pay phone in the hall. "You're not a prisoner."

189

Leo arrived just as Bette and the detective were coming out of the office. Rod introduced them and told Rabinovitz they would be staying at his apartment for the night.

Rabinovitz said to Leo, "This nutcake, Guy or Brendan, has he ever been to your apartment?"

"No," Rod interrupted.

"I asked *him*."

Leo shook his head and asked Rod, "You ever tell him where I live?"

"I said he doesn't know."

"Okay, okay." Leo's face was drawn and tired looking. He knelt down beside Bette, who was sitting on a narrow bench, leaning against the dingy green wall. "How are you doing, sweetheart?" he asked gently.

Her eyes were dry but red-rimmed. She shrugged but didn't answer. When he put his hands up to her shoulders, she shrank back slightly. He dropped them to his sides. His glasses winked up at Rod. "Has she been to a doctor yet?"

Rod nodded.

"First thing," Rabinovitz said.

"I'll be okay, Leo," she said, in a small voice. "Lori's dead, you know."

"I know. I wish you and Rod had called me sooner. I would have sat with you, all this time. It must of been hell, going over it all."

"It wouldn't have helped," she said. "That's the thing about it. The person I want to talk to is Lori, but thinking about her scares me right now." She tugged at the sleeve of her hooded red sweatshirt. "This is Lori's. That's what Rod grabbed for me. It makes sense; it was her room, her closet. I can smell her perfume, you know; it's funny how that makes me feel good and makes me want to scream, all at the same time."

Rod put his hand on hers, but she pulled it away.

Leo said to the policeman, "I should take them home now. I

have an unlisted number, so the address isn't in the book. She needs to get out of here."

"Unlisted number, thanks for small mercies," the cop said. "You've met this Brendan how many times yourself?"

Leo pulled at his lip, then said, "Three, four times. When he stopped by looking for Rod."

"And he took the diving lessons."

"Right." Leo's face grew excited, but Rod spoke before he could.

"Forget the photo, Leo. We've already gone over that. He didn't give us one."

"What do you mean? You couldn't have given him the certification card without it."

"I didn't."

"Damn it, Rod, why not? He went out on that checkout dive, I know he did."

Rod's voice rose. "Goddamn it, Leo, he didn't pass. I failed him. So no card, no photo, get it?"

"Whoa," Rabinovitz said. "He probably never would've let you take a photo. No matter what."

"That's not the point. Leo thinks I screwed up again, that I cut a corner and this is the result."

Leo shook his head, looking away from Rod. "Sorry. That's not true, I just thought we had something there. Sorry. This is worse for you, of course."

"It's nothing compared to how Lori feels," Bette said.

Rod swung to face her. Rabinovitz took his elbow and said, "Let's have another word before you go, Rod."

"Just a minute."

"Now." The detective closed the door behind them. Rod found he was relieved to be away from Bette for a few minutes and immediately felt ashamed.

Rabinovitz sat on the edge of his desk. "I called the Ithaca police. They had the same opinion as me. Whole column of Kirks in the phone book, but I bet not one has a son named Guy or Brendan. I'll work on them, get them to check it out. They already woke the school principal. No knowledge, no record of a high-school teacher with a name or a description even close. Same thing with Boston University. Nobody named Brendan Kirk registered for this fall semester. Nobody in the education program with a first name of Guy. All you remember about his previous roommate he was supposed to have had was that he was divorced and kind of cranky about women, right?"

Rod nodded wearily.

"Okay. I'm going to have this drawing distributed among the patrols, and we'll go to B.U. with it. We've got a description going out over the wire and circulars. I've got somebody checking the M.O. file, we might pull something there. We've got his blood type, we've got clean fingerprints. We'll be using the state police computer system. If he's ever been printed, either for a crime, or maybe if he's been in the service, we're in good shape for identifying his real name. If not, at least if we get him in custody, we'll have a good case."

"If."

Rabinovitz continued as if he didn't hear. "We'll have officers out talking to your neighbors, and your girl's. You'll probably get approached by the newspapers on this, but keep quiet. We may need to turn to them, get the public to help look, you know, but for now I'd just as soon not scare him off. Somebody who keeps moving from city to city, is basically small-time, low profile, doesn't use credit cards, write checks, have many connections like that, is hard to trace. How do you think he's fixed for money?"

Rod shrugged. "He always seemed to have some."

"Any idea how?"

"He told some story about selling his house back in Ithaca. Probably just bullshit."

The detective just nodded, staring away for a second. He grunted. "Okay. That's about it for now. We'll probably pick him up soon, if he hasn't skipped the state already."

"He hasn't."

The detective looked at him silently for a moment and then said, "So you broke her out of the closet."

Rod nodded.

"That was hard to do, wasn't it? The way the rope was tied. Broke that rod, and it was oak. Not easy when the rope stretches."

"What's the point?"

"Think you can take him?"

"I can kill him."

"You think so, huh? Well, think all you want. *Do* it, we'll have *you* up on murder charges. Don't go looking for him. Just look after the girl, stay with her."

"I can't just sit on my hands."

"You damn well better," Rabinovitz said sharply. He stepped closer, and Rod could smell his sweetish bad breath. "Don't go running around playing hero. You haven't got a clue as to where he is, but he might be able to figure out where you'll be. We'll just find you with a knife in your back in some alley and then he'll be after her alone. He's cold, this bastard. The medical examiner puts the girl's death somewhere around midnight last night. She had soap in her hair. I figure he followed her into the bathroom with her belt, killed her, cleaned up the mess, stuck her on that hook in the closet, and waited all day for your girl to come home. He's way out of your league. Unless you're not telling me something, there's no way you can know he's not out of the state by now. Not that I'm going to assume he is."

"He isn't."

"What do you know?" Rabinovitz stepped even closer. "Or do you just want it to be that way, because she's digging at you."

The color drained from Rod's face, but he didn't give any distance. "He just hasn't left. You saw his clothes, the same style as mine, you know what Bette and I told you. This was about me and Bette. It's personal. He tried to be me, and part of that was having Bette. And she kicked him in the balls and he had to run away when I came up the stairs. He's all pride. He's not going to just forget about us."

Rabinovitz lifted his eyebrows. "Maybe. It's the safe way to think. And it lets you figure you'll have a chance at him."

"What would you think, if you were me?"

Rabinovitz nodded his head toward the door. "I'd plan how I could make her feel safe again. You got your work cut out, we've got ours." Rabinovitz backed off. "We'll want to talk to you tomorrow. The dead girl's parents are going to want to talk to you too. They'll be flying in from California."

Rod grimaced. "What the hell am I going to say?"

"Can't help you there." Rabinovitz held the door open. As Rod started out the door, he grasped him lightly by the arm. "Making phone calls to next of kin is part of the job—part I hate. You got a strong girl there, a good one. She's got to be bitchy now, or else she'd be blubbering. You look out for her. Stay in your friend's apartment. We'll have someone outside tonight anyhow. Outside your place and hers, too. Plan on staying away for the next few days."

"He's not going back to my condo now. He's not stupid."

"You'd be surprised. Any case, we'll have somebody there." The detective picked at his teeth with his thumbnail. "Like I said, he could've stolen a car, hitched a ride, and be moving in with somebody in L.A. next week for all we know. If he hangs out in Boston, our chances are good."

"What about Bette's chances?" Rod's voice was harsh, but he kept it low.

Rabinovitz brushed his fingers on his pants leg. "We'll do our bit. You do yours and sit tight. When I want to get in touch with you, I'll call. Don't open doors for people you don't know. In a few days, we don't have any more questions, maybe I'll recommend you two take a vacation. I got an idea of something to do. You'll just need to be ready to come back quick to identify this scumbag."

■ ■ ■

Leo lived alone in a large one-bedroom condominium on Beacon Hill. To Rod, even though he had been there dozens of times, the place looked altered. Bette followed him as he walked through each room, taking in the layout, the good furniture beginning to go thread-bare—Leo's ex-wife had kept the newer pieces.

"I didn't know you would be doing a formal inspection," Leo tried.

Rod's lips moved, but the smile didn't work. "It's just that everything seems different."

"It's not. Same old dump."

"That's not it," Bette said. It was the first time she'd opened her mouth since the police station. "It's us. Like the people on the street."

Rod looked at her. "Yeah."

"Who?" Leo was perplexed. "Somebody you saw? Somebody following us?"

Bette shivered. "Who knows?" She rubbed her hands over her arms and said, "I'm going to take a shower. I need to wash." Her eyes flicked to Rod, and he stepped closer.

She took a step back and put her hand on his chest. "Please. Could you stay just outside the bathroom door? Don't come in, though."

"Sure." Rod's voice was husky. "Anything you want."

■ ■ ■

After changing the sheets on the bed, Leo joined Rod by the bathroom door. They could hear the shower running, and steam was coming out from underneath the door. Leo put his hand on Rod's arm and squeezed. "How you taking it?" he asked quietly.

"Just dandy. I didn't almost get raped and killed." Rod put his head in his hands and ran his fingers through his sweaty hair. "I'm just the carrier." He snorted. "The guy who made the introductions, that's how the fat old police lady who took Bette to the hospital described me."

"Bitch."

"She's right."

"Fuck you," Leo said patiently.

"It's true, Leo. It started with me when I was racing the boat. The day I cracked it up with Bette. I could've killed her and that kid."

Leo crossed his arms. "Listen, I already did the connect the dots, and I've got some guilty feelings here. Like maybe it's my fault, some, for pressuring you to pay for the boat repairs instead of using the insurance, and you needed to get a roommate."

"Oh, come on," Rod said. "That's ridiculous."

"Course it is." Leo looked at him evenly. "Now you want to tell me that it's more your fault? Want to argue over it?"

"No."

"My mistake. I thought that's where we were heading: 'I have the right to feel worse than you.' "

"Get the hell away from me, Leo. I don't want any psychological crap about my selfish guilt. My roommate just killed the girl I introduced him to, and tried to do the same to the woman I want to marry. Excuse me please if I feel like shit."

"Go right ahead. Just remember who did the killing here. Brendan. Guy, I guess his name is. Not you. Not me. And it wasn't Bette's or Lori's fault either. He fooled all of us. And maybe he's been doing it for a while, and he's good at it."

"Well, he's not getting any more practice."

"Meaning?"

"Meaning I'm not going to just sit here and let him come at her again. He's going to try, you know. That detective thinks he's on the way to L.A. or something. There's no damn way. He's going to be around, he'll be one of those faces on the street, and if I'm not ready, I'll look right over him, and then he'll be on her. He'll hurt her, do something, kill her if he can. He's for real, and he's not going away."

"So you'll stay here. Lay low. Let the police do their jobs."

"No." Rod began pacing. "I have to do more than that. You've got to loan me your gun."

"The hell I do." Leo shook his head. "Not a chance. It's a year in jail, mandatory, to carry a handgun in Massachusetts without a permit."

"After what's happened to us? Bullshit."

"Maybe. Maybe not."

The bathroom doorknob turned. Rod leaned closer, his eyes hard. "Never mind the damn counseling, Leo. What if Brendan shows up again, with a knife or a gun of his own? Bette and me, at the morgue. You want to identify us? Give me something I can use now."

Bette came into the room wearing Leo's robe and a towel wrapped around her hair. Her eyes flitted uncertainly to both their faces. "What are you two glaring at each other about?"

"Nothing," Rod said to her. To Leo, he said, "Think about it," and stalked off to the bedroom.

After he closed the door, she said to the older man, "Thanks for helping us, Leo."

"Oh, shush."

Tears welled in her eyes for a moment, and then she seemed to regain control. "I *know* we can really count on you. And that's not something I'll be accepting too easily for a while." She laughed, brokenly. "It's quite a responsibility."

He put his hand out, and after a moment she took it. "I'll be glad to accept it."

She looked to the bedroom door and then back at him. Her eyes widened, and now a tear did spill down her cheek. "I can't even trust myself," she said. "All I want to do is call my mother and father and have them come down and take me away."

"Do it." Leo gestured to the phone in the kitchen. "The call is on me."

"No. No, I don't dare. I don't dare involve them. I will *not* take the chance that Brendan might find out about them. Because he'd kill them too, if it suited him."

Leo squeezed her hand. "He's not so powerful. You kicked him where it counts. The police are probably right, he's probably long gone."

Bette shook her head. The tears were streaming more freely now. "No, I don't think he is. That's what I mean about people, Leo. You can't trust them, you can't even trust me. I won't risk my parents by letting them come to town. But I'll risk you by living here. You see what I mean?"

. . .

An hour later, Bette and Rod were still awake. Rod lay on his back, hands behind his head, she on her side facing the wall.

"I've never made love with anyone as soon as I did with you," she said. "And you're only the third."

Rod turned his head toward her. Bette's back was to him. Leo's striped pajama top on her contrasted sharply with the white painted wall. She had wanted to sleep close to the wall, far from the door and window. She had insisted he shut the closet door firmly.

Now he said, "I know that."

She shrugged. Rolling onto his side, Rod placed his hand lightly in the curve of her waist. She shifted away, and his breath stopped.

"What did you say about me to him?" she said.

For a moment, he was confused. Rabinovitz? Then, "You mean Brendan?"

She said, "Don't turn stupid on me, Rod." She turned over. Her eyes glinted in the faint light from the street.

Rod felt a bead of sweat trickle down his side. He said carefully, "Not the way you're thinking."

"And what am I thinking?"

"Don't do this, Bette."

She gazed steadily at Rod and then said, "What about Lori?"

He took a deep breath. "I told him to watch out."

She sat up abruptly. "For what?"

Rod hitched up and leaned against the headboard. "Take it easy. I just said that Lori wasn't as aggressive as he might think."

"And what did he say to that?"

"He made a comment. A crude comment."

"But you didn't think anything of it."

"That's right. It was the usual, you know how guys talk. Plus, lately, it seemed like he and I weren't getting along as well as before. Now, looking back, I think it was like he'd grown tired of me, kind of impatient. Part of the reason I'm so angry with myself is that I knew something was going on, but I didn't really look at it. You know? Like things would be different in my room sometimes, if I was over at your house all night. I think he might have been sleeping in my bed. Maybe even wearing my clothes."

Bette's tone sharpened. "You knew that was happening?"

"I didn't *know* it." Rod looked down. He rubbed his thumb into the palm of his left hand and said, "I love you very much, Bette. You have every right to hate me for what I brought into your life, and if you walked away from me after this is all over, that'd be your right too. You don't deserve any of this."

"Deserve it?" Bette began to cry but kept her head up. Rod reached out to pull her close, but she pushed back, her arms surprisingly strong. "Goddamn it, of course I don't deserve it. He told me to turn on the light and get a preview of what was going to happen to me. And when I did, I just started screaming and flailing around, like my body knew why I was scared before I did, and I'm hitting at the rope and pushing at the door, and I'd still be there now if you didn't let me out. And the whole time there's this little part of my brain that knows this isn't just some fright-night horror, with bugging eyes and the tongue out. It's my best friend, and he's got her strung up in the corner with a belt, and I'm *mad* at her for scaring me so, I'm screaming at her to *stop it*, Lori, stop scaring me, and I'm alive and she's dead. And all the time he was trying to pull the door open and kill me, she was just inches away."

Bette suddenly swung out and hit Rod across the face, then began to cry even harder. She clutched at his arm, and he could feel her fingernails sink into his skin.

"Damn you, I hated you while I was at the hospital, when that little part of me looked down at the nurses and doctors all starched and clean, taking care of me, a squalling mess that got herself into trouble. With that ugly policewoman, talking about me like I couldn't hear—and I'm thinking, 'Look what comes from fucking Rod.'"

He blanched and swayed away from her. She pulled him back and said, "But you don't get off that easy. Unless you absolutely want out, you're still stuck with the crybaby." Bette smiled faintly. Her cheeks were wet. "I figured that out before I left the hospital. But when I saw you at the police station, I started getting angry again. I wanted you to hurt as much as me, I wanted you to *look* the part. The fact is, I'm as much to blame as you are. We both introduced him to Lori. She wanted us to. And we were all fooled."

"First off, I absolutely don't want out," Rod said. "I told you that. And I'll tell you what Leo told me. Brendan killed Lori. Not you, not me. You want to hate somebody, you spend it on him. I am."

"Things are going to be different," she said. "And not for the better. I'm in a different place now. The things I needed before—your kindness, your fun—don't mean as much now. I still love you, but I'm so scared I can't breathe without the air shuddering in. I'm afraid to open a bathroom or a closet door. I'm terrified of what's at my back, but I'm afraid to turn and look, too."

Rod clutched a fistful of her hair and gently pulled her closer. "Didn't I tell you I'd take care of you?"

"I'm not just talking about moral support in a courtroom, or meeting with Lori's parents," she said. "He's still out there. And he's going to try and kill me, and probably you."

"I know," Rod said quietly. Their eyes were only inches apart. "It's my mess. I'll clean it up."

ONE NIGHT AT dinner, about a month after
the opening of the play, Chucky announced
he had a date with Andrea. Ginny squealed
delightedly and slapped the table. "That's
wonderful, Chucky. The two of you will be
able to put all that unpleasantness aside."

Chucky hid his grin by wiping his mouth
with a napkin, his eyes on Guy. "Yeah. It took
some doing. All that unpleasantness."

Their father glanced quickly from Chucky
to Guy to Ginny. He pursed his lips.

Ginny's face was glowing. "This is such a
relief. It's been such a blight."

Art cleared his throat.

"What?" she asked, irritably.

"There will be even more talk, actually.
The fact she's going out with either of the
Nolan boys again."

"Oh, is that right, Mr. Emily Post?" She
sniffed and waved her hand at him. "Why
don't you limit yourself to things you know
something about?" To Chucky she said
sweetly, "When are you going out, dear?"

18

"Wednesday."

"Not Saturday?"

"That's amateur night."

She laughed. "Amateur night, you're too much." She turned her attention to Guy. "And for you, let's not have any more difficulty. This will be better for everybody, make us all look like we forgive and forget. I don't want to hear you whining about her, there will be other girls for you. Do you understand me?"

From inside his head, Guy watched himself say calmly, "Sure, I understand. I expected it."

■ ■ ■

And he did, too. He knew how Andrea thought. She was rebuilding. And that didn't include him. It could have, but it didn't.

He'd tried to talk with her, once.

It had been during the second week after the opening night. He hadn't gone back to school yet, had stayed in his room. He probably would have been able to finish out the rest of the semester there, but Mrs. Bennett had called and talked to Ginny. His mother came to his door immediately afterward and said, "This hiding in your room is ridiculous. Makes your father and me look like child abusers. You're going to class tomorrow, end of conversation."

Andrea was on the way home. Guy had waited for her for over half an hour in the corner booth of a deli near the school, looking out the window, rehearsing what he would say to convince her at least to put on a show for the others, to face them down together. The other walkers from school had passed by, and the big yellow buses were long gone. At last, she appeared at the end of the block, and he dropped four dollars on the table and went to stand near the door. Her head was up, and she strode along easily, looking in at the store displays. To anyone watching her, she was just a pretty girl window shopping on the way home from school. But Guy was willing to bet this wasn't the only day she'd left a half-hour later than everyone else. He stepped out beside her. "Going my way?"

She was startled. Her yellow hair flew across her face as she looked up and down the street.

"Nobody we know to see us," he said.

Her face hardened. "I don't like you following me, Guy."

"I wasn't."

"Of course you were!"

He pointed to the restaurant. "I just had a sandwich there. I saw you coming up the street and wanted to talk to you, so I got up and walked out, all right?"

"No!" She shook her head. "It is *not* all right. Let me make this clear. I don't want to see you. I don't want to be seen with you." She started away.

He stepped in front of her. "Andrea, don't do this. This is me. I didn't do anything to you."

"It would've been better if you had. If you could've." The color was high on her cheeks now. "Do you know the jokes they make about me? Call me an Andreasicle? Sweet but frozen? Kids who would've been *glad* to have me even talk to them before insult me right to my face!"

Guy nodded. "Yeah. I'm going to be open season for everybody. It's not so bad for a girl, it really isn't."

"What do you know about what it's like?" Andrea slapped her thigh. "How dare you say it's not so bad! You haven't even had the nerve to come in."

"I know what it's like," he retorted. "I goddamn well know what it's like—the comments, people laughing about you, pointing, staring, acting like you're just some *thing*, some creature that anybody can poke or push if they want. Yeah, you're a nice girl, Andrea, you were being fair, right? You were just slumming with a geek, that's all."

"That's right, Guy, you've got it." Her voice took on a savage edge. "I'm not used to it, and I'm not going to get used to it. Stop whining at me." She jerked her thumb toward herself and said, "I made a mistake. I felt sorry for you, and I figured I've always been lucky, things have worked well for me, maybe I can spread it around.

Show you a few things. I thought you were going to surprise everybody, I really did. But now I know, it was so obvious, but I thought I knew better."

"What? What was so obvious?" She started to push past him, and he grabbed her arm.

"Let go of me." She swung her arm out of his grip deftly and tapped him on the chest, hard. "You keep your hands off me."

"What was so obvious?" he asked more quietly.

Her eyes met his and, momentarily, her face softened. But she spoke briskly enough. "People have always picked on you, and I guess there's a reason. The only difference, when I tried to help you out, they have me to pick on, too."

He felt a pressure in his heart snap. "What your dad said. That I'm a loser."

She frowned quickly, reached out as if to touch his shoulder, then withdrew her hand when she saw his expression. "Listen, I've got to go."

"You're wrong. He's wrong."

She shrugged. "Yeah, well, maybe." She shaded the late afternoon sun from her eyes and observed him. "I've got to go now. I guess it's good we had a chance to talk. I guess if we see each other in the hall, it's okay to say hi sometimes, but otherwise, you know, I'll just be going my way. Okay?"

He watched her walking away, her clean girl smell already blown away by the breeze, the sun in her hair. She was the prettiest girl he had ever seen, and his wanting her was all mixed together with hating her.

Why does she have to do this to me?

His despair hardened into a resolve before she turned the corner. But it wasn't until the night she went out with Chucky that it was clear how he was going to carry it out.

■ ■ ■

He went into Chucky's room before leaving the house. Ginny and Art were already upstairs. He had turned the volume on the television in his own room just high enough to suggest his presence but not to attract demands to turn it down. He went through his brother's drawers and picked out a black cotton short-sleeved shirt, one of Chucky's favorites. It was a little small on Chucky, tight enough to show the muscles in his arms and chest. On Guy it fit comfortably, a little loose, but not too bad. He was surprised how close in size they actually were. Next he pulled on a pair of white corduroys. The belt needed to be only one hole tighter. The sneakers were fine.

He took a pair of his mother's disposable rubber gloves from below the kitchen sink. In the garage he picked up the newspaper-wrapped package from behind the freshly swept workbench, strapped it to the bicycle, and headed off for the car he had picked out the day before.

■　■　■

Guy's fingers were sweaty inside the rubber gloves, but when the ignition wires sparked, the red Mustang with the black hood scoop roared to life. The lights in the house it was parked in front of remained off. He jammed the Hurst shifter into reverse. On the road, he headed out of what passed for the tough side of town toward the Beacon movie theater to wait for Chucky and Andrea.

He had picked the car not only because it looked as if the owner was away, with the newspapers piled up in front of the house. No, he knew from Bob Ernson's motor-head rhapsodies on the bus that a Mustang with a 351-cubic-inch engine with a four barrel and dual exhaust would walk away from his brother's Camaro as if it were sunk in quicksand. And Bob had spent more than one morning bus ride going over the various methods of stealing the car of his dreams. Not that he'd ever actually do it. Guy had listened dutifully, thinking it was the price to pay for having what appeared to be a friend.

Guy imagined Bob seeing him now, driving this car that would slam him back into the seat at just a slight jab of his right foot. Stealing the car was nothing. Driving the four on the floor was nothing, and Guy had only driven a column shift before. *Screw worrying about it, just do it.* He said the words aloud in the car. "Do it." The sick feeling he normally carried in his belly was gone.

"Fuck with me now, Chucky," he said aloud in the empty car. He pulled a cassette from the glove compartment and slipped it into the tape deck. The Stones' "Get Off of My Cloud" crashed onto the speakers. He grinned and rolled down the window, not caring who saw him. Let them look. If he got caught, that would be too bad, but he was certain he could do some damage along the way.

He pulled into the theater's parking lot and wound through the rows of cars, looking for the Camaro. At idle, the exhaust sounded ragged through the twin glass pack mufflers. He spotted his brother's car in the back row, angled to take two spaces. Guy grunted. Typical.

Parking along the side wall of the theater so he could watch both the car and the exit door, Guy unwrapped Chucky's present. He stuffed the newspaper behind the passenger seat. When he looked up, the movie had let out. Andrea and Chucky were strolling toward the Camaro. He had his arm around her, and she looked stiff.

But she was there, and that was all that mattered.

Chucky opened the passenger door, took her by the shoulders, and kissed her. Her arms stayed by her sides until someone in one of the cars filing out yelled, "Go for it, Chucky!" She put her hands on his back.

Guy inhaled sharply.

He followed them out of the parking lot, staying several cars behind. When they came to River Road, Chucky pulled a hard left and sped down the dark lane. Guy did the same. Into the windshield, he said, "You going to your favorite spot, Andrea?"

Guy slowed and followed them at a steady pace. They passed the entrance of the little clearing and continued on for several miles before reaching a series of winding turns. Guy almost lost them; the red lights of the Camaro winked off in the bushes to the right just as he came around a corner. When he was parallel to where his brother's car must have been, Guy looked over. From the road it was invisible. The entrance was just a dark shadow in the undergrowth. Guy continued around the bend and pulled over.

The exhaust muttered and popped. Guy dimmed the dashboard lights and waited. Ten minutes passed. A smile began to tug at his lips. Guy put his hand to his face, feeling the curve of his jaw, the wet of his teeth. It was both familiar and alien to his touch. There was a pounding in his head, but it felt good, a steady, hot pulsing of blood flowing through his body like high-pressure hydraulic fluid in a dangerous machine. He twisted the rearview mirror down and turned on the overhead light. In the narrow band of silver he gazed at himself, unblinking. *That's me. Am I crazy?*

"Could be," he said aloud. He snapped off the light, slipped into first gear, and spun the car into a tight U-turn. With a wail of protesting rubber, the car leaped forward. The tires squealed for the next two gearshifts, and by the time he was around the corner he was going seventy-five and the speedometer needle was climbing fast. The bellow of the engine hammered at the trees. Then he stood on the brakes.

The back end started to fishtail, and he corrected with quick jabs at the wheel. Where the road widened after the curve, Guy spun the car around and jammed the shifter back into first. He roared along the dirt shoulder, nosed into the narrow path behind his brother, and skidded to a halt. He stomped on the high-beam knob on the floor, and the Camaro was bathed in harsh light. It was about three car lengths away. White faces appeared at the plastic rearview window.

"Ten goddamn minutes," he said and popped the clutch. The Mustang jumped forward, spinning rocks and grass under its wide rear tires before he slammed on the brake. He did it again. Chucky stuck his head out the window and bellowed, "If I have to get out of this car I'm gonna bounce your head off the bumper."

Guy slipped the shift into neutral and raced the engine, drowning his brother's words. The smell of the exhaust was hot and oily, the roar of the engine an angry sound.

His brother pulled his head back into the car. Guy immediately let the engine idle down. He could see hurried movement in the car, his brother twisting and turning, getting dressed. In the right-hand corner of the rear window, Andrea looked back at his blinding glare of light. When Chucky's door opened she turned away, and Guy could hear her over the loud muttering of the Mustang.

"Don't. Chucky, get back in. I want to go."

His brother wasn't wearing a shirt, only jeans and sneakers. He shaded his eyes with his hand, and the big bicep of his left arm swelled. He approached Guy's open window slightly at an angle, his right arm behind his leg. "What's your problem, buddy?" he said into the darkened car.

Guy stuck the épée into his chest.

He had honed it to needle sharpness on their father's grindstone and had cleaned and polished the rusty steel, so Chucky probably had just the faintest sense of the silver glint shooting toward him before the tip plunged into his flesh. The daily regimen of push-ups and weight lifting in Chucky's life of football, wrestling, and baseball saved him from dying right there. As the blade sank into his tough pectoral muscle, he reflexively parried with the tire iron he had been holding alongside his leg. The tip of the épée gashed his chest open to the ribs, instead of sliding into his heart as Guy intended. Chucky cried out and stumbled into the glare of the stolen car's headlights.

"Chucky!" Andrea screamed.

Bright red blood poured between his fingers, down his belly. Suddenly he didn't look so big to Guy. Chucky's face was amazed, and he looked down at himself and back at the car, mouth open, tears glistening on his cheeks. The tire iron hung loosely from his fingers. *What are you doing?* Guy thought. But he got out to finish what he'd started.

"Guy!" Chucky said. Pathetic hope crossed over his face. Then he saw the weapon in Guy's hand.

You don't have to kill him, the voice said inside his head. Then Guy's jaw clenched, and he shot his arm out, sending the sword point toward his brother's jugular. Chucky jerked his head back and swung the tire iron in a wide circle, pushing the blade away and clipping Guy on the chin.

"Stop it!" Andrea cried. "What are you doing, Guy?" She stuck her head out of the passenger side of the Camaro.

He backed off and rubbed his jaw. "Ten minutes," he said, quietly. "Ten minutes and you're crawling in the backseat. I'm going to do you tonight too."

"Guy, you hurt me bad." Chucky extended a bloodstained hand, palm out. "Let's cut the shit, okay? Put that thing down, you got to get me to a doctor."

"You don't get it. I'm killing you now, and her next. Ginny's going to be identifying her darling Chucky at the morgue sometime tonight, tomorrow, or whenever they find you. Probably when you start to stink." He looked at Andrea. "And your dad is going to know firsthand what being a loser is all about."

Chucky's back straightened. He brushed under his eye, replacing tears with a streak of blood. "Start the car, Andrea," he said, keeping his eyes on Guy. "You're a fucking loony, Guy. You're doing this because of that trick I pulled? It was just a joke, like goddamn 'Candid Camera,' for Christ's sake." He jerked his head toward his Camaro. "Andrea knew it was a joke. She let it go, why can't you?"

"Maybe because you've been fucking me so much longer than her."

"Back off, Guy." Chucky raised the tire iron in his right hand. "I'll split your head wide open. So help me, I'll do it." His eyes narrowed, and he straightened slightly. "Why're you wearing my clothes?" Behind him the Camaro's starter ground but didn't catch.

Guy flicked the point of the épée near Chucky's face and said, "It's the combination. I figured it out. You, me, Cyrano. We can beat just you any day."

"Pump it!" Chucky yelled to Andrea. He jerked his head back to Guy. "Cyrano? You're totally soft, Guy. You come any closer, I'm going to have to kill you. There's no damn choice."

Guy set his legs.

The Camaro hadn't fired yet, and Chucky risked a glance over his shoulder. "Pump it twice, leave the pedal halfway down!"

Guy lunged. He jabbed the épée deep into Chucky's right upper arm and felt it grate against bone. Screaming, Chucky dropped the tire iron and clutched at the blade with his left hand. But Guy tugged it out of his arm and through his fingers. He played the point, dripping red, in front of Chucky's eyes. "Should I make a poem about it?"

"Stop it, Guy, please," Chucky pleaded. "I'm your brother, for Christ's sake." Guy dropped the point to Chucky's throat. The Camaro started just as he lunged again. Chucky pushed the blade aside with his forearm while Andrea spun the rear wheels and shot backward. Chucky jumped back. "Hit him, Andrea!"

Guy slipped in the grass, and the rear end of the car loomed over him, hot exhaust fumes blowing in his face. He rolled under the front of the Mustang as she cut the wheel. The Camaro spun at right angles to Guy's car, the Mustang's headlights only a few feet from her door. Guy stood up quietly between the two cars. He could see Andrea's gold hair shimmering as she bent over the stick shift. The gears clashed as she tried to find first. Grasping the épée tightly, he edged over to her open window. She shot a wide-eyed look over her shoulder, not seeing him until he blocked the headlight.

"Did you have a good laugh, Andrea?"

"Don't, Guy, don't!" she screamed, and then popped the clutch. The car lurched forward. He shoved the épée at her face, but she ducked, and it slid through her hair to plunge into the seat. She got the car moving again, and the pommel of the weapon hit him on the chest. Guy ran alongside, holding on to the door handle.

"Leave me alone!" she screamed, hitting at him with her left arm. He yanked the blade out with his left hand. Her eyes widened and met his for a split second. He was aware of Chucky moving off to his left, but concentrated on her.

That's the spot, he thought savagely, and was drawing the épée across his body when a numbing blow to his chest knocked him off his feet. He rolled along the car, pushing away to avoid the wide, spinning tires. Then it was gone, and he hit the ground, the exhaust of the Camaro blowing on his face. The breath was knocked out of him, and his chest felt like it was on fire. There was a fist-size rock on the ground in front of him. He got to his feet, clutching the épée, looking for his brother's next attack.

But Chucky jumped onto the hood of the Camaro and yelled to Andrea, "Go, go, go!" He grabbed hold of the windshield wipers and jerked his head toward the narrow path. "Through there!" She pushed through the light brush beside Guy's car. Sparks flew out as the mufflers scraped rock.

"No!" Guy raged. He tossed the épée in the back of the Mustang and got into the driver's seat. "No!"

THEY'RE GOING TO TELL! his mind raged, *THEY'RE GOING TO TELL!*

He lost time finding reverse in the dark and then was shoving through the path backward. Branches whipped at the car, and he bottomed out in the deep ruts. Twisting around in his seat to look directly out the back window, Guy stared at the bouncing rear lights of the Camaro. And then it was on the smooth pavement of the road and gone. Guy lost more time turning around. They were around the bend before he got started.

He floored the gas pedal and smelled burning rubber until the rushing wind blew the air clean. He caught up to them within a mile and followed, staying right on their tail with his high beams on, steadily pushing the speed up. Under the glare of his lights, he couldn't see through the Camaro's plastic back window. When he saw the streetlights over the highway abutment a half mile ahead, he pulled alongside them, pounding out a hundred and ten miles an hour. He had to laugh. Andrea was too scared to stop and let Chucky into the car. He was still holding on to the windshield wipers.

Guy honked the horn and waved. Andrea turned his way, the dashboard lights dimly highlighting her features in a horrified mask, mouth drawn down, eyes wild. She put her hand out the window as if to make friends.

Chucky lay on his stomach, hair whipping over the back of his head. As they passed under a streetlamp, Guy could see his brother looking at him. His mouth was moving.

Guy waved at him and said, "Chucky, if you must speak, *enunciate.*" He jabbed the wheel over. Andrea cut too hard to the right and hit the curb. Guy saw his brother in the air for a second before the rolling Camaro landed on top of him. The car slammed into the abutment, and then Guy was past. He slowed easily, not wanting to leave a tire mark. He backed up. The wheels were still spinning on the overturned car. The ragtop roof was flat. Andrea was certain not to be pretty anymore. The bundle of rags in front of the car wasn't moving. Guy was about to get out to make sure that it couldn't when the Camaro exploded with a billowing crump. Flames soared over the wrecked car, and Guy took a few seconds before leaving to roll down his passenger side window and feel the purifying heat.

Using the back roads, Guy returned the Mustang to its driveway and cleaned it out. The owner would be able to tell it had been hot-wired, but that couldn't be helped.

At home, he slipped in quietly and looked at the kitchen clock. He had been gone a little under an hour and a half. He turned off the television in his room, put Chucky's clothes in the bottom of the hamper, took a shower, and called a cheerful good night to his mother and father. Alone in his bed, Guy had an uncontrollable fit of laughter. He covered his face with a pillow, giggling over the thought that had been tickling him all the way home.

Some people just couldn't take a joke.

GUY HAD TRIED Ericka first. Right after he heard Rod pounding up the stairs, Guy hurried down the back way into the alley and around to the sidewalk along Bay State Road. Police cars raced by, blue lights swirling. He didn't look their way, didn't run either. He had been in situations like this before and knew the best thing was to find a quiet place and stay there. Tony's place might still be vacant, he figured, but the thought of sitting in the apartment alone made the sickening tension in his belly spread into his arms and legs.

19

Those four walls, alone, thinking, thinking, Rod and Bette knowing about him, talking about him, telling about him, their hatred written on their faces, their contempt . . . it was a tangible pressure in his heart. He didn't want to live with that, didn't want them to continue living either. He glanced back at their window, then turned the corner toward Kenmore Square. "It's untenable," he said to no one in particular. The words had a nice ring, a nice finality. "It's an untenable situa-

tion," he said, louder. "And I'll just have to do something about it."
The small comfort the words inspired didn't even last to the end of
the block.

Why can't they tell? he wondered about the other people on the
sidewalk. *Why can't they smell it on me?* He stared covertly at a young
woman with short bangs who was walking his way. What would she
do if she knew? Gag? Run to the police? What would he do? Would
he cut her down in time? Push her into traffic? Stand there and do
nothing?

Anything could happen. He had no base, no confidence. Bette
and Rod were talking about him by now. His hands and legs trembled.
The girl looked his way, frankly, and he looked at the ground.

Lori had pushed him, the bitch, pushed him right out of the life
he had spent weeks developing. She got just what she deserved.
Choked off her snide comments with her own belt. "Well, I guess
we're just not a couple made in heaven after all," she had said. "No
biggie. It's not like we put a lot of time in before we found out."

Eyes bulged as wide as Popeye's. Surprised the *hell* out of her.

Stepping into the traffic in Kenmore Square, he almost got his
left leg taken off by a taxi. He jumped to the island just in time and
glared after the taxi but didn't dare to flip the driver off. Partly because
he didn't want to attract attention when the police could already be
looking for him. But mostly because he felt empty and afraid.

Ericka had made him feel good. She wouldn't discount him the
way Lori had. And he was betting she was the type to take the slap
he had given her as encouragement. He followed a man about his
age into the lobby of her building and took the elevator to her floor.
Music was playing behind her door. He knocked.

"Who is it?" she called.

"Brendan."

"Who?"

He knocked again. "Come on, open the door, please."

She opened it against the chain and peered out. Her eyes were
glassy. But her face was even prettier in the daylight, and he found
himself responding to her immediately. *Why did I waste my time on
Lori?*

"Having a few White Russians?" he asked, trying to smile.

Recognition came into her eyes, and he thought he saw fear also. She slammed the door shut.

He knocked on the door quietly. "Ericka, please, I want to apologize."

The door snapped open against the chain. "Come to try for the other cheek?" The glassiness in her eyes was replaced with a smoldering defiance.

"I came to say I'm sorry about that." He felt out of step and clumsy. "It must have been the coke and the drinks, but there was no excuse, really."

"I didn't say there was."

"I want to make it up to you."

"How?" She stood on her toes, trying to look behind him. Her brow wrinkled. "How'd you get in, anyway? This building is supposed to have some security. Keep out guys who like to hit women."

"I don't like to." He gave her the most sincere look he could muster, even though his insides were trembling. He desperately wanted her to take him in now, and take care of him as she had before. That would set him right, take care of the talking that Bette and Rod were doing about him. "It was a mistake, my head was in a bad place. Please, Ericka, let me in."

"Why should I? I don't know anything about you."

It was enough to take me in you before, he thought, but he said, "Sure you do. Come on, we danced. We made love."

"Huh," she snorted. "I wouldn't call it that. Brendan, go away. Guys like you are too easy to come by, without the trouble, too." She started to close the door.

He put his foot in the door. "Please, Ericka. I don't have anywhere to go."

She looked at his foot pointedly and said, "Go play with your roommate and his girlfriend."

"We're not friends anymore." His voice was tight, and he could feel the blood rise in his face.

Her eyes widened mockingly, and she said in a little girl voice, "What's the matter? You try to make it with her?"

215

"No!" Her words stung all the more as he realized she was not just a little automaton, but a woman who had given him what he wanted.

"Uh-huh." She started to lean on the door.

He slammed his palm against the door. "Damn it, Ericka, I want to come in. Please. I need you."

"You need me, huh? I *told* you, I know practically nothing about you, and what I do sucks. So, go away. I'm warning you."

He controlled his breathing, smiled again, and said, "What do you want to know?"

She stared at him, her face hard to read. Her chin lifted and she said, "Okay. How about your last name, Brendan?"

The tension eased in his chest. He laughed. "I see what you mean. Kirk. The name's Brendan Kirk."

She smiled now, slowly. "All right, Brendan Kirk, where do you live? And don't tell me 'here' or the doorknob will hit you in the balls."

She is tough. What was I thinking? Rod and Bette would've gotten to like her. Lori ruined everything. He said, "The South End."

"Where in the South End?"

"Why?"

"Good-bye, Brendan Kirk." She started to push against the door again.

Quickly, he said, "Off of Columbus."

"Which street?"

"Why?" He was losing his patience. She was so *close* to letting him in, but this pleading outside the door was exactly what he didn't need. "West Newton," he lied. "Why do you want to know that?"

Her pretty mask contorted suddenly, and she hissed, "Because now I know your name and where you live, you son of a bitch. Enough to send the cops if you ever come around and bother me again."

He braced himself and was about to slam his shoulder against the door when she said, "Look at this, Brendan Kirk." It was a little gun with a silver barrel, and she was pointing below his belt. "I bought it from a guy I know right after you hit me," she said. "If I'd had it in my room that night, you wouldn't have made it out the door."

He backed away. "You couldn't."

"Oh yes I could, you cowardly boy. Run away now, and keep on running. Because if you ever come around me again I'll empty this thing right into your limp little cock."

He left.

■ ■ ■

An excruciating week passed. Ericka's words mingled with those of Bette and Rod. If he closed his eyes, he could hear all three of them talking about him, telling everyone his secrets. His hatred settled on Rod and Bette. Ericka he would take care of later. Rod and Bette had failed him first.

He tried to drown their whispering with the television, sitting up close with the volume just loud enough to hear but not enough for the neighbors to notice. Tony's answering machine held nothing but calls about overdue bills. Same with his mailbox, plus the latest *Penthouse*. One of the bills was a notice that the rent was overdue and eviction was imminent. July had been paid before he left, and he knew from when he'd lived with Tony that he could go until the latter part of the month before the rental office would really put the pressure on. Tony had been that late more than once. Guy figured he would be all right until he took care of his business.

■ ■ ■

Late Saturday afternoon he walked out to Tony's car, carrying a long package wrapped in an orange plastic poncho he had taken from the closet. He didn't think the Thunderbird was going to start at first— it hadn't been driven in the past month and a half. But the engine churned over reluctantly and started. Seemed that Tony was good for something after all.

After letting the engine warm up for a few minutes, Guy headed down Massachusetts Avenue and took a left onto Beacon Street. The pink shirt and chinos he'd worn on his date with Lori were wrinkled and sour-smelling. But he didn't want to wear any of Tony's clothes, even if a week *had* passed.

It was a muggy evening, and Guy had the Thunderbird's air conditioner going full blast. He passed the dive shop, took a U-turn, and parked across the street, in front of the deli from where he had first watched Rod and Bette. After a twenty-minute wait, he saw Leo come out carrying a big orange canvas bag in one hand and a toolbox in the other. Neither Rod nor Bette appeared, but Guy had promised himself he was going to be patient this time. He put on a pair of Tony's tinted glasses, which he'd found in the glove compartment, and flipped down the visor.

After locking the gate, Leo loaded the toolbox and canvas bag into a beige Volvo sedan. He got in, turned the car around, and headed intown, apparently not noticing the Thunderbird a few cars back. He parked in front of a brownstone on Beacon Hill, stepped into the lobby to push the buzzer, and came back outside to unload the bag and toolbox. Rod stepped out a few minutes later.

"Bingo," Guy said. He reached into the backseat for the poncho.

■ ■ ■

Leo kissed Bette on the cheek. "How did it go with Lori's parents this morning? They're heading back today, right?"

"Awful," she said. "I just kept crying and telling them how sorry I was, and how much I missed her. But they both just stared at us. Their eyes were red, they had been crying, but they sure weren't going to do it with us."

Rod nodded. "Mr. Reed stared at me with this look on his face like he'd like to jam a gun down my throat and pull the trigger. I felt like such a screwup."

"It wasn't your fault," Leo said, mildly.

"I don't think they'd agree," Bette said, as she hopped up onto the kitchen counter and ran her fingers through her hair distractedly. She was wearing the new clothes Leo had bought for her—jeans, a red cotton shirt, and white sneakers. "I don't know if Brendan is still out there or not, but I've got to get outside. Go to work, leave Boston, do something. Maybe Rabinovitz might let us go visit my parents if he puts a policewoman in my apartment." She said wryly, "Of course, then I'd have to tell them what happened."

"Still haven't yet?" Leo said, dropping his keys onto the bar.

"They'd insist on coming down, and I can't take the chance. Maybe it'd be okay if we went up there, though. Rabinovitz said we had to give it at least a week before he puts a policewoman in my apartment, because it wouldn't look logical if I went right back home."

"Yeah," Rod said. "He mentioned it two days ago. We haven't heard a thing about it since." He knelt down, unzipped the orange bag, and began to untangle the mess of regulators. "Haven't heard about *anything*. I'll have these overhauled by tomorrow. I can't stand another day sitting around."

Bette said, "Maybe that's what Guy wants. He's going to drive us insane."

"I guarantee you he's around someplace, and he's figuring we're going to get bored and stop worrying about him," Rod said. "Well, I haven't stopped worrying, but I'd sooner be out looking for him than turning into an earthworm here."

Leo mixed a whiskey and soda. He took a sip. Quietly, he said, "If you've got any consideration for Bette, you should do what the police tell you. Let them do their job."

The knock at the door interrupted Rod's answer.

"Who is it?" Leo said. Bette clutched at her throat, and her face paled. Rod set down his wrench.

"Police," a muffled voice said. "We've got a cruiser outside. We need the both of you down at the station to make an identification."

Leo beamed back at the two of them. "What'd I say?" In two strides he was at the door.

"Don't!" Rod stood, spilling a set of wrenches to the floor. Leo opened the door to the limit of the chain. From behind, Bette could see the brown hair of a man slightly taller than Leo, and a patch of orange. "Leo!" she screamed.

Then Leo said something and tried to close the door, but it wouldn't shut all the way, and red gouts of blood splattered the wall.

219

Leo made a gargling sound and clawed at his throat. Rod ran over and caught him as he fell, and Bette saw that something was sticking in his throat, something long and green. And she was screaming, and mercifully her head suddenly became light and her body heavy.

It hurt when she hit the floor.

Her last thought before she lost consciousness was, Leo's hurt, not me. I should help . . .

It wasn't until later that Rod told her Leo was killed by a steak knife bound to a broom handle with electrician's tape.

CYRANO WAS GONE. Gone from the moment the phone rang in the middle of the night and Guy's mother started wailing. Gone later, during the funeral, during his first day back at school. Gone.

But it was all right, because Chucky was in his place. Guy felt his brother moving within himself, a little surprised, a little chagrined, but it was still him. And it was better than it had ever been with the fictional character. Because Chucky was real. He *knew* things, how to act, what to say, what to wear. He wasn't stuck in the trappings of honor, as Cyrano was. He wouldn't waste his time mooning after one girl.

Guy started exercising. He worked his way up to twenty pull-ups on the bar in Chucky's bedroom doorway. One hundred sit-ups and seventy push-ups. Within two months he was running five miles every other evening. The muscles in his chest and arms began to swell, as Chucky became more pronounced in him. At first his mother was too wrapped up in her

20

grief to notice anything he did. Then he began to see her hollow eyes questioning him, as she shuffled through the house, wearing the same pink robe from morning to evening.

He ignored her.

Until one day when he was in Chucky's room, pressing weights. One hundred and ninety pounds trembled in his arms, a new record. He had only been able to press 150, once, when he started. The part of him that was Guy was impressed, but the Chucky in him was disgusted. He should be able to knock off at least 210.

"Who said you could do that?"

He let the bar hit his chest and exhaled for another all-out push when she appeared above him. He noted how she had aged, the crepiness under her neck, and a streak of gray in her hair that hadn't been there before. She smelled of old sweat. A feeling he hadn't known since childhood welled up inside him that he realized was Chucky's affection for her. It was tinged with a secret contempt. "Don't worry, Ginny," he said. He concentrated on his breathing.

"Don't call me Ginny." Her eyes narrowed.

"Mother?" He shoved the bar up, and let it back down to his chest. "How about Mommy?"

"Shut your rotten mouth." Tears welled out onto her cheeks, and he was shocked to find a touch of shame coming from Chucky. But Guy was in control. He said, "It's not like Chucky's here to use the stuff."

But she wasn't listening. Her eyes had turned down from his face, and a red flush spread up her neck. "You're wearing his clothes!" Her voice was low, incredulous. "Oh, my God, what's the matter with you? You're wearing his clothes, he isn't even dead two months."

He had pulled on Chucky's shorts and a gray sweatshirt with cutoff sleeves without even thinking. Not that he would have had any compunction about it—he was more relaxed in Chucky's clothes than in his own. But he probably should have closed the door.

"Yeah. It just seemed the best thing, when I was working out." He started to push again when she grasped the bar and pushed down.

With the weight against him, she overpowered him easily. The bar pressed against his breastbone, and he could hardly bring in a breath. Keeping his voice calm, he said, "Ginny, I'm not going to hold back when I get up."

"I told you not to call me that," she grated. The smell of gin billowed down on his face, and wildly he thought, *She's switched her drink.*

"Let me up."

"What are you up to, little mister?" Her voice shook, and she pressed the bar harder. "Just what are you up to? I've been watching you. You're in his room, acting so cocky, strutting off to school like you're so damn special. Like you're happy! Happy! It's like blood is coming out of my eyes, I'm crying and hurting all day long, and you're whistling around the place. Didn't your brother mean anything to you?"

His ribs burned, taking the full brunt of the weights. He reached around with his right hand and struck her across the face. She shrieked and backed away, hands over her face. Quickly, he marshaled all his strength and thrust the weights up onto the rack above his head. He stood up and towered over her, his muscles bulging, well oiled with sweat.

"You hit me," she breathed. The mark of his hand was etched in red on her right cheek.

He moved closer, until she backed up. "Try something like that again, and I'll break something. Send you off to a bridge game with a big black eye to hide under two pounds of makeup."

"I'm going to tell your father!"

"Not Papa!" He grinned. "Guess I'll have to do the same for him. But, between you and me, Ginny, you know I won't have to."

She backed toward the doorway. "I don't know what's gotten into you. You've never been like this."

"You'd be surprised. You *will* be surprised." He sat down in Chucky's chair. "By the way, Ginny, I'm moving into this room." Locking his hands behind his head, he looked around critically at the stereo, the posters, the sunlight streaming through the window. "Yeah, the light is better, the furniture and the bed, too."

She put her hand to her mouth. He could hear her gag, and he grinned. "It's just more me, you know?"

■ ■ ■

He made them buy him a car. He chose a green Mustang with fifty thousand miles on the odometer, wide tires with Cragar mags and the same 351 eight-cylinder engine that was in the car he'd run Chucky and Andrea off the road with. It made him laugh, his parents' paying for virtually the same car that had killed their beloved firstborn, but he kept the joke to himself. That was hard. It was all he could do not to stand up in class and do Show and Tell: How I Killed My Brother and His Girlfriend.

But there was plenty more to show them.

He had been wearing Chucky's old steel-toed boots for a week, but the opportunity to use them didn't come until one morning in Mrs. Bennett's class, before she was in herself. Chucky hadn't worn them for a couple of years. Unlike T.D., after he'd established his reputation he'd put them in the closet. Now it was T.D. who gave Guy the chance to build his own. "Take a look, ladies and gentlemen, so you can tell your kids. With Chucky a cinder, this is the last Nolan on earth. There's no way, no how *Guy's* ever going to reproduce."

The others laughed, uneasily at first, until Laura Teason joined in. The blood began pumping in Guy's arms and chest, but along with it an icy calm descended. Marveling, Guy let his brother take over. He walked directly up to T.D., who sat apparently waiting for some sort of answer, some defense. The fear came into his eyes at the last minute, a sudden recognition of a Guy he had seen before. But before he could stand up, Guy hit him.

He tried to smash through to the back of T.D.'s skull, putting all his weight and newfound strength behind his fist. There was a satisfying chunking noise in T.D.'s face. He put T.D. in a headlock and pulled him over, tangling him in the desk and chair. When T.D. tried to stand, Guy stepped back and kicked him in the balls. T.D. made a sound like a girl screaming.

"You're out," Mr. Terault said. "Your brother's death must be up-setting you. That and what happened before. But that still doesn't allow you to assault people in my school. Think about that until I let you know you can come back."

"Got it," he said, and went home to lift more weights.

Terault let him come back after a week. It took two more fights to get the message across. One in the locker room after gym class with Jerry Palmerson earned him two weeks' expulsion and Jerry a broken knee. The other with Scott Racowsky, a huge denim-clad biker who never spoke much and who fought only when severely provoked. Guy provoked him by walking up to him in the hallway and using his boots the way he had on T.D.

It was Guy's worst fight, but he won. His mouth was bloodied and one eye was swollen shut. Scott's nose and two ribs were broken, and, most shameful of all, he was crying when the gym coach and his assistant pulled Guy away.

• • •

For the rest of his high school career, nobody met Guy's gaze in the hallway. He put Chucky's boots back in the closet. When they finally let him back into school, he set to work finishing out the rest of his junior year, with better grades than his teachers at first believed possible. But it was for real. He found that the work came so easily to him that he only needed to listen once to a lecture, or read the assignments quickly, for the framework of the information to be clear to him.

He saw how Chucky had been able to take on such an attitude about himself. He really *was* superior.

And I killed him. ✦

• • •

That summer, he decided it was time to make love again. He didn't use the word *try* to himself. In him, Chucky chose the best partner. Guy watched and approved. She would be the best challenge.

Laura Teason.

He called her at home during the Fourth of July weekend. It was a hot Saturday. The sun was beating off the street outside, but there was a steady breeze blowing. He used the phone in the kitchen, not caring if his parents could hear.

"Who?" Laura said, when her mother put her on the phone.

"Your mother got it right."

"What are you doing calling me, Guy?"

"I'm driving up to the beach at Watch Hill this morning, and I figured you might want to come along."

"You figured wrong."

"I don't think so. I'm leaving in fifteen minutes."

"Have fun."

"We will."

"What is this 'we' nonsense?"

"We as in you and me. In the car, with the radio playing. On the beach. Suntan lotion, hot dogs, the whole thing. We."

The line was silent. Then she said, "Let me give you a clue, Guy. I never liked you before, and lately you've turned into a thug, beating everybody up. What makes you think you can call me up like this and ask me out?"

"Because you're curious."

"That's not enough of a reason."

"Sure it is."

"Besides," she said, archly. "What I'd be most curious about, I already know. The whole school does, remember?"

He laughed aloud; his confidence was never so high. "Sure I remember, but that's old information."

"You say."

"You can find out."

"Who says I want to?"

"Me. I'll be there in fifteen minutes. Bring your bathing suit."

He hung up.

■ ■ ■

She came. It took him a few more minutes, sitting in the car, idling outside her parents' house. But Guy could see the outline of her bathing suit underneath her halter and knew it was just a matter of saying the right words. And Chucky knew all of those. For the hour-long drive, she stayed as far from him as she could, leaning against the passenger door, looking at him as if he were a failed laboratory experiment.

He didn't care.

Chucky taught him that. Not caring was the key.

Sure, he cared about how her plump breasts looked in her halter. The full hips pressing against her shorts, the glow of her nicely tanned skin. Her high cheekbones, her eyes, the sexy pout of her mouth. The bitchy look of her that made him want to pull off the road and take her right there. He cared about those things, and how they looked when they finally reached the beach. But it was just as pleasing looking at the other girls, nearly naked in their brief suits. Several had bodies as good as hers.

So there was no real need to care about *her*.

"So tell me," she said.

"What?"

"You know. Your 'new information.' How you got the balls to call me up like this, why you've been starting fights with everyone lately. All that."

"Don't you want to know what it's like living without my older brother? I mean, you used to hang around with him, you must be curious." He spread the blanket on the sand, peeled off his shirt and shorts, down to his bathing suit. He pulled the suntan lotion from the athletic bag he had carried and sat down. She stood there looking at him. He thought she was blushing slightly. "Really," he said. "Shouldn't you be asking about stuff like that? How's my mom taking it, my dad?"

She pursed her lips and shrugged. "Sure. I suppose." She took her halter and shorts off to reveal a tiny white bikini. Her honey-colored skin had a faint sheen of perspiration.

He patted the blanket. "Come on, lie down. I'll put some lotion on you."

"I don't need it." She lay down though, on her stomach. Flipping her caramel-colored hair to one side, she observed him suspiciously.

He pulled out another bottle. "Baby oil, then. I want to rub it on, anyway."

Her face tightened again, but she didn't stop him. He started on her shoulders, rubbing the oil in slowly, enjoying the feel of her smooth skin.

"You don't act the way you're supposed to," she said.

"How's that?"

"Oh, please. You know what I mean." She sat up, pushing aside his arm. "Like you asking me out. What're you up to? Why do you think you have the right to do this?"

"Who says I have the right? And why haven't you asked me those nice, sincere questions about my family yet?"

She made a face. "Screw. I don't have to be nice and say a bunch of stuff I don't want."

He grinned. "That's one of the reasons I asked you." He squeezed a palmful of oil onto his hand and rubbed it into her chest, down the sides of her breasts on the way to her belly. "This is the other."

Her eyelids lowered, and she began to breathe more heavily. "Stop it."

"Why?"

"There are people all around."

"Since when did people watching you stop anything?"

"You shouldn't."

"Yeah, well, that's a green light for you, too." He put his hand on the back of her thigh and pulled her close. The oil was hot between their skin, and just before they kissed, she said, "I still don't like you."

"So what?" He kissed her again.

■ ■ ■

Guy drove through Westerly, looking for a spot to pull off. Finally, he found a side road near the Route 95 access ramp. They made love in the car, the passenger seat pushed all the way back. Laura's nails cut into his back, and his mind turned off entirely, lost in her slippery heat. When it was over he lay on top of her, his brain slowly ticking back to reality.

Laura said, "You're as good as your brother was."

He brought her into focus and grunted, "I ought to be." He stepped outside and pulled on his jeans and shirt.

"What if somebody sees you?"

"What if they do?" He got in, started the engine, and turned the car back toward Connecticut, feeling very warm and good. He enjoyed the small things, the feel of the sunlight pouring through the window on his hands, the taste of air flowing in and out of his lungs.

She pulled her shorts back on and said petulantly, "You could've waited until I was dressed."

Irritation tugged at his sense of well-being. Suddenly he wished he were alone to enjoy the glow in peace. He said, "Why? I don't want to give you the wrong impression."

"What's that?"

"That I care about you or anything."

She stared at him a moment, then laughed.

That surprised him a little, and he looked at her quickly.

"You watch too much TV. Who said I wanted you to care?"

"I figured . . ." He shut his mouth and the black crawling feeling that had been absent for weeks crept into his belly.

"You figured what? That because of this one time, you're on top of everything? And that you can just throw me away?" She shook her head. "Uh-uh. Takes time. Takes time before anyone else is going to notice you the way you want. I was curious, and, yeah, you surprised me. But I'm not saying a word to anyone about today, and I'll tell everyone you've gone off the deep end if *you* try to tell them."

He tried to talk to her. But as the ride lengthened, her strength grew. By the time he was in front of her house, Chucky had withered away to nothing inside him. Laura got out of the car without kissing him. She leaned into the open passenger-side window. "I'll tell you the truth, Guy. If I just met you, I'd be as impressed as hell. But I know what you were, and no matter what happened today, I can't believe you've changed that much." She blew him a kiss. "Bye-bye, Guy."

Chucky was gone. Guy sat alone in the Mustang until her door closed and then drove away with tears blurring his vision. In spite of himself, he missed his brother terribly.

He pulled over before turning onto his parents' street and pulled some Kleenex from the glove compartment. He dried his eyes and blew his nose and considered his options.

He could kill her. But that would be useless. The whole thing just couldn't work with people who knew what he really was, not for very long. Short of killing everyone in town who knew him, there was nothing to do but go home and start over as Guy.

Or leave.

He drove onto the highway, heading toward New York. He figured he could sell the car there for at least a couple of thousand.

That was the last time he was ever in his hometown.

"WHAT ARE WE going to do, Rod?" Bette said. He was at the wheel of her car, driving away from Leo's funeral.

Rod took his wallet from his inside jacket pocket and thumbed through the bills. There was three hundred dollars, in fifties and tens. Abruptly, he said, "I think it's time for you to visit your parents for a while."

"You think they'll let us?" Bette jerked her thumb over her shoulder at the unmarked four-door Plymouth following one car back. Rabinovitz had said that the funeral would be the easiest place for Guy to pick them up again. And if Guy was there, the detective wanted a reception committee.

"Don't worry about that." Rod glanced at her. "Do you want to go, or not?"

Bette gave him a sidelong look and crossed her arms. "Sure. I need to get away from here. I think I'll be less scared there. But I don't want him following me to my parents."

"I'll take care of that," he said. She looked back at him sharply but said nothing.

21

He caught it and said, "Like I took care of Leo, right?"

"I didn't say that."

"Right." They rode in silence for a while. Rod took a left up Chestnut Hill Avenue and a right onto Beacon Street just as the light turned red. He looked into the rearview mirror as the Plymouth eased its way into the traffic. "Taking it slow back there," he said. "Brendan isn't stupid enough to go to the funeral."

"Guy," she corrected. "You proud of him?"

"I'm not going to waste my time with that one." When they were parallel to the dive shop, he pulled over and said, "I'll be right back." He put on his suit jacket. The police car glided past and double-parked on the next block as Rod crossed over to the store. He opened the gate and went inside. A few minutes later he came out, holding a large piece of cardboard. Wiping sweat from his forehead, he quickly fashioned a sign with a Magic Marker: CLOSED. DEATH IN FAMILY. After locking the gate, he walked back to the car, folded his coat, and put it in the backseat. "Let's go."

■ ■ ■

The police were three cars behind the BMW. Rod braked as the light turned yellow at the intersection of Harvard and Beacon streets and shifted into first. Just as it turned red, he popped the clutch and peeled through an illegal left-hand turn, cutting off a huge blue garbage truck. The trucker blasted his air horn. "Good," Rod said, checking the mirror. The police were effectively blocked off as the truck roared in behind him, edging past double-parked cars.

He sped up Harvard Street, after weaving around a teenage girl in a pink tank top who ran across to join the line in front of a movie house.

"What's gotten into you?" Bette twisted in her seat to look back.

"I'm not sitting on my ass this time, that's what," Rod said, harshly. "Waiting for him to pick us off when he feels like it." He took a hard left a few blocks before Commonwealth Avenue, downshifted, and pushed the BMW to the top of third gear. He hit the brakes, took another left, and slowed down considerably. "That should do it for a while."

"Not for long. They know the car."

"We won't need it for long."

"Why not?"

"In a minute. Now do your part. See if anyone is following us."

Bette stared at him hard for a second, then folded her legs underneath herself and looked out the back window. "You think this is the thing to do?" she asked, carefully.

"I don't know exactly the right thing to do, damn it. This is a first for me too, Bette. But I know last time I did what Rabinovitz said, and Brendan found us. We wait here, couple of weeks, the cops are going to lose interest and we'll be right back where we started. If I'm sitting in a room, just watching you, I can't do anything about him."

"And what are you going to do if I'm not around? You're not a detective."

"No. But if I'm out, walking around, going through my usual routine, he's going to turn up. I know it. He's after me too, it's not just you. I began to feel like I was an intruder in my own house toward the end, even though we were still acting friendly. There wasn't any reason I can possibly figure for him to kill Leo, other than because Leo was my friend." Rod took a right onto Beacon Street, heading back the way they had come.

"And he was there."

"Right."

"So take me up to Maine, but we'll rent a cabin someplace for a few days. If he doesn't show, then maybe we'll go to my parents' house. But you stay with me, don't go back to Boston. We'll phone Rabinovitz when we get there. Maybe he'll put the policewoman in my place."

Rod turned right onto Washington Street and parked in front of a silver Firebird. He said, "That's ours. I rented it."

Her mouth opened. "When?"

"Last night. You were asleep. I took a cab to the airport."

She stared at him and then got out and slammed the door. He walked around to the passenger side of the silver car and opened the door. She got in and yanked the door out of his hand.

He slid into the driver's seat. "Bette—"

"Thanks for telling me," she interrupted. "Thanks for sticking around."

"Cops were out front as usual."

"So how did you get in and out?"

"Bathroom window."

"Which is the way he'd get in, too."

"Uh-uh." Rod shook his head. "Guy is more cautious than that. He'd see the cops, he's not going to take the chance."

"So you say." Her eyes narrowed. "Or were you just hoping he was going to try something with you while you were alone? Driving back from the airport, catching a cab back here."

"The thought crossed my mind."

"Did the thought occur to you that maybe he might just take that time to slip in the bathroom window the way you left and slit my throat?"

Rod's face was white. "That's the scene I kept playing in my mind all the time I was gone. But really, he's got more fear than that. He's smarter too. Me alone, sure, but no cops. I can't believe that."

"The cops could have shot you climbing in the window, too. Damn it, were you thinking?"

He didn't raise his voice. "Yes, I was thinking. I was thinking that I didn't want to trust your life and mine to some guy sitting in an unmarked car who doesn't even bother to keep an eye on something as obvious as that. What's *he* got to lose? 'Sorry, I blew it'? That's why we've got to take care of this ourselves."

Bette stamped her foot. "So don't keep me out of it! Tell me what you're going to do. Maybe for that matter, *I* should go back to my routine, live in my apartment. I'm not a coward."

"I know you're not."

Bette's lips tightened. "Really. I'm sorry I fainted, and didn't help you. It just happened. It won't again."

Rod put his finger to her lips. "You're not going back there alone. Period. We'll go to Maine."

"And you'll stay?"

"That misses the point. I want you safe so I can move around and help end this. Look, he doesn't know where your parents live, right?"

"I don't see how he could. Unless Lori mentioned it. I never talked to him all that much, and I doubt he even knows they live in Maine, never mind Harrison."

"Lori and he had other things on their minds besides where your parents lived."

"So good. We'll rent a place up there for a few days. I'll call my parents and tell them what's going on, and that they need to keep the dogs out front and the guns loaded. They'll be upset, but they'll keep an eye out, and my dad and brother are good shots. If it works, the police here will take care of Guy."

"We'll see. I can't leave the store closed forever. Besides, we'll always have that feeling at the back of our necks if they don't find him."

"Better that feeling than you find him and he kills you," she said. She took his forearm and squeezed hard enough to leave a mark. "You want to fulfill your responsibilities to me, you get both of us out of here. I'm ready to let you and my father watch over me and drive each other crazy."

He started the engine and stared intently out the windows at the cars around them. "I don't see him, but we'll be working on it all the way up."

"Anything else you're not telling me?" she said.

"One thing." He nodded toward the backseat. "Leo's gun. I picked it up at the store. It's in my coat."

22

DIAGONALLY ACROSS the street Guy hunkered down beside the stolen motorcycle and tightened the tank bag. His heart was beating quickly. He'd thought he had been recognized back when Rod had hauled off onto Harvard Street. But then he realized the guys in the blue sedan with the big whip antenna were caught off guard too. Real masters of disguise, those two.

So he'd taken a chance and made a U-turn, twisting the throttle on the Honda. Sure enough, he had only waited a few minutes before Rod and Bette drove up to the Firebird on Washington Street. He had wondered when the car was going to tie in, ever since he'd followed Rod to and from the rental agency the night before.

They were all so stupid, both the cops and Rod and Bette. It took so little. They look, they expect to see Rod's former roommate, wearing the same clothes, sitting in a car behind them.

No, Guy thought, *you take away what they*

expect to see, and you're invisible. As long as he didn't ride on their bumper all day, the motorcycle leathers, the bike, the helmet—that was all it took. That and enough brains to recognize what happened next.

Getting the motorcycle in time to follow Rod and Bette from the police station after he'd killed Leo had turned out to be the most difficult job. He hadn't planned to kill Leo, had expected Rod would be the one to answer the door. It had been fine though, seeing that about-to-crap-in-his-pants look on Leo's face when he recognized who was on the other side of the door. Leo had tried to slam it. But by then, the point, as Mrs. Bennett used to say, was moot.

Guy had cupped the end of the broom handle in his palm and shoved it through the O of his thumb and forefinger. The blade hit bone and he twisted the stick, and all sorts of screaming broke out in the room. Blood everywhere. Good idea bringing the poncho. It would have been something, watching Rod bawl over his surrogate dad, but he knew better than to stay around. Down the stairs, poncho off and wrapped in a ball. Out the back door to the alley, and to the car. Walk quickly, don't run, and Rod was too busy trying to save his friend to look for him. And if someone noticed him, noticed the car, that wasn't good, but at least it was a stolen plate.

Still, he decided that evening it would be too risky to use the Thunderbird any longer. Certainly not to follow Rod and Bette away from the police station. He decided on a motorcycle. Hide out in the open. Plus, he just wanted one. It went with his mood.

At Tony's apartment that night, Guy put a fist-size rock in the toe of a double layer of socks. He slapped it in his palm. The heft was impressive. Checking himself in the bathroom mirror, he washed his arms one more time, making sure he was clean of Leo's blood. He saw no choice but to take one of Tony's sport jackets, because the makeshift sap would bulge too much in his pants pocket. He chose a light tan one. Then he took a subway out to a bar off of Commonwealth Avenue that sold Mexican food and was well known for attracting bikers.

It was surprisingly full for a weeknight. "Pink Cadillac" boomed out of wall-mounted speakers, and Guy pushed into the crowd of denim- and leather-clad customers. He felt overdressed but saw no one pay him any real attention. Eyes slid past his face without stopping, as always. Guy found an empty stool near the door and ordered a draft beer. The bartender held up a single finger, and Guy slid a dollar across the scarred wood. The old man dropped the beer in front of him with a clunk.

Looking through the steel grate window, Guy could see the crowded little parking lot. After downing two beers, he saw what he was looking for roll in. The 900-cc bike had been painted solid black and modified as a cafe racer, with a bullet fairing, clip-on handlebars, and a single black exhaust pipe. The rider was about the same height as Guy, and maybe a little heavier. He wore a full-face helmet with a plastic visor. From the way it reflected in the dull light of the streetlamp, Guy thought it might be tinted. Perfect.

The biker swaggered in and ordered a beer. He walked as if his tread was very heavy. The leather jacket creaked, and Guy stifled a laugh that swept up inside, seeing his own reflection beside the biker's in the bar mirror. He was a dandy, in comparison, wearing Tony's sport jacket.

Leather Jacket had dirty blond hair and pitted, sallow skin. He took a swig of draft beer and leaned back on the bar with overt nonchalance. He wore a gray T-shirt underneath the leather, and oddly enough, a gold earring. A pretty blond girl wearing designer jeans and an open expression started by him, and he drifted away from the bar, blocking her way. He said something, and her back stiffened. She looked over her shoulder, and Guy and the other male patrons at the bar took a sudden interest in their beer. She sniffed and stalked angrily among the tables around the biker to the ladies' room. The biker watched her and then stared across the room, beaconing his challenge to anyone who cared to accept. His heavy-lidded gaze passed Guy without stopping. His eyes were startlingly blue. Guy took another sip and turned his head to hide his curving smile. The biker ordered another beer.

By the time Leather Jacket finished two more, Guy didn't have to fake the need to follow him down the stairs and around the bend to the men's room. Inside, there were two stalls and three urinals against the wall. The biker walked over to the urinal farthest away, next to the stall, and unzipped his fly. He hunched his shoulders and didn't look back. Guy went to the toilet, relieved himself, and slipped the sock out of his jacket pocket. He wrapped the slack around his hand and stepped out of the stall just as the biker shook himself and began to zip up.

Guy drew the sap back and swung. The whistling arc ended just behind the biker's ear, and his knees buckled.

But he was tough. He grunted, pushing back from the wall, and put his elbow in Guy's stomach. He swung a right punch, but Guy stepped inside him and lifted his knee. The biker made a gagging sound, and Guy could smell his warm, beery breath. But before Guy could draw back his arm again, the biker lowered his head and butted Guy in the chest. Guy felt a thrill of terror run through him as he fell back. He took two hard punches to his ribs, and then, without uttering a word, the biker stepped back and reached into his jacket. There was a click and a flash of silver.

Switchblade.

Time to stop this right now. He feinted toward the doorway, and the biker staggered in his way, eyes unfocused from the first blow. He swung his knife viciously at Guy's face. Guy ducked just in time, straightened, and lashed out with the sap, knocking the biker's front teeth right out of his mouth. Guy spun him around with a quick backhand. His head hit the porcelain urinal with a solid thunk, and he stayed down.

Guy's breath rasped in and out while he locked the door. His hands were shaking, and he had to admit the biker had surprised him badly. His ribs didn't feel too good either, but he was pretty sure nothing was broken. Guy moved quickly, stripping the unconscious man of his jacket and chaps, ignoring the sweat stink. The underarms of the coat were wet to the touch. Guy put it on anyway, then laced the chaps on. He made a surprising discovery when he bent over to drag the biker into the stall.

Those blue eyes were contact lenses. Guy sat back on his haunches, amazed at his luck, and his ability to choose the right people. He lifted the man's lids between thumb and forefinger, took

239

the contact lenses, licked them, and popped them into his own eyes. They provided no correction. Apparently, Leather Jacket just didn't like the muddy brown that was his real eye color. Guy could understand that.

Then came the part of the plan he felt queasy about. The guy's pants had to be around his ankles for people to see when they came in. He pulled them down and horsed the biker into the stall and onto the toilet, sweating profusely for fear that someone would somehow see. Then he locked the stall door on the inside and climbed out.

The rest was easy. Tony's jacket was light, so he twisted it into a narrow length and stuffed it under the leather jacket. Then he walked upstairs and out of the bar, looking straight ahead. No one appeared to notice. He figured he'd been in the men's room no more than five minutes. The helmet was locked to the bike, and it took him only a few moments to find the ignition, choke, and starter button.

He had learned to ride a motorcycle one summer while working with a construction company. A lot of the guys had them. There wasn't much else to do with your money in that little Georgia town, and fast cars and motorcycles were two of the four staple diversions. Guy didn't drink much. And while he didn't admit to himself that he was afraid of girls, he knew better than to be with one if he couldn't run away afterward.

But there was a guy named Nick who had a beautiful tawny-haired girlfriend named Chloe. Nick rode a gleaming black Norton Commando, perfectly restored. So Guy looked through the paper and spent seven hundred and fifty dollars on a Triumph Bonneville, knowing that another Norton would be a mistake. The Triumph needed work. And soon he had a friend. They spent long nights restoring the bike in the shed behind Nick's rented house, drinking beer, talking about Nick's days as a Ranger in Vietnam. They stayed tight until one day a few months later, when Guy tried to make it with Chloe even though she made it absolutely clear she wasn't interested.

Nick came riding up just as she started screaming. He ran straight into the house, forgetting all his beer talk about guerrilla training.

Guy waited for him behind the door with Nick's own knife, the one with the brass knuckle guard.

He was tired of them by then anyway.

■ ■ ■

Once Guy had the bike, there was that jangling period of indecision, waiting for Rod and Bette outside the Berkeley Street station, not knowing if they had already left, or if one of the cops walking by might ask why he was fiddling with his bike so long. But when they finally hurried out to the car, he was ready, and he followed them to that dive Beacon Street motel, and then he *stayed away.*

Two days festering in Tony's apartment, until Leo's funeral was announced in the paper, and *then* checking out what they were up to the night before. He had ridden past the motel when he saw the two guys sitting in a car outside. Two in the morning and they were just sitting there—who could they be?

He would have called it a night then, but when he swung around the block, who did he see strolling along but Rod? He had a good opportunity to take him right there, waiting for a cab by the phone booth. Or later, after Rod dropped off the Firebird and started hiking up Beacon Street to the motel.

Guy could have roared past him on the bike at fifty and clipped his head right off with the tire iron.

But it wouldn't have been the same without her being there to watch. Wouldn't have been the same at all. Guy lived for these times: The dripping acid in his chest burned and filled the emptiness with purpose.

Oh, *such* a purpose.

Rod and Bette first, Ericka second.

Later, the feeling would slip away and he would need somebody else. But that was far off. Now was now. Rod and Bette were in his arena. And it felt awfully good to be back on a bike, with a plan and the tools to carry it out. Without the police chaperone.

He let several cars get between them and started after the Firebird up Washington Street.

241

23

"HOW DO YOU KNOW Brendan isn't following us?" Bette said to Rod. They were on Route 95 North, just entering Maine.

"I don't. But it's time to find out."

"How?"

"To start, tell me if you see anyone else driving like an idiot." Rod pushed the gas pedal deep into the carpet, and the speedometer needle climbed to eighty, eighty-five, ninety. The car slipped into a shallow decline, and their speed slipped up to a hundred. Without taking his eyes from the road, Rod said, "We've switched cars. He doesn't know where we're going. So if he's behind us, he's going to have to hustle to keep us in sight."

Bette peered out the back window. "You seem to be leaving everyone behind. There's a motorcycle way back there that looks like it's going a little faster than everyone else, but it's hard to tell when it's coming straight on like that." She settled back against the door and braced herself. "Motorcycles go fast all the time anyhow. If this is the only way we're going to check, we might just save him the trouble of killing us."

"This is just a start. I figure it's going to take us all day to make the three-hour trip to your parents', the route I have in mind. Convoluted. Twisty roads sometimes, the highway others. For no particular reason. Taking exit ramps and circling back again. Going too fast, going too slow. If there's a car behind us now that's behind us by the end of the day, then the driver's name is Brendan to you and me."

"You've got it all figured out." She winced as Rod swept into the left lane around a Volkswagen Rabbit, then cut back in to avoid a tractor trailer with a silver oil tank. "What are you going to do if we make it to the end of the day, and there is somebody behind us?"

"Damn it!' Rod hit the brakes.

Bette inhaled sharply and twisted around in her seat. Then she clapped her hand over her mouth to keep from laughing. "I'm sorry, it's not funny, I know, it's just . . . not what I expected." The lights of a state police car filled the back window.

Rod slapped the steering wheel as he pulled the car off to the breakdown lane. "He must have been coming off that entrance ramp." He pointed to the glove box. "Pull out the rental agreement and stop laughing." Rod reached into the backseat to pull his wallet from his suit jacket. The wallet caught in the inside pocket, and he could feel the dead weight inside his coat when he tugged harder. Rod felt the blood drain from his face. "Did you see his face?"

Bette caught her breath. She slid down in the seat to get a better view.

Rod glanced in the rearview mirror. The police car was empty. A shadow fell over the backseat, and Rod's hand closed over the wooden gun butt under his coat. His heart beat furiously. A cop or Brendan? His finger found the trigger.

Then Bette's face relaxed, her mouth softened. Rod let go of the gun, pulled his wallet free, and rolled down the window. A cop wearing reflector sunglasses and an impenetrable expression stared down at him. "What the hell are you running from?" he said.

Neither Rod nor Bette noticed the motorcycle which passed at a sedate fifty-five miles an hour, the rider's full-face helmet turned their way.

■ ■ ■

At a rest area two miles ahead, Guy turned off the engine, took off his helmet, and peered into the bike's right-hand mirror. Then he checked the contents of the bag strapped along the gas tank between his legs. He unzipped the flap partially and tucked it out of the way.

It was a hot day, and the heat from the ticking motorcycle engine only caused him to sweat more. It was getting hard to stand himself, his own perspiration mixing with the ancient sweat soaked into the leather jacket. He took a paper sack from the tank bag and walked into the men's room.

When he returned a few minutes later, he thought, *Maybe I should just go on to Bette's parents' house.* He strapped the helmet back on. *Be sitting there with Mom and Dad when they get home. That'd give Bette a shock. "Mom, Dad, you don't look so good!"*

Of course, the thing wrong with that was he couldn't be *positive* that's where they were heading. Could be they were going to a motel someplace. But he doubted Bette would come to Maine without dropping in to see Mom and Dad. After putting Lori in the closet, Guy had read Bette's mail. Her mother wrote these chatty letters all about her little sister in the lacrosse league, and Dad and his gall-bladder.

Mom and Dad. That's what they called themselves. Sounded like something from "The Brady Bunch." Stepping in on them right at dinnertime could be very entertaining. Especially with the tire iron he'd lifted from the Thunderbird. Put Dad on the couch with that sticking out of his head, and see what Bette said.

Guy straddled the bike again. He wanted to wipe the sweat trickling down the back of his neck but was unwilling to take the helmet off again. Rod and Bette might be along anytime now. And they might want a break after talking with the cop and pull into the rest area. He hoped Rod didn't lose his license; he must have been going over ninety. That would screw everything up. But it looked like the cop was just coming off the ramp and saw them hauling by. Good chance he didn't have them on radar.

Guy craned his head to see if they were coming. Frigging trees were in the way. Be a bitch if he lost them just sitting here. Then he would definitely have to go visit the family. There was only one real problem with taking the time to visit Mom and Dad.

Guy wanted to do it *now*.

A fat woman with a pink blouse and pastel pants waddled in front of him on the way to the bathrooms. She stared, her mouth pursed. He started to say something—the guy who owned the bike certainly would have mentioned her pig heritage—when he saw a silver glint on the highway between the pine trees, and the Firebird flashed past the small clearing. Guy slapped down his visor, hit the starter button, and the hot engine roared to life. He popped the clutch, and smoke poured under the rear wheel. The fat woman squealed and fell back as he left a black patch of rubber inches from her pink tennis sneakers. The Honda snarled powerfully through the gears, and he was after them, laughing aloud at the woman behind him. It would've been a real pleasure running over her, but he figured he'd have gotten stuck somewhere around that big fat belly.

He eased back on the throttle to keep his distance and almost missed them turning off an exit just outside Portland. He trailed them heading west through a small town that had traded clean air for jobs at the local paper mill. Guy tried to hold his breath.

Once he was out of town he opened the bike up and screamed down the winding road. He caught up to them quickly. It looked as if they were definitely heading for her parents' house, from what he remembered of the road map.

Then they turned down an even narrower road. Guy bit at his lower lip. Either they'd realized it was him behind them, or they were trying to find out.

One way or another, this looked like his best opportunity. He hit the brakes and leaned the bike hard through the turn. He ran the bike through the gears quickly until he was right behind them. Standing on the pegs, he could see a brief straightaway in front of the car, then a sharp left turn through a stand of pine trees. Before the trees there was a shallow ditch and a gray stone wall. His speedometer was sitting right at sixty-five. Perfect.

As they entered the turn, he toed the gearshift down two notches, twisted the throttle all the way back, and the high-performance engine really began to wail. He clamped his knees hard against the gas tank and reached with his left hand into his bag of tricks.

■ ■ ■

"It's that biker," Rod said, looking in the rearview mirror.

Bette whirled and saw the motorcyclist lean out to pass. As he pulled past them, she saw him take something from the bag strapped to the tank. She grasped Rod's elbow tightly. "What's in his hand?"

For Rod a jumble of unrecognized images came together in an instant: the single headlight several cars behind him on the way back from the airport with the rental car, the whine of a fast-accelerating motorcycle when he was being dropped off by the cab near the hotel, a bike with a bullet fairing leaning on its side peg across the street from the police station. "It's him," Rod said and almost cut the wheel to the left.

But a sudden doubt frozen him: he'd almost shot the state cop thinking he could be Brendan.

Then Guy threw a bag of blood onto the windshield.

That's what Rod thought it was. He saw something leave the biker's hand, and there was a soft explosion of red across the window.

"Leave us alone!" Bette screamed and hit her fist against the windshield.

Blood. Can't see. Rod desperately tried to remember the road.

Curve.

Ditch.

Stone wall.

The wipers only smeared the viscous fluid.

Rod hit the brake and eased the wheel to the left, praying there wasn't another car coming around the corner. He started to roll down the window when suddenly the black motorcycle and rider fell back beside the car, tauntingly close. "Bastard!" Rod cut the wheel harder to the left and punched the gas pedal to the floor. The back end of the car started to slide, the rear wheels scratching for traction along the dirt shoulder.

The biker dipped away, then straightened. With his left hand he drew something out of his bag and flung it across his chest.

A tire iron crashed through Rod's window, the sharp end jabbing into his arm. Agonizing pain shot through his bicep, and he yanked the steering wheel all the way over to the left.

The car slewed around, and through a small patch of clear glass Rod could see they were heading straight for the biker. He braced for the impact.

But the rear wheels of the car hit a patch of sand, and their traction was gone. "Damn it!" Rod gave up on the biker. He kept his foot on the gas and steered into the skid. A glance at the speedometer told him they were still going over fifty. Skidding blind beside a ditch. He pumped the brake pedal once before the front right wheel rumbled over the shoulder and the steering wheel went loose under his hands.

They were airborne.

Bette drew breath sharply.

Rod snapped off the ignition; he had only a heartbeat to meet her wild-eyed stare.

The shoulder strap yanked his breath away, and his face slammed into the steering wheel. Bette cried out, but Rod needed his hands for himself, holding on to the wheel. The windshield shattered, there was a flashing patch of blue sky out his side window, and then the ground rushed up at tremendous speed outside Bette's and he took his right hand off the wheel, grabbed her by the hair, and pulled her across the seat. Then they were upside-down, the roof crumpled down flat near the headrests, and he braced against the ceiling with his elbow. The shoulder strap cut into his neck—they were supposed to save you not cut your head off—and they were still rolling—goddamn, goddamn, isn't this going to stop?—and still they rolled, upright, bouncing on the tires and shocks until they slammed into the stone wall and it was over.

247

Rod sat holding his head for a few moments. The smell of pine needles mixed with that of hot oil and gasoline, and it came to him slowly that he was still alive. He uncovered his face and took a deep breath and instantly wished he hadn't. Pain shot down his neck and back.

Bette's head was down, her hair covering her face. Rod tried to say her name, but it came out all wrong. Touching his mouth, he felt wet teeth and his hand came away bloody. Bette moaned. He parted her hair, his fingers leaving red streaks on her cheeks. There was a knot just under her hairline. It was pulpy to the touch. She winced and jerked her head away. Her eyes fluttered open, and she said, "Stop it," and then drifted out. The ceiling was too close for Rod to see well, and the steering wheel was pushed against his legs, but he could move them. He lifted the door handle and shoved with his shoulder. The door creaked but didn't budge. His window was broken, but the space was too narrow and edged with glass to crawl through. The windshield lay across the hood like a crystalline rug, the frame reduced to no more than a foot and a half high. It was going to take a gymnastic feat to twist out from under the steering wheel and crawl out of there. Particularly the way his back was beginning to throb. Blood dripped from his mouth down his chest onto his lap. Rod began to fumble for his seat belt. Better to get it over with before he knew *how* badly he was hurt.

Then the muttering sound of the motorcycle drew close, and he nearly lost control. His breath began to rush, and sweat made his finger slippery on the seat belt button. *It's not over, you stupid bastard, he's coming to pull your arms off, stick you in the face with a pitchfork if it's his whim.* Rod twisted around and jammed his thumb against the button, and the pressure across his chest released. He heard himself whimper slightly as a fresh bolt of pain ripped down his spine. He clamped his teeth shut abruptly and reached back for the gun.

His seat had slid forward in the impact. Jammed up like that, he could only slap around with the back of his hand, his eyes straight ahead. The gun wasn't on the backseat; at least he couldn't find it with his nose stuck in the steering wheel. Rod pulled his seat's slide lever and pushed back with his legs. The bucket seat slid back about an inch, then stopped. He pushed harder, but the seat wouldn't budge.

The sound of the motorcycle was switched off. He bit down on his damaged lower lip involuntarily, and the sudden pain cut into his panic. He forced himself to relax, the way he taught his diving students, exhaling slowly. Big damn hero in the blue wet suit, standing there pontificating, telling them, "You can handle *anything* if you train right and keep calm. *Make* yourself be calm."

How do you train for this? he thought, savagely. He shoved back quickly with his legs, but the seat remained stuck.

Rod could hear boots on the gravel.

"Bette," he whispered thickly. "He's coming." He slapped her lightly on the cheek. She came to groggily.

"What?"

"Brendan. He's here."

He saw the panic rise behind the glazed look in her eyes.

"No, Bette, easy now."

"No." She shook her head closing him out. "No. Not trapped in here, no." She pulled at the door latch and shoved her shoulder against the door. "Damn you," she said, her voice low. "Open, you damn door." She drew back against Rod and lunged against the door. She cried out and he winced for her.

"Easy," he whispered, taking her by the shoulders. "We don't want to go out there just yet, anyhow."

She stared at him blankly, then closed her eyes and hugged herself. "I'll kill him first. He's not going to do to me what he did to Lori."

Rod scrunched down to look out the narrow slit that had been the window. Leather-covered legs. Boots. He looked back at her. "You've got it. Talk to him in the meantime."

"I'm not going to beg." She opened her eyes.

"You bet you're not going to." Rod took her chin in his hand and looked directly at her. "We're not going to give him that. No matter what he does."

Unbelievably, a faint smile touched her mouth. "Watch me."

His mouth hurt when he returned it.

Bracing his legs flat against the floor, Rod pulled the seat lever and shoved back. The seat caught again. He exhaled in short, hard breaths and brought all his strength to bear. It slid past the obstruction.

The headrest hit the cumpled roof and forced him to lean forward. He kept his eyes on the boots standing in front of the car as he ran his hands over the backseat, feeling for his coat and gun.

I don't expect it to be where I left it, not after rolling, he bargained. But let me find it, and I'll put an end to all this. I'll put a bullet right into Brendan or Guy or whatever name he's using today and we can go home.

Bette leaned down near the windshield. "Brendan, is that you out there?" Her voice sounded remarkably clear in the tight space.

Rod's hand closed on his coat behind his seat. He tugged it onto his lap, the adrenaline pumping, his thumb eager to pull back the hammer on the revolver. This nightmare is going to end, this bastard is going to die.

But the coat pocket was empty.

GUY LOOKED DOWN the road both ways. No traffic yet. It couldn't last long, but he could take a minute or two. He slid the helmet off and walked up to the crumpled car, enjoying the gravel under his boots, knowing how it must sound to them inside. Assuming they were still alive.

Standing in front of the car, he idly fastened the chin strap of the helmet and listened. Whispers, then pounding on the passenger side door—must be Bette. He grinned. They'd made it! There was a rumbling noise inside the car, then Bette asked if it was him standing out there.

Her tone wiped the grin off his face. Acting as if she wasn't scared, too cool. He swung the helmet down onto the roof, just over where her head should be.

Silence.

"Stupid question, Bette." He put the grin back on and leaned in to inspect the damage. And to give them a good look at his face.

Bette put her hand to her mouth. It was

24

the contact lenses that did it. Changing the hair color was nothing. People could figure that out in an instant. But with the makeup and the eye color, she was looking at Rod, both inside the car and out.

She was looking pretty good herself, he thought, considering. Her face was pale, but she stared right back at him, not anywhere nearly as beat up as she could have been. Rod looked worse, face all bloody, bent over in a position that looked none too comfortable. Like he was peering out from under a giant's boot. "You're just the two to consult with about my new face." He rested his chin on his fists, turning toward Bette. "How do you like it?"

"Look at that, Bette," Rod said. "I've got a fan club of one."

Bette laughed. "Pretty poor club, Rod." She raised her voice slightly. "Your makeup is cracking, Brendan. Couldn't you get one of your girlfriends to tell you how to apply it?"

Guy smiled. "You're *tough*. I'm so proud of you. Too bad nobody else is around to see it."

"I guess he's a fan of yours too, Bette."

"Probably wore my underclothes after he killed Lori."

"Could be. I know for a fact he wore mine."

Bette nodded. "No telling what a man like him does alone with a drawer full of panties. A man who needs to kill women and dress up like another man."

"I can make it hurt worse than it has to," Guy said, making his tone casual. They were making him angry, partly because they just didn't seem to realize how much trouble they were in. "You want to think about that."

"Fuck you, Guy," Rod said.

"That's probably exactly the invitation he was waiting for," Bette said, staring straight at Guy.

Guy felt his face go hot.

"Bette," Rod chided. "You made him blush."

Guy stalked off to the bike and unzipped the tank bag. In the mirror, he saw that his lips were compressed in a white line. He made his face relax, and he felt it throughout his body. No matter what they said, he was in charge, fully in charge. He took a plastic Pepsi bottle out of the bag and walked back to the car quietly. He walked around to Bette's side and saw that she was bent over, reaching behind Rod's seat for something. Rod was looking back as well. Guy reached in through the front window and grasped her knee. "Miss me?"

Bette recoiled instantly, screaming.

Rod lunged over and caught Guy's wrist. But it was slick with perspiration, and Guy deftly twisted his hand away. "Ah, ah. No holding hands."

Rod didn't answer. A vein in his temple pulsed angrily.

Bette rubbed her knee.

"Know what's in here?" Guy continued, setting the Pepsi bottle on the hood. "You've got one guess, then I'll give a demonstration."

Rod's expression remained stony. He reached behind the seat again. Guy felt impatient. "I'll give you a hint, Bette. It's not lemonade."

Rod leaned over and kissed her on the cheek and spoke into her ear.

Guy unscrewed the Pepsi bottle's top. "Ah, that's nice, the two lovers kissing good-bye. Where are the cameras?"

Bette said, "What do you tell yourself, Brendan?"

"Trying to figure it out?" Guy shook his head.

"He's crazy," Rod said. "Why bother with what he thinks?"

Guy smiled. "Rod's got a point. You're hoping that somehow this is going to turn out to be fair, you'll razz me out of it. Out of hurting you, because you haven't done anything wrong. Fact is, though, you're both losing to me and that's it. The two of you have been just skimming along, bright smiles, good looks. Fucking television commercials, the both of you. A dress buyer and scuba instructor, shit. Well you're going to be ugly real soon. The cops might actually puke when they find you. And you know what? It *isn't* fair. You didn't really do a goddamn thing to deserve it. Who wouldn't want to be you? Fact is, it's just my turn. Stepping into somebody else's life—greatest secret in the world. It's like stealing a car. You put your foot to the floor, make it go a hundred, see what it can do. It's not worth much when you're done, but the ride's great."

"Is that why you killed Lori?" The edge in Bette's voice was still sharp. "Is killing women part of your big ride?"

"None of your fucking business."

"I'm sure fucking has everything to do with it."

Guy threw gasoline in her face.

"Stop it!" Rod tried to grab his arm, but Guy stepped back.

"I can't see," Bette said, digging her knuckles into her eyes. She gagged and coughed.

"Something wrong?" Guy said.

"I'm going to kill you, Brendan," Rod said. "You don't know it, but I'm going to rip your heart out." Rod threw himself back into the seat and reached behind.

"You think so, huh?" Guy squeezed the bottle, spewing a froth of gasoline over Rod's lap. "What the hell you squirming for, you looking for the tire iron I gave you? Just give up, Rod, there's nothing you can do, short of begging. You might want to try that. All your struggling and threats, and you'll still just be a memory of a long-ago barbecue by the time it's my turn to die." He took a red cigarette lighter from his pocket.

"Stop it, Brendan. I won't say it again."

"Why should I? Because you say so? You're about to be a one- or two-day item in the *Portland Press*, and that's the end of your story. Bette's mom and dad will probably spill some crocodile tears, and from the sound of things, your dad will feel guilty for a morning and go back to making airplane parts in the afternoon." Guy shook his head dismissively as he adjusted the lighter for maximum flame. "You just don't have that much influence with me right now, Rod. I am curious, though—what did you think of the Baggie of transmission fluid I threw at your windshield?"

"I thought it was blood."

"Really?" Guy looked up, grinning happily.

"Really. Now let's take a look at yours." Rod held a gun in two hands, aimed directly at Guy's face.

Guy's knees went weak, and he had to touch the hood to keep from falling. He wet his lips and said, "Gasoline. You're covered in gasoline. You fire that gun with all the fumes in there, it'll be no different than me using this lighter."

"The only difference is your brains will be all over that tree."

"We can do something on this. I can just walk away. That car would go off like a bomb."

"That's what you were counting on seeing. I'm going to do it anyway."

Bette lifted her head and turned her face in Guy's direction. Her eyes were still squeezed shut. "Don't let him get away. This will never end."

"No," Guy said, quickly. "Think about it, you touch the stove with your hand, that's what fire feels like. You don't want that all over your body." Guy set the lighter down on the hood of the car. "Here. I'll just walk away. I'll get on the bike and go."

"Stay there, Brendan. We'll all stay right here and wait for whoever comes along."

A tentative smile touched Guy's face. They were so weak. "Sorry. Don't want to be difficult, Rod, but I can't do that."

"You don't have a choice." Rod carefully thumbed the hammer back. "I'll blow that face you're so proud of right off."

Guy looked directly into Rod's eyes. He shook his head slightly and made his smile fade away. He kept his tone even, respectful. "I don't think so. You don't want to be like that monk. Flames five feet off your body. Bette's too. And both of you are in there screaming, alive for a long time." Guy drummed his fingers lightly on the hood and tensed his legs. "And you don't really want to shoot me, do you? It's a mess, you know. Little hole in the front. But the whole back of my head would blow out. I know you, Rod—you can do it, but you don't want to."

"I want to. You keep talking, I want to all the more."

"No." Guy shook his head. "You don't even like to spear fish. I walk and we all get to live. That's a better deal, and you'll take it." Guy pulled the pocket liner out of his leather jacket. "No matches and there's the lighter on the hood."

"Rod," Bette said warningly.

Guy dropped suddenly in front of the car. He scrambled along Bette's side of the car, figuring that Rod would not be able to reach past her quickly enough to get off a shot. The shattered back window was opaque, and he was certain Rod would not risk putting a bullet through that, with all the fumes in the car. Guy hurried over to the motorcycle and dug through the tank bag. He kept an eye out toward the car. Rod had reached outside his window with the gun, but Guy figured he was beyond Rod's field of vision.

Matches, Jesus Christ, there must be some matches in here, Guy thought, going through the side pockets of the tank bag. His heart was pounding from the near miss, and sweat poured into his eyes. To blow it when he was that close made him sick to his stomach; it was as if they *were* truly superior. He knew that could not be true; he knew he was far more dangerous, far more intelligent than they were—but by not being ready he'd almost got himself killed.

No matches. And time was passing. He glanced at his watch. Over five minutes had passed since he'd first walked up to them. *Why did I waste it talking?* He listened. A sinking realization settled into him—something was coming. It sounded like a truck. Frustrated, he reached down, grabbed a rock, and threw it at Rod's arm. It glanced off the doorframe and hit Rod's forearm. Guy felt a small stab of pleasure at the sound Rod made, and he held his breath, hoping he had provoked Rod into pulling the trigger and igniting his own funeral pyre.

But the feeling was dashed when Rod called out calmly, "You can throw all the rocks you want, Brendan. But I'm not going to pull the trigger until I can take your head off."

Guy heard the engine noise grow suddenly louder, and he figured the truck was approaching the straightaway before the curve. He swore softly, put the helmet on, and hit the starter button. The hot engine roared to life. He reached down, grabbed a rock the size of a grapefruit, and dropped it into the open tank bag. He spun the bike through a quick turn in the dirt, dipped down into the ditch, and kicked up gravel as he charged up the incline behind Rod's car. He clamped his knees to the tank, and just before he swept past the Firebird, he flung the rock with all his strength through the top left corner of the back window.

He slipped down through the ditch again and out onto the road before the truck rounded the corner. Guy thought that maybe his luck had held after all. There was no bullet to meet the itchy feeling in the small of his back, and that could mean the rock had flown true. If so, only Bette and Ericka were left for him to deal with.

25

TWO MONTHS LATER, Rod awoke in his room and sat up quietly, heart pounding. The dive knife was in his hand. Bette moaned in her sleep and rolled closer, her head and knees touching him. The room was faintly visible in the green glow of the digital clock, and he realized he had been dreaming again.

He released pent-up breath and slid the knife back into the sheath wedged between the mattress and box spring. Three thirty-five in the morning. A time to consider your mistakes, Rod thought. Wonder if Brendan is somewhere doing that now? Rod still couldn't think of him as Guy.

It was a cool morning, and the sweat on his body chilled him. He lay back and pulled the down comforter up over himself again. He slid the edge of his hand gently along Bette's thigh. She made a faint noise and parted her legs slightly, and he grasped her just above the knee.

Feeling comforted, he looked up at the ceiling and tried to relax. It was the dream he had told Bette about. She'd tried to dismiss it, joking that he was unimaginative, having the same old nightmare, again and again:

> *Brendan following up his rock with a burning branch, grinding the jagged point into Rod's chest. The flames brush up the cloth of his shirt like a hand, followed by searing pain as the flesh underneath blackens and peels away. From behind, Bette screams his name, but he can't help her. He struggles to get out, trying to open the door with fingers that are burning together, turning his hands into useless talons.*
>
> *Shoot Brendan, his mind screams. Shoot him and it will stop. He struggles to grip the gun in his lap. But his arms won't do what he wants. He strains, willing them to rise and shoot at the laughing face outside the window—the face that really does look like his own, the face that merrily grins and crows at his anguished cries. Then with a muffled thump and a crackle of sparks, his shoulders are suddenly light, and his arms roll onto his lap and burn like logs in a fireplace. The laughter outside the window is louder, and when he turns to Bette helplessly, he can read the reproach in her eyes. "You promised me," she says, as the flames run up her blouse and over her face.*

∎ ∎ ∎

Rod couldn't bring himself to form words about the other ones. Where *he* was the laughing face outside the window, standing, watching Bette burn down to the size of a large dog.

Or about the one with Lori.

> *Dragging her naked body by the belt around her neck. Heaving her against the closet wall and raising the belt to the hook. Her bulging dead eyes suddenly roll and meet his, and she says past her thickened tongue, "Why did you do it, Rod?"*

That dream had started two weeks before. Now, Rod wiped the sweat that had formed on his forehead while he'd been reviewing his list of horrors. He supposed a psychiatrist would say it was just guilt. And it probably was. But knowing that didn't make it any better. Rod looked at the clock. Fifteen minutes had passed. He needed to go to the bathroom, then he would try for some more sleep. Bette didn't move as he slipped quietly out of bed. He took the revolver out of the nightstand drawer and looked back at Bette. Outside, the clouds released a bar of moonlight, and he could see her clearly. The covers were pulled close under her chin, and she slept with her lips slightly parted. Her eyelashes lay against the white of her cheeks, unmoved by the type of dreams that kept him awake, night after night.

It was ridiculous. Two months after the "accident," Bette was sleeping easily, while he had to be armed for guerrilla warfare to take a piss. She seemed confident Brendan was frightened of them. One morning after Rod had had a particularly bad night Bette said, "If you're just feeling scared for me, don't. Brendan's a coward. You're probably the first one to ever make him think *he* was going to die. You saw the look on his face—he's in another part of the world." She had shuddered. "I only worry about whoever he's with."

Disgusted with himself, Rod lay the gun down on the nightstand and hurried across the cold hallway to the bathroom. After urinating, he washed his hands, rinsed his face, and looked into the mirror. There were dark pouches under his eyes, and his tan had faded. His mouth had a sour taste, and he brushed his teeth quickly. Why couldn't he let it go? Rabinovitz certainly didn't appear to be losing any sleep over the problem.

■ ■ ■

He had met them at the New Hampshire state line in an unmarked Ford the morning after Guy had left them in the overturned car. The police car dropping them off said GREEN MILLS TOWN POLICE on the side in gold lettering. The driver, a hefty cop in his midtwenties, checked Rabinovitz's badge and said, "Any of what they said true?"

"What do I know?" Rabinovitz said, eyes on Bette and Rod. "Dumb shit that I am, I thought they were staying in Boston."

The patrolman opened the back door of Rabinovitz's car for Bette while Rod walked around to the front. "Unlicensed gun, totaled car, and Chief Strider tells me to chauffeur them down here. You know him, huh?"

Rabinovitz nodded. "Well enough. How's he like it up there in Maine?"

The cop shrugged. "Doesn't confide in me, tell you the truth." He bent down and looked across at Rod and then back at Bette. He smiled cheerfully at her, and then said to Rabinovitz, "You wanted them, you got them."

"Lucky me." Rabinovitz snorted.

The town cop got in his car and merged back into traffic. Rabinovitz started toward Boston. He glanced in the mirror at Bette. She sat with her arms crossed, looking out the window. Rod stared straight ahead.

"I know the scenery is fascinating," Rabinovitz said. "But I'd like to know what happened."

"Let's get something straight," Rod said. "We're not doing this to be a pain in the ass for Detective Rabinovitz of the Boston Police. This is being done to us. So I appreciate you helping us out and all, with the cops in Maine, and picking us up. But don't expect me to go apologizing for screwing up your plans. Way things were going when I left, my best friend got a knife in his throat."

"And that's my fault? So you're the hotshot, what'd you do when you had the chance?"

"What'd you cops do about picking him up? I was out cold, but Bette gave the cops a description twenty minutes after the truck driver found us. How'd he get away?"

"They did what they could, soon as they believed she was making sense."

Bette interjected furiously, "I couldn't see, with the gasoline in my eyes and all. I'm trying to tell them what happened, to go after Brendan before he gets too far! But no, they've got to do it their way.

Asking my name, where I lived, can I count backwards from a hundred. I'm trying to tell them he's getting away, they're trying to decide if my head is cracked!"

Rabinovitz put a cigarette in his mouth and offered the pack to them vaguely. Both shook their heads. "You're not complaining that they rushed you to the emergency room, too, are you? Besides, they did what they could. Put out an APB. Had people staked out at the tollbooths, pulling over bikers. Lot of bikers this time of year. But from what you've told me about this guy, I wouldn't be surprised if he stashed that bike in the woods fifteen minutes after leaving you and stole a car, or hitched a ride. Maybe hid in a truck. There aren't that many cars stolen in the Portland area, but some. I'm getting a list of the vehicles missing in the Portland and west area. None reported missing right in Green Mills so far. They checked the airport, bus station, you know. We'll keep an eye out here too, see if a car stolen from Maine shows up in Boston."

Rod said, "More likely he snuck into somebody's house, bashed their head in, and is sitting in their kitchen right now."

Rabinovitz tapped the cigarette in the ashtray and eyed Rod speculatively. "I thought of that. And I've talked to Strider about it. Now why don't you tell me what happened?"

So Rod did, leaving nothing out from the time they left the cemetery.

"Figured that's why you stopped at the store," Rabinovitz said. "Strider gave me the registration number. At least Leo had a license."

Nodding, Rod said, "You can count on it. He always played by the rules."

"Give it a try. Your way didn't work so hot. Guy still walked."

"So what was I supposed to do?" Rod said. "Blow ourselves up to shoot him?"

"No, I never tell citizens to shoot each other. So this time we do it my way." Rabinovitz took his eyes from the road to look at Rod. "That clear?"

"If that means you're going to give us a hand, great. But I want a gun too. I can't just leave it to you to look after us. Bette and I have a little too much invested to just leave it to someone else. Brendan's going to try again, I know it."

Rabinovitz snorted. "You're lucky you weren't charged with unlawful possession. Don't talk to me about another gun!"

"He poured gasoline in my face," Bette said, "or weren't you listening? If Rod hadn't brought the gun, Brendan would've burned us alive in that car!"

Rabinovitz shrugged. "There's that." They drove in silence for a few minutes. Finally he said, "All right. You fill out an application and I'll talk to the chief. We'll see what we can do. But I call it from here. Deal?"

Rod turned to Bette and their eyes met. "Deal," he said. She smiled and touched Rabinovitz on the shoulder. "We *do* appreciate this."

Rabinovitz returned the smile sourly and said, "You ought to." Idly, he asked, "Either of you know a woman by the name of Susan Russell?" He looked across at Rod and into the mirror at Bette. For all his apparent indifference, his eyes were sharp.

Rod shook his head and turned to look at Bette, his face grim.

"No," she said in a low voice. "Why?"

"You ever go to Copley Place with Guy?"

"Who is she?" Rod said, harshly.

The detective ground his cigarette out. "Who was she," he corrected. "She was found strangled in one of the rooms about a month and a half back. We found a partial print of his, and the skin sample under her nails is the same blood type as the ones taken from Lori and you." He jutted his chin toward the rearview mirror.

Bette shrank back into her seat.

"What does that mean for us?" Rod said. "Does that put you any closer?"

"Not much. We've got his prints, not him. We still don't know his real name."

"How old was this Susan, and what did she look like?" Rod said.

Rabinovitz described her, glancing curiously at Rod as he drove.

Rod turned to Bette. "I was thinking of that girl he was with at the Dance Factory. But this happened before he even met us."

Rabinovitz hit the brakes. "What girl at the Dance Factory?" Rod rubbed his face tiredly. "I forgot all about it."

"Damn it. And you want to do this on your own."

He told the detective about meeting her. "She's a good bit younger than this other woman. Around college age. I have no idea if he ever saw her again."

"What was her name?"

Rod covered his eyes and leaned back in the seat. After a moment he said to Bette, "Irene?"

"No. It was like a man's name, I remember."

"Eric . . . Ericka," he said.

"That's it!"

"Last name?" Rabinovitz asked.

Rod shook his head.

"Not a clue," said Bette.

"All right," the detective said. "You can help us find her in the evenings. This is how it's going to run for the next few weeks . . ."

■ ■ ■

Bette moved in with Rod. They drove out to the Dance Factory several nights, with undercover cops following at a discreet distance. They didn't see Ericka.

Before going to bed, they worked out the next day's schedule over the telephone with Rabinovitz. A detective stayed on the couch in the living room each night. In the morning he was relieved by an undercover policeman or woman who would be walking past the front door of the apartment building when they came out. Rod felt apprehensive, leaving Bette on the subway in the care of the seemingly indifferent officer, only to go into the shop and find himself churlishly defensive at having his own baby-sitter already sweeping the floor.

The first day back, Rabinovitz had him put a help wanted ad in the *Phoenix*. Rod felt a heavy sense of déjà vu, wishing he could somehow retract the earlier ad and make everything as it had been. After a few days of screening interested customers and applicants from the ad, he selected a wiry thirty-year-old man with several years of sport diving experience. He was also an undercover cop. Rod started him with filling tanks. To handle the boat dives, Rod hired Shelley, the burly cabdriver who had helped on many a checkout dive. He would have to make decisions later to bring more people in. He couldn't run the store by himself forever.

And they waited. Bette was nervous, as if all the preparation made Brendan's appearance a given. Rod felt itchy and depressed, picking up the business without Leo. Nothing happened. After two weeks Rabinovitz called and said, "I don't know what to tell you."

Rod said, "You're going to back off."

"We can't do this forever. I'll be straight with you. This is costing a fortune, staking you two out like this. I got people to report to, and I don't have anything to show he's still in the same state, never mind trying to whack you."

"Yeah."

"Look, you got the gun."

"Yeah." Rod's voice was flat. "Thanks for arranging it."

Rabinovitz was silent for a moment. Then he said, "Do *you* still think he's coming back?"

Rod paused, then said, "I think he is. But he'll never come by with you guys waiting around. He's smarter than you think."

"I never thought he was stupid, just crazy."

"I'm not even sure he's that. He knows exactly what he's doing. If I could, I'd send Bette away. But if I did, put her on a bus or a plane, somehow he'd find her. But who knows? Maybe I'm just being a chickenshit."

"No, neither you or Bette are that. I've watched the two of you."

"Thanks."

"Well." The silence hung heavy on the line again. "Well, okay then. I'll have the patrol cars swing by your place, same as before."

"Same as when he killed Leo."

"Yeah, I know."

■ ■ ■

Leaving the bathroom, Rod felt a draft coming down the hallway. Goose bumps formed on his bare arms and chest. He looked in at Bette, sleeping peacefully. She had hugged a pillow to herself in his absence. Smiling to himself, Rod walked back toward the kitchen to see if he had left a window cracked open. Bette looked too good to leave alone for long. But he knew he would never get to sleep if there was an open window in the apartment.

The windows on each side of the breakfast bar were latched down. In the living room the skylights were secure, as were the windows. That left only Brendan's room.

Rod's mouth went dry. He had always used that room basically for storage. Since Brendan, Rod regarded it as tainted ground, and reason enough lately to consider selling the condominium. Now he didn't want to go in it. He considered going back for the gun. Why had he woken up? Had he heard something? Rod listened now.

Nothing.

Disgusted with himself, he strode past the kitchen to the short hallway leading to Brendan's room.

It's the dream, same as every night. Some fine night you'll work yourself into a terror and shoot Bette on her way to the bathroom.

The hair along his arms and the back of his neck lifted. Cold air brushed against him from the partially open bedroom door. In the faint light, he could see the door was caught on the rug.

He had not left it open.

Rod hesitated, then said, "Chickenshit," aloud to himself, stepped in the room, and turned on the light. The window was wide open. Blood began to pound in Rod's head. A rope hung outside the window, slapping lightly against the sill. There was yellow masking tape just above the latch, and Rod could see where a rectangle of glass had been cut out.

A door slammed at the other end of the apartment. Bette was screaming by the time Rod reached the hallway, sprinting.

THE HALL CLOSET was open. That's where he was, Rod thought, pushing the bedroom door.

"Rod!" Bette cried. "He's got the gun!"

Rod fell to his knees behind the door as the gun exploded. The gun flash filled the room with a brief orange light, and splinters stung his cheek. On his belly in the hallway, Rod pulled the door by the bottom edge, leaving it slightly ajar. It vibrated in his hand as another bullet ripped over his head and into the bathroom, shattering the toilet.

26

Water sloshed across the floor, cold against his bare skin. Rod shivered. He strained to hear past the ringing in his ears. Inside, the bed creaked and Guy made a loud grunting sound as if he had been punched.

"You bitch," he said.

Rod stood and put his hand on the door, the memory of Lori's bulging eyes and tongue pushing aside caution.

But a slap of skin on skin made him stop. Bette started crying in steady sobs.

Rod took his hand from the doorknob. If she could cry, she was clearly breathing. Rod found he had been holding his own breath.

"What are you doing out there, Rod?" Guy's voice rang out. He was breathing heavily, but it was the same smug voice as when he'd been pouring on the gasoline. Rod looked down the hall. Police? Neighbors even? Where the Christ were they? Then he realized only a few seconds had passed since the gunshot. Both Rod and Bette could be dead a dozen times over before the police arrived.

"Answer me. I know I didn't hit you," Guy said. "You would've made some noise, you're not that tough. Not that bright, either. What did you do, tell yourself I'd never come back? Convince yourself? Must have, to leave her here for me all cozy and warm, with a gun too. You didn't need to do that, Rod. I brought my own. You remember the girl you introduced me to—Ericka. First person I went to see when I came back to town tonight, knocked on her apartment door, and she wasn't cautious anymore either. But, shit, I hardly gave her any reason to be scared of me. You should've known better. She gave me this little bitty thing, but yours is a lot better. A real fighter, that girl, you'd never expect it. Just like Bette here, you should see us, we're having a great time in your bed, isn't that right?"

"He's going to kill you, Brendan," she said, her voice shaking.

"Is that right?" He grunted, and Bette cried out. "You know my name. Say it."

"Guy. It's Guy."

"That's right. Guy and Bette are having a great time in Rod's bed, isn't that right?"

Rod stood up quietly and started toward the kitchen, walking near the edge of the hallway, where the floorboards were less likely to creak.

Guy apparently heard anyhow. "You leave the apartment, I'll spread your little chickie's brains all over the room before I come for you. Or were you just going to make a call?"

In the kitchen, Rod hit his thigh. The line to the wall phone was cut. He pulled open the drawers, looking for the butcher knife.

"I'm gonna count to five," Guy called. "You don't answer me by then, I'm messing up the sheets. . . . One!"

Spatula.

Forks.

Spoons.

Dull-edged knives.

"Two!"

Remembering, Rod slammed the drawer shut and ran to Guy's room. He threw the closet door open.

"Three!"

He snatched up the spear gun with its loosely hanging rubbers and grabbed one of the barbed shafts.

"Four!"

Running back down the hall, he screamed, "Wait, all right, Guy. I'll come in, don't hurt her, please!"

Bette's sobbing became louder inside the bedroom. "Don't, Rod, no!" her voice insistent. Then she was cut off, strangled.

"Please," Rod said, hitting the doorjamb with his fist. "Don't hurt her anymore!"

"Did I hear the magic words, Rod?" Guy mimicked in a whining, effeminate voice. "Please don't hurt her, please. I don't like my girlfriend's face when she can't breathe. I don't like it when it's all bloody." His voice hardened. "Five it is, Rod, and I don't see you."

"I'm coming in," Rod said and stepped quickly past the bedroom door into the closet. There was a space clear of shoes to stand. Even past the fear pounding through him, Rod noticed the dank smell of perspiration in the closet. *I should have smelled him*, he thought, and then pushed it away.

"I'll come in. Just don't shoot her." Rod let his voice shake. It wasn't hard to do. "You don't want to hurt her. What's the point? It's me you want to get rid of." Rod set the shaft in the spear gun and pulled the first rubber back.

Guy snorted. "Listen to him, Bette, some man you've got out there. He's going to just stand outside the door and say 'please, pretty please' right up until the time I blow your face off." Louder he said, "Rod, both me and Bette are getting sick in here, listening to you."

Rod quietly pushed the closet door all the way open, until it touched the wall. He set the second and third rubbers and figured his attack: if he kicked the bedroom door open and loosed the spear, he might still have time to pull back behind the wall before Guy fired. The protection of the wall and the closet door might stop a bullet.

But the one spear was his only chance—if Rod missed, Guy would certainly kill Bette before Rod could load another. Rod saw no choice but to charge in directly with the goal of bringing the spear within a few feet of Guy before pulling the trigger. Guy could undoubtedly pull off at least one shot before then; Rod was acutely aware that he most likely would be hit.

He crouched slightly and was bracing himself to kick the bedroom door when he noticed a glimmer of light from inside the closet wall. Buying time, he shouted, "You've got the gun. Why don't you have the balls to come out and get me?"

Putting his fingers against the wall, he found the rough edges of the peephole. He pressed his eye against it, the significance of it digging icy fingers into his belly. The room was clearly visible in the moonlight. Guy was sitting up against the headboard on the far side of the bed, where Rod normally slept. Bette was pulled against him, her back to his crotch. His legs were wrapped around her torso. Rod could see her left arm pinned to her side. Her right seemed to be off the edge of the bed. Around her neck there was something dark. Rod squinted.

Suddenly she was gasping, and Rod could see it was a belt Guy had twisted around her neck. Guy spoke loudly into Bette's ear. "I think you've been hung out to dry, Bette. You not giving him enough lately? Huh? Your brave man just ain't coming to your rescue, and that's a fact." She struggled to reach her throat, but he just chuckled and clamped his legs tighter. He pointed the revolver at the door. "Come on, hero, we're getting lonely here. I'm not staying until the cops come."

"You bastard," Rod said, and Guy suddenly jerked his head to the right, looking directly at the eyehole. His face split into a wide grin.

"That's the place for you," he said, and put a bullet through the wall.

GUY WAS TWISTING the belt tighter around Bette's neck when Rod kicked in the bedroom door and lunged forward with the spear gun extended. Guy shoved Bette forward and shouted, "Her first!"

Rod froze.

Guy reached around with the revolver and pulled the trigger. Rod put his left hand out reflexively, and, even in the poor light, Guy could see Rod's little finger disappear. The bullet continued on to take Rod in the shoulder, lift him off his feet, and slam him against the wall.

Bette cried, "Rod!" and half-pulled Guy off the bed trying to get to him.

Guy hit her a glancing blow across the head with the gun and said, "He's not dead yet, Bette. I'm going to give you a chance to say good-bye. I'd like to talk to him too."

He tugged her back across the bed by the belt around her neck, until he was sitting up against the headboard again. "Just want to give a little distance there, Rod. So it'll make your aim that much more difficult." He loosened his grip on the belt so Bette could breathe.

Rod tried to lift the spear gun up, but he didn't seem to have the strength. Blood poured down the wall behind him, and a small pool was forming at his feet.

Guy said to Bette, "Take a look at that, girl. Your hero is trying to shoot a spear gun with one hand. What do you think the chances are of him hitting me but not you? I bet if he tries it, you'd thank me for shooting him first."

Guy raised his voice and spoke slowly, as if to a stupid child. "Now Rod, what's it like, getting hit with a bullet like that? I mean it, I want to know."

He waited.

Guy felt the familiar impatience creep back, but he tried to keep it from his voice. "Rod, you've got to know you're dead. Your blood is pouring out on the floor. And anything you could try at the last second, I could beat. You know that. So tell me, what's it feel like? Did you think you would win? Are you angry, are you thinking this is not how you expected to go? That you were going to get more time, more life? Or are you just thinking about me, wishing you could kill me. Is that it?"

Bette started crying again. Guy could feel her shudder as she drew in breath.

Rod said something that Guy strained to hear.

"Shhh," Guy shook Bette, and leaned forward. "What's that?"

Rod licked his lips and said in a hoarse whisper, "I'm thinking about Bette."

"Ah, isn't that nice?" Guy said. "It's hard to believe, but if you say it's true, why not? You're both going to be dead in minutes, why should you lie?"

"I'm thinking about Bette killing you. I'm thinking about Bette cutting your heart out."

"Just like a woman," Guy said, cocking the hammer. "But she isn't going to have the chance this time."

"Do it," Rod said.

Bette slammed her head back into Guy's face, threw herself to the right side of the bed, and reached over the edge of the mattress, apparently trying to drag herself off. Guy was jarred for a split second, and she kicked at him, but he was too close for it to do much damage. He rolled up onto his knees and yanked her back. He put the gun back on Rod and said, "Nice try, but all you've done is piss me off. Maybe I'll just have to use all these bullets to finish the job. Say good-bye to Rod."

Bette rolled onto her back as he took aim, crying, "No!"

Guy saw a faint gleam in the moonlight in his peripheral vision, but she had plunged the seven-inch knife into his belly before he realized what it was. He shrieked and let go of the belt. He clutched his stomach and swung the gun on Bette just as Rod pulled the spear gun trigger. The bands snapped loudly, and the barbed spear ripped through Guy's throat. His fingers twitched, and the revolver belched flame. A bullet thumped into the mattress by Bette's head.

His life spewed out of him, a black fountain in the moonlight. Guy slumped back against the headboard, holding the shaft between his hands as if caught in dark prayer. Rod staggered toward him and said something. But Guy could not understand him at first through his own agonizing pain, his inability to catch his breath, and the confusion of other voices. There was a rising babble in his head, and he was choking, choking on the shaft, and all the questions, all the people talking, people he knew so well . . .

"Oh my god, what's happening?"

"It's happened to him. . . ."

"You should not have used the name of Cyrano de Bergerac in this manner . . ."

"What should we do?" Bette said.

"I'm in you, that's right, I was always in there, remember me? I'm Carter, you don't want to admit . . ."

Rod said, "He's dying. There's nothing we can do for him."

"It's Nick, you son of a bitch, you hid behind that door. You'd never have had a chance if I knew you were there. . . . You killed Chloe, you cut her and she never did a thing to you . . ."

"You've lost so much blood." Bette tried to tug Rod away.

"You were wearing my clothes when you killed that girl,

you were acting like me, you fucker, you didn't have the right. Tony Bernetti never hit a woman in his life. There was nothing wrong with her, you didn't need to do that . . ."

"Please, Rod, lie down," Bette said. "I've got to go for help." Rod shook his head and looked into Guy's eyes.

"Slog, it's me. You did it, man, you did me in, oh man, you killed your own brother. . . . You surprised the hell out of me, but shit, you showed me some things, you did show me some things . . ."

Rod's face suddenly appeared to be a great distance away, as if Guy were moving abruptly backward. Rod's voice was saying,

". . . I don't want to be in here. I had to kill you, but I won't go with you . . ."

Darkness.

Rod said, "So now you know."